THE *heartbeat* HYPOTHESIS

THE *heartbeat* HYPOTHESIS

LINDSEY FRYDMAN

Entangled Publishing, LLC
2614 South Timberline Road
Suite 109
Fort Collins, CO 80525
Visit our website at www.entangledpublishing.com.

Embrace is an imprint of Entangled Publishing, LLC.

Edited by Jenn Mishler
Cover design by Letitia Hasser
Cover art from iStock

Manufactured in the United States of America

First Edition March 2017

embrace

For all the dreamers out there, this one's for you.

Chapter One

Everyone called me a miracle. I guess they didn't understand the concept. My heart was the miracle. I, however, was an aerobically challenged basket case trying to hoof it ten blocks from campus without fainting.

Halfway there, I stopped, bracing my hands against my knees. My body heaved, lungs burned, and Pete's Coffee Shop loomed in the near distance.

The universe didn't owe me another favor, but damn. If I could just make it there looking semi-normal—not covered in sweat, huffing and puffing, ready for a nap. That was not the impression I wanted to give Jake.

Maybe he wouldn't show. Or worse, maybe he *would* show and refuse to help me.

I placed a shaky hand on my chest, running my fingers over the bumpy scar hiding beneath my shirt, and trudged on, calming myself by humming an annoying jingle. I even sang the alphabet in my head—anything to slow my frantic pulse.

A light breeze tickled my skin, blew the scent of freshly cut grass past my nose, and I breathed it in, steadying my twitchy fingers.

But my sense of calm evaporated the moment I saw the baby-blue sign for Pete's Coffee Shop. My quick pace became a measured shuffle, the soles of my shoes clinging to the pavement.

Holy fucking shit. I couldn't do this.

There was nothing casual about this meeting. Jake was not just *some guy*. His sister's heart beat furiously beneath my rib cage, and all the pleasantries in the world wouldn't change that she was dead—and I was not.

Still, as I stood paralyzed in front of the door, which was a putrid shade of yellow, I silently mouthed my lines. "Hey, happy to meet you." No, "happy" wasn't appropriate, and "hey" was too offhand. So I'd say…what? "Sorry we're meeting under these circumstances." No, that was crap, too. My stomach tightened, and a mix of anxiety and dread bubbled into my throat. I leaned forward, swallowed hard, and blinked at the dirty welcome mat, watching a giant ant cross some artistic rendition of a coffee mug. Then I slapped my thighs, stood up, and squared my shoulders.

Okay. I can do this. I want *to do this.*

The door rattled a high-pitched chime when I pushed it open. I instinctively ducked, flinching like it was gunfire, and I almost scurried back outside. But I didn't, because I was okay. Everything was going to be—

There he was. I'd know that dark blond hair and strong jawline anywhere—thanks to some Facebook stalking—but Jake was no longer just pixels mashed together on a screen. He was an actual guy wearing jeans and a T-shirt, hunkered down in a booth fifteen feet away.

He lifted his head, scanning the room slowly. My feet cemented to the tile. Holding my breath, I waited. He shifted his jaw when his eyes found mine, and the pressure in my chest, combined with the lack of oxygen, made me dizzy.

I opened my mouth, but still hadn't moved, and now he stared at me like I had a time bomb strapped to my chest. *Tick, tick, tick.*

Finally, after watching him watch me for what felt like an entire espresso production, I dipped my chin and walked to the booth.

"Hi," I said, slinking into the brown leather seat across from him.

Jake's hair fell in semi-waves across his brow, framing an angular face. He ran a hand over the faint stubble covering his jaw, and even though his lips were pressed firmly together, I couldn't stop thinking about how gorgeous he was.

"Hi." His voice was deep, guarded.

While he assessed my face, I wiped sweaty palms against my jeans and forced a smile. "I'm…Audra Madison."

Jake leaned back in the booth. "If you weren't, this would be pretty awkward, huh?"

I would've laughed, if not for the gravel in his voice and the coldness in his eyes.

"Yeah." I cleared my throat.

The faint sounds of people chattering and clinking their coffee mugs on the tables weren't enough to disguise the tense silence between us. I aimed my gaze at his chest to avoid an unnerving staring contest. His shirt was pitch-black with the words "I'LL FIX IT IN PHOTOSHOP" in white.

"Thanks for meeting me," I said.

"Sure." He looked down at my chest before angling his head toward the window.

Oh God, was he wishing it were Emily sitting here? I wanted to tell him I was sorry for his loss, because I was, but that seemed mendacious—if Emily were alive, I'd be dead. And I certainly couldn't say *that.* As the silence stretched, his fingers tapped the empty tabletop, and I panicked.

"Don't you like coffee?" I blurted.

His brows slid upward. "Yeah. Don't you?"

"Yes. But you don't have one. This is a coffee shop, and you wanted to meet here so...I thought you'd have a coffee, I guess."

"I was waiting for you."

Warmth spread across my neck. "Oh."

A shadow of a grin lifted the corners of his mouth. "How do you like your coffee?"

I fidgeted against the soft material of the seat, twirling the silver bracelet around my wrist. "With a little cream and no less than three packets of sugar."

"So you don't like coffee."

Before I could respond, he was out of the seat and headed for the counter. I waited, rubbing my hands together and staring at the brown tabletop.

Don't freak out.

Ever since he'd agreed to meet me, I'd thought about how this day might go, what I'd say, what he'd say. It was a two-month fantasy of every possible conversation we could've had. He could've been an ass. He could've been weird or creepy. *I* could've been weird or creepy.

Wait. Maybe I was.

Oh man, this was like a blind date.

It's not a date, you idiot.

Jake set two coffee cups on the table. He slid one toward me.

"Thank you." I pulled the mug closer, breathing in the rich aroma, trying to find comfort in the smell.

No such luck.

He ran a hand across his jaw, shrugging one shoulder. "Sure thing. I'm always happy to enable another caffeine addict."

"You assume I'm a caffeine addict?"

Jake smirked. "No. I *know* you are. Every college student

is."

"Fair enough." Although he was right, and I did love my caffeine, my indulgences were severely limited since the transplant.

Silence settled between us again, and I gripped the mug between my palms, stealing glances at him when I thought he wasn't looking. As soon as he caught me, his shoulders tensed and I took to staring at the mocha-colored liquid, trying to remember the advice my best friend, Kat, had given me.

Oh, she'd had a perfect break-the-ice line, but I couldn't remember it. All I heard was my heartbeat—or rather, Emily's heartbeat—pounding in my ears.

I shifted, digging my fingers into the booth seat. "I want to do something for your sister. To honor her…thank her."

When Jake looked up, his eyes had softened and so had the hard set to his jaw. "You do?"

"Yes." I swallowed my nerves and decided my words carefully. "Have you ever seen Emily's Tumblr account?"

"Ah, no."

"They're full of your photographs. You've really never seen it?"

His forehead creased, one eyebrow rising slightly. "What?"

I pulled out my phone and set it on the table. Sixty daunting seconds later, I'd found Emily's page and twisted the display so he could see.

Jake tapped on the phone, scrolling for only a moment before removing his finger and looking at me. "Why would you think these are mine?"

"Most of them share the same hashtag: my favorite photographer Jake. That's you. Right?"

He returned his attention to the phone, this time picking it up, interest lighting his face. "Oh. Yeah, I took these. There's so many damn hashtags, I didn't even see my name."

"Well, her whole page, it's a done-it list."

His gaze lifted, along with the corners of his lips. "A what?"

"According to her, she never understood why people made lists of the things they were going to do, so she made a page dedicated to all the things she *did* do."

"Sounds like Emily."

Now that is a smile. "Well, it's inspired me to start my own done-it list, but I want to start by re-creating her list."

Jake set the phone down and slid it across the table. "Re-create it?"

"Yes. Like this one…" I scrolled until I found the photograph. "She threw glow sticks in a pool and went swimming." I assumed he remembered, since he'd been behind the camera. "I'm going to do that, then put it on my own done-it Tumblr list. Emily only had sixteen done-its, so I plan on redoing all of them."

After taking a slow sip of coffee, he leaned forward like he was going to share a secret. "Can I make a suggestion?"

I winced, instilled with a burning desire to flee from the coffee shop. There I was, alive and well—with a perfectly functioning heart—and Emily lay six feet under, dead and gone. Jake probably thought—

"You should name it something else," he said. "Done-its sounds like Cheez-Its, and that's a little weird, don't you think? Don't get me wrong, kudos to my sister for the idea, but, uh, she could've been more original with the name." His smile grew, crooked and adorable.

Relief washed over me, and I smiled, too. "I agree *done-it* is unoriginal, but I can't think of anything better that isn't also weirder. Can you?"

With a considering expression, Jake leaned back in the booth, and while he thought, I took a sip of my coffee and cream mixture.

"See. Not as easy as it sounds." I laughed, warming my fingers around the mug.

Jake chuckled, shaking his head. "Guess I'll have to get back to you on that one. But where do I come into this?"

I let go of the ceramic and splayed my hands across the tabletop. "I want you to photograph my...poorly named list."

"Why me?"

Opening up Emily's Tumblr again, I inhaled deeply, reminding myself this was going better than I'd expected. *Look on the bright side*—that's what Kat would tell me. "I tried to re-create this photo." I tapped on the image and turned the phone around.

It was a picture of Emily lying in the middle of a road, hands behind her head, one leg crossed over the other, blissfully unaware of her surroundings. Two yellow lines trailed beneath her, narrowing down and out of the frame, and a golden horizon burned across treetops in the background.

"I had my friend take it," I explained. "But there wasn't a photo app in the world that could make it half as awesome as the one you took." His lips quirked, and I took that as a sign to go on. "Since you're Emily's favorite photographer, it only seems right to hire you for the job. I mean, if that's something you'd be comfortable with." Even though his sister's death was two years ago, it wasn't the kind of pain that simply faded away. "I'll completely understand if it might be...too much to ask of you."

He tipped his head, saying nothing. I looked down at my coffee and wrapped my fingers together in my lap to keep them from twitching.

Maybe this had been a bad idea.

I chanced a look at him, still waiting for a reply. His stone face gave nothing away.

No.

No, this wasn't a bad idea. This was a *good* thing.

Finally he said, "Why?"

Swallowing, I shifted against the seat. "Why what?"

"Why re-create the things Emily did when you could start with your own list?"

Maybe because when I saw the photos, it was like being let in to a significant part of her life. The done-its weren't extraordinary feats, but they were random and quirky. Re-creating them would allow me to step into her shoes and hopefully find whatever it was that made those moments magical for her—whatever made her beam so brightly in those photographs. But I couldn't bring myself to tell Jake all of that so I said, "I want to get to know her somehow, and this feels like the best way."

After a moment, he nodded. "Okay. I can understand that. So…I'll do it."

I wrapped both hands around the mug, sucking in a breath. "You will?"

"Yeah. But you don't need to hire me. I don't want your money. I'll just do it."

I wanted to jump up and down, clap my hands, then run off singing down the street. But I chose to smile instead. "So great."

We spent the next few minutes silently drinking our coffees. I tried stealing more glances, but none went unnoticed. Maybe if I'd gone on more than two real dates in high school, this would feel more natural.

This is not *a date.*

Jake's phone buzzed against the table. He tapped the screen before looking up. "I have to go, but before I do…you want to try what real coffee tastes like?" he said, lips twisting with amusement as he slid his mug toward me.

"I know what real, unaltered coffee tastes like — it's gross."

Lashes lowering, he shook his head and laughed. "But you've never had Pete's special brew before. It's the best damn coffee in Fort Collins. I promise."

I peered at the black liquid inside his cup. "Uh. You make a compelling argument, but no thanks. Maybe next time."

"All right. If we find ourselves together in a coffee shop again, I'm holding you to that, deal?" Before I could respond, Jake slipped out of the booth. "I'll message you later. We can set up a time to meet."

"Er—wait."

He stopped, confusion lurking in his gray eyes. I waved one hand. Faked a smile. Prayed he didn't notice my desperation—I didn't want him to leave. "I'm sure we'll have plenty of chances to talk later."

As he headed for the door, he glanced back at me—was that a wink?—and said, "I'm sure we will."

Chapter Two

The door smacked shut behind Jake, and I blinked twice before turning back to my mug. I couldn't tell if I'd flirted with my heart donor's brother…or made a complete ass of myself.

Or both.

With only the soft reggae music keeping me company, I stared at my hands, playing his words over in my head. *Why?* Jake wanted to know, and although I offered explanations, it wasn't the entire truth. Frowning, I twisted the bracelet around my wrist. The one piece of jewelry I never took off. The one labeling me a heart transplant recipient.

I needed to clear my head. The hike back to my dorm would do the trick—if it didn't kill me. Colorado State lay in the foothills of the Rockies, so no flat, even land for me. Sadly. But at least the cyan-colored sky casing the backdrop of the green-and-brown mountains made the exhausting trek worth it.

As I walked, I considered all the things I didn't tell Jake. Like how when I found Emily's Tumblr, I'd been smacked in the face with reality. A girl I didn't know, could never know, was dead, and her tragedy had suddenly become my blessing. It felt…wrong. And it would've been foolish to sit around and do nothing about it.

Hours later, I was still stuck with my own thoughts on repeat. I pressed my ear against my pillow until I heard my heartbeat — hauntingly similar to the tick of a clock, warning of time gone by.

Lub-dub.

Eighty-six thousand, four hundred seconds in a day. How many was I wasting?

I rolled over until the taunting noise ceased. "What are we doing tonight?"

Kat, my closest friend since the glue incident in fourth grade, spun in her computer chair a few feet away. "We could always—"

"No frat parties." I leaned forward on my bed. The two of us had done everything together for years, and she'd always been my go-to person, so choosing the same college and becoming roommates was a no-brainer. Even if she enjoyed the party scene more than I did. "I can't smell any more stale beer breath for at least…a few more days. Okay?"

"Fine." She pulled her legs up and spun the chair again. Since it was cheap, plastic, and cost two bucks at a yard sale, it only rotated once before stopping. "We can watch a movie, or some trashy reality TV." Kat laughed, and it made me smile. It always did. "Have you heard from the heart guy yet?"

"Don't call him that. His name is Jake."

That nickname had to go, mostly because it made no sense. I was the one who had a heart transplant two years ago. The heart pumping blood through my body belonged to his sister, Emily. His heart had nothing to do with this.

She waved off my comment. "Have you heard from *Jake*?"

Even though it'd only been a few hours since I saw him,

I'd been checking my Facebook messages non-freaking-stop. It was becoming something of a problem. "Not yet."

Kat leaped off the chair and lunged for my twin-size bed. She rolled onto her side, propping her head on her hand. "You could always message him first, you know."

I pulled my computer onto my lap, leaning against a boring white wall. "He said *he* would message *me*."

She gave me a look that I took to mean: *you poor, naive thing.* "Did you get his number?"

I tapped at the keyboard and logged on to Facebook. Again. "No."

"Did you give him your number?"

"Um. No."

Kat only rolled her eyes, shoving her hand into the bowl of popcorn next to the bed. "You can't wait on other people for the things you want. Especially guys. Now tell me what he said. Tell me *everything.*"

She always wanted to know everything about any interaction I had with a guy, starting back in middle school, and I always obliged—not that there was much to tell. But this wasn't the same. "It's not like we went on a date."

"No shit, Sherlock. That meeting was way more important than any old date could ever be. So I gotta know, was he excited about your proposal?"

I pulled on a piece of my hair, twisting it, inspecting the dark red strand like it held the answer. "I don't think 'proposal' is the right word. And neither is 'excited.'"

"M'kay. Well, what's the right word then?"

Letting my hair fall back down around my neck, I rubbed my cheek and shook my head. "He was…hesitant."

"But he agreed," Kat said, her blue eyes widening. "So obviously whatever you said convinced him."

I fixed my gaze on her. "Obviously."

She tipped her head, sending long blond curls swaying.

"What *did* you say?"

After giving her the shortened play-by-play, I checked my messages, just in case Facebook failed me and didn't give me a proper notification.

"It sounds like it went well," she said. "You didn't take any of the advice I gave you, but whatever, you still got Jake to say yes. Plus, he bought you coffee. Bonus, right? Now. Have you decided which done-it to do first?"

In my head, all I could think was *Cheez-It*, and I tried not to laugh. "Negative."

"Seriously? Okay, you're not sleeping until you decide."

"Whatever you say, Katarina."

She glared, and even with her face scrunched, she still looked pretty. "That's a low blow."

I grinned. Kat stopped using her full name when she turned thirteen and demanded everyone follow suit. She claimed *Katarina* belonged to someone bitchy and stuck-up and that it didn't jibe with her desire to be the nice, bubbly girl. "You might not like it. But I do."

"I cannot be the future 'nurse Katarina.' It sounds like a superhero name or something."

"But nurses save lives, right? I think the superhero name fits."

Her glare dissipated. "I never thought of it like that. It does sound…kind of badass. Shit. Maybe I should change it back."

Shrugging, I tapped on the keyboard. "You don't have to decide now."

"You're right. But *you*, my friend, *do* need to decide on a done-it."

While she searched Emily's Tumblr on her phone, I scrolled through Jake's Facebook page, hunting for something I didn't already know. He shared little about his personal life. Basic info filled out. A few pictures of himself. No status updates aside from his photography and a link to his Instagram. He was a junior at Colorado State—where I was a freshman. He didn't like smiling for pictures. Or maybe he simply didn't like smiling.

Kat leaned against the wall beside me, thumbing the screen. "This pie thing…where people nominate you to get a pie thrown in your face, and then you do it and nominate someone else? I wanna know who the hell came up with that crap. There must be an easier way to raise money than pies to the face and buckets of ice-cold water dumped on your head."

"Sure, but something easy wouldn't be entertaining." I shut my laptop and shoved it onto the bed. It wasn't doing anything besides making me crazy.

"How old do you think she was in these last posts?"

"In her teens, I would guess."

"So…right before she died?"

"Probably." I frowned, trying not to think too hard about it.

"I still want to know how she died," Kat said.

I shook my head slowly. "It was probably a car accident. It's the leading cause of death for teenagers, right?"

"Yeah, maybe."

Six months ago, I decided to learn more about the girl who gave me this second chance. I wanted to know who she was. So I Googled her, and there was nothing that Google did not know—well, almost nothing.

Eventually I stumbled onto her Tumblr account. The photos were breathtaking, and each event was something unique, something meaningful to only her. They had to be meaningful—why else would she broadcast those things she'd done for all the world to see? All of the images listed a done-it, and a few even had quotes or short notes. Oh, but they *all* came with a ridiculous number of hashtags.

It was weird to me, to see these clichéd tags like

#bluehairdontcare combined with a deep quote about life, love, or the stars coming from a sixteen-year-old. I'd scoured every bit of Emily's internet presence, but still couldn't get all the pieces to fit.

Emily, to me, was a juxtaposition I wanted to understand. Most girls her age used social media to showcase selfies, coffee pictures, and cute clothing. And even though she seriously abused the ridiculous hashtags, the rest of her online presence was deep, presenting herself as older and wiser than the typical teenager.

Kat's voice snapped me out of my blank stare and back down to reality.

"There you go," she said, holding my own phone out to me.

Confused, I pulled it from her hand and glanced down. My Facebook page filled the screen, and a slimy feeling slithered its way into my gut. "What did you do?"

"I helped you out. You're welcome."

I opened the messenger app and read the message sent from me to Jake—the one I didn't write.

Me: *When's our first appointment?*

Shaking my head, I glared at her. "You bitch." I stared at the message, and a buzzing electricity surged through my veins, creating an unexpected panic in my pulse. "This seems awfully forward."

She snorted, chomping on popcorn. "What, are you afraid he'll change his mind?"

"He could, but I don't think he will."

"Then what're you afraid of?"

My phone vibrated in my palm before I could answer her question.

Jake: *I'm free Tuesday after 5.*

Kat pulled the screen closer, grinning madly. "See. Being forward gets you somewhere."

She nudged me with her shoulder, and I laughed halfheartedly.

Six months after I'd gotten out of the hospital, I wrote a letter to the Cavanaughs acknowledging their loss and expressing my gratitude. I'd been warned that I might not receive a reply, but a few weeks later, I did. My simple paragraphs didn't feel like enough. And it wasn't until I'd decided on CSU and discovered Jake went to school here, too, that my plan to re-create Emily's done-it list began to form. The universe had given me a sign, or so I liked to believe, and I couldn't just ignore it.

College was supposed to mean freedom, and freedom was supposed to be awesome. The life every teenager dreamed about, right? No parents. Away at college. No rules. (Okay, maybe some rules.) I should've been jumping up and down, planning to stay up all night and make terrible decisions.

Instead, I thought about the heart in my chest and how it wasn't always mine, how it used to belong to a girl with a name and a face, a family and a *life*.

Now I had her heart. Her life.

A debt I'd never be able to repay.

"This is the one you should do first," Kat said, shoving her phone into my line of sight.

I looked at the last photograph Emily posted. The last done-it she ever did. *God, that really does need a better name.*

"If you're going to re-create them all, you may as well get the painful one out of the way. Plus, Jake needs to know you're serious."

I cringed at the idea, but as usual, Kat had a point. Nothing says serious like a tattoo.

Emily's sixteenth done-it was a blurry cell phone photo, clearly taken by one of her friends. Some guy with two full sleeves and neck tattoos hovered nearby as she showed off the new blue flower on her ankle. She beamed at the camera as though she were the winner of a game show, and not in any pain at all. Below the image, a succession of curious hashtags followed a short quote.

We live with the scars we choose. *#FirstTattoo* *#FlowerTattoo* *#NoPainNoBeauty* *#ForgetMeNot* *#JakeTakesBetterPhotos*

I'd sent Jake the address and told him to meet me Tuesday night at six. At five forty-five, I walked to the front doors of Twisted Image Tattoos and Piercings to find him already there, leaning against the brick building as though he were a decoration. A fluttery sensation filled my gut and I bit my lip, unsure whether the fluttering was a good thing or not. But the sight of him calmed the nervous adrenaline I'd been carrying around all day at the thought of how painful getting this tattoo might be.

His brows raised as I approached, and though half a smile pulled on his lips, he didn't exactly look happy. "You're not serious."

"Actually, I am."

Jake rocked back on his heels, his voice turning rough. "What I mean is, there's no way Emily had a tattoo. She wasn't even eighteen."

"I'm sure there's ways around that. Didn't you see it on her blog yesterday when I showed you? She definitely had a tattoo."

He cocked his head and laughed, low and taut. "I definitely didn't take a photo of any tattoos."

I smiled. "Nope. Not yet."

My distraction and nerves about meeting with Jake again

had been enough to override any thoughts I had about letting someone pierce my skin with a thousand tiny needles. Now the entrance was one foot away, the OPEN sign lit up a neon-green in the window, and a slow burn started in the center of my chest.

"I've, uh…never gotten a tattoo before," I said, crossing my arms. "But this is probably going to suck, huh?"

He pushed off the wall, took a step forward, and then shoved his hands into his pockets. "Nah. There's a lot of things more painful than a tattoo."

I laughed, though I was hardly amused. "Not sure if that makes me feel any better."

"I only have one. It didn't suck that bad, but then everyone's different." His shoulders lifted. "I don't want to lie to you."

With a nod, I looked at the grayish-white door, my chest still burning. Guess I could appreciate the honesty.

Suck or no suck, I wasn't going back to the dorm without the ink I'd spent days thinking about. I breathed in once, and then again before steadying my shaking hands against my jeans.

Jake strolled forward, casting a sidelong grin at me, then gave the door a substantial yank. "After you."

Thirty minutes later, I sat in a stiff chair, admiring the heavily festooned walls as a guy named Alex tattooed my left wrist. At first it felt like a blowtorch against my skin, but after ten minutes my arm went numb, and now all I felt was warmth, like I was sitting too close to a fire.

Alex was short and had equally short hair. Not a chatty guy, but I was okay with that. If he didn't talk, maybe he'd finish faster.

"You doing okay over there?" Jake said, and I could hear the amusement threaded into the question.

"Uh…huh." I glanced over, planning to send him a scowl,

but his cheeky grin kept my witty retort locked inside. My lips pressed together while my pulse sped up. Maybe I should've picked a first done-it that wasn't so…embarrassing. If I didn't make an ass of myself in the coffee shop, I was certainly doing it now.

"What did she have a tattoo of?"

"A flower."

He frowned. "Don't tell me she got it on her ankle."

"What's wrong with ankle tattoos?"

"Nothing really. I didn't think my sister was *that* clichéd."

"She was probably trying to hide it from your parents. And in that case, her ankle is the perfect place. Seems like she was being smart, not clichéd." I lifted my brows, hoping my expression said *I'm right and you know it.*

Jake smirked, leaning forward to rest his elbows on his knees. "Yeah, maybe."

"It was pretty, though," I said. "And blue. That's unique."

"Don't get many requests for blue flowers," Alex said, his words lazy and his voice calm.

"See." I smiled at Jake, though the longer I sat, the harder it was to do anything but grind my teeth and pretend I was somewhere else. "She gets points for being original."

His dark eyes assessed me slowly, and his beautiful frown returned. I breathed in the scent of something orange and woodsy and aimed to steady my pulse.

Jake rubbed one hand across his jaw, breaking eye contact. "A five-petal flower with a yellow center? Darker blue on the outside, lighter blue on the inside?"

"What, now you remember the photograph from her page?"

"No, I… It's just a guess."

I narrowed my gaze, but Jake was staring at something—anything—that wasn't me.

One hell of a guess.

Maybe Emily drew flowers like this all the time, or maybe she had a bedspread with blue flowers that was her all-time favorite. Maybe it was her preferred flower. Whatever it was, that wasn't a guess, and Jake clearly didn't want to talk about it.

"So." I cleared my throat, then winced as Alex dug into a sensitive spot. "You can just take the picture and leave. I mean, you don't have to stay through the whole thing if you don't want to."

"Don't you want a picture of the finished tattoo?" he said, eyeing his shoes.

"I only need one picture. You're the photographer. You decide what kind of shot you want."

He nodded an agreement and finally looked at me with a twisted smile that was phony and obviously forced. But he didn't pull out his camera and hightail it out of there like I expected. Instead, he sat silently with his elbows still on his knees.

Time passed slowly, and I'd spent so long staring at a framed Marilyn Monroe photo that I could draw it from memory—if I had any talent for drawing. But I could either study Marilyn or study Jake, and I was self-conscious enough already.

"All done," Alex said in a dry monotone. He wasn't as happy about this as I was.

Thank you, thank you, thank you. I lifted my arm, wiggling my fingers around in hopes that the numbness would fade. "It's…" I inspected the deep purple and black ink that I chose for the largest portion of the tattoo: the old-school pocket watch displaying the time as 10:24. The date of my heart transplant. The date that Emily died. Running artfully across the center of the two-inch tattoo was a thin red line—the sharp peaks and valleys of a heart rhythm. My skin burned and tingled, but the end result was stunning.

I looked up, grinning like an idiot, and Jake's attention was focused on the back of his camera. I hadn't seen him pull it out of the bag.

"What's the verdict?" he asked, raising his gaze to meet mine. "How much did it suck?"

"A lot." I laughed, light-headed and giddy. "But it was worth it." My endorphins would eventually fade and my wrist would feel like a terrible sunburn, but right now I felt like I'd done something right. I was going to bask in that warm and fuzzy feeling for as long as I could.

With a small smile, Jake lowered the camera into the bag. "Good."

Alex cleaned off my wrist and wrapped it up. When he was done, I inspected the tattoo again, then looked up at Jake. "You got the shot?"

"Yep."

"Can I see it?"

He shook his head and stood, pulling the camera bag over his shoulder. "I'll send it to you. Don't worry."

"Tease." I stood, too, ready to say thanks, pay, and get out of the tiny, overly decorated room that smelled like a candle gone wrong.

Half a grin showcased his charming dimples. "I think someone once said something about patience and virtues."

"I think you made that up. I've heard no such thing."

"You're probably right." Jake stuck his left hand into his pocket and took a slow step toward the exit. "Pick up some unscented lotion on your way home. Some Tylenol, too. You'll thank me later."

And then he was gone.

Chapter Three

A little after midnight, while I was rubbing lotion on my tattoo, my Facebook messenger pinged, and Jake's profile picture popped up on my cell. With my whole body tingling, I opened the app to see what he said.

Jake: *What's your email address? I have your photo.*

I sat on my bed, tapping my toes, anticipation fueling my quick reply.

Me: *AudraMadison@gmail.com*

Leaning back against the pillows, I stared at my screen, and while I waited, the excitement I felt shifted to nervous energy. What if the image was nothing more than a boring, standard snapshot because Jake didn't actually care about how my pictures looked?

Jake: *How original. ;)*

Oh...I never pegged him for the kind of guy to use an

emoticon, especially a winky face—but wait, was he calling *me* clichéd?

Me: *It's professional and appropriate. Would it be better if my email was HeartsNLove@gmail.com?*

Jake: *Ha! No. I'm just giving you shit. I'll send the photo in a few.*

Chuckling to myself, I rolled onto my stomach before looking over to Kat's side of the dorm. She was still fast asleep, hidden between her overly plump pink duvet and a mountain of pillows. She'd always been a heavy sleeper, always the first to pass out during our childhood sleepovers.

Me: *How come it took you three weeks to reply to my first message?*

I gnawed at my lower lip for a few long, anxious minutes until he typed something back.

Jake: *I didn't want to meet you.*

Ouch.

Jake: *I think if you were me, you'd understand not wanting to meet the person who got your seventeen-year-old sister's heart after she died. Right?*

Double ouch.

Me: *Right. So why accept? Why agree to meet me? To do this.*

Jake: *I saw your name, saw your face, and changed my mind.*

Me: *You changed your mind because of my face?*

Jake: *I didn't say that. Don't let anything go to your head.*

My cheeks burned, and I was thankful he couldn't see it.

Me: *So you changed your mind? Just like that?*

Jake: *Just. Like. That.*

My pulse thrummed much too fast as I attempted to dissect his answer, but got nowhere. And pressing him to explain likely wouldn't get me far, either.

Me: *Thanks again for doing this. And for sitting through my entire tattoo session.*

Jake: *No problem. I like tattoos. But I'll admit, watching someone else get one is more fun than getting one yourself.*

Me: *Because someone else's pain is enjoyable for you?*

Okay, probably not the best thing to say, but I hit enter before thinking better of it. And the longer it took for him to reply, the more I worried I'd said the wrong thing.

Jake: *It was actually a first for me, the whole watching someone else get tattooed. I wish Emily had asked me to tag along when she got hers.*

I heaved out a sigh, but before I had time to type a single word, he sent another message.

Jake: *But being there with you almost felt like being*

*there with her. It was…nice. Comforting in a way, I
guess. You know?*

An ache filled my gut, because I did know. I touched a
hand to my chest, felt the rough scar through my shirt, felt my
heart *lub-dub* below my palm.

Me: *I'm really glad you came with me.*

All he said back was "incoming," and a second later, my
email notification went off. It took only seconds to open my
laptop and download the image he'd taken inside the tattoo
shop.

It looked eerily like Emily's, and despite being in pain for
a solid two hours, I appeared to be nothing but *happy.*

Pulling the laptop closer, I brought up my newly created
Tumblr account. I uploaded the photo and finished it off with
a quote and a few hashtags.

*How can you sleep at night when the sound of the
clock is ticking away our time? #FirstTattoo #ThatHurt
#Artsy*

Get a tattoo—done.

Me: *It's perfect. Thank you.*

Jake: *No problem. What's next?*

Me: *What about this one?*

I attached the photo I'd saved from Emily's page. In it, she
sat in front of a gorgeous black piano, thin fingers stretched
over black and white keys. This was Jake's photograph, and it
was striking.

His response came fifteen minutes later.

Jake: *If you're free Thursday, meet me at the Student Rec Center at 7 p.m. Second floor. Near the purple-and-gold chair.*

· · ·

He wasn't kidding about the chair. Gold stripes shimmered next to the deep purple velvet.

I was still staring at it with a silly grin when I heard a voice.

"You're early." Jake's words made me jump. I turned in time to see his steely eyes brighten a bit. "A good start."

He was leaning against the far wall, arms crossed, straight-faced and still as a statue. My heart thumped erratically, and I rubbed my palms against my jeans as I walked toward him.

"What would late have meant? A bad start?"

He licked his lips, then twisted them to one side. "It's, well…I decided I would wait nine minutes past seven and then I would leave. People are always late. Figured you would be, too." He cocked his head. "Come on. Let's get this over with."

I stepped back, clamped my hands together in front of me, and squeezed my fingers tight. "Hey, wait. If you don't want to do this, you don't have to, you know." That was why I asked first. I thought yes meant yes. "You don't need an excuse if you don't want to take any more photos." Maybe I did freak him out after all. Or maybe he'd decided being around me reminded him too much of Emily and it wasn't *nice* like he'd previously thought.

Part of me wanted to turn around and leave before he could respond.

"It's not that." He pushed off the wall, took a few slow steps toward me. "Sorry, it's—" One hand ran through his hair. "It's a bad habit."

Either I was completely stupid or…he wasn't making any sense. "What's a bad habit?"

His eyes bounced back and forth from the ceiling to my eyes, narrowing all the while. "Sometimes I give people deadlines I know they won't keep."

I always thought that jaw-falling-open expression was bullshit, because really, who lets their jaw hang open like that for more than two seconds? "Why would you do that? To prove a point?"

Jake tipped his head, and his cheeks dimpled with a slow smile. "Guess I don't know."

"Oh…okay."

"This way." He placed a hand gingerly against my lower back, nodding down the hall.

His fingers fell away and before I had time to react, he took off walking, and I hurried to catch up. "Where are we going?"

"You didn't know there was a piano on this floor?"

I shook my head, but he wasn't looking to see anyway. "I've only been on campus for two weeks." There were a lot of things I didn't know yet. And I'd only been to the Student Recreation Center twice so far.

We rounded a corner, and Jake nodded, sticking his hands in his pockets. "There is."

I'd been too busy staring at him to notice the area we'd arrived at. Two of the walls were glass. Long couches lined the sides, and a black piano sat in the back corner. It was a weird thing for a university to have. At least in the rec center. If it were in the arts building, then sure, it might've made sense.

Jake slowed his step, but continued moving. "Students will come in here and play sometimes. Some are amazing. The rest suck."

"Like karaoke."

He looked at me, his lips twitching. "Exactly."

I did a slow turn, taking in the artwork on the walls. It was a fancy-shmancy, out-of-place living room—that probably cost way too much money.

He meandered toward the back, where the hulking instrument sat. The muscles in his jaw tightened. He looked sad—like his Facebook photo. "You're really going to do all those things on her website? Dyeing your hair, camping, graffitiing?"

He must've looked at Emily's Tumblr more since I originally showed him. Those were a lot of specifics to remember from her posts. I nodded, then averted my gaze toward the ground, taking in his dark jeans and dark boots. "Yes," I said. "All of them. But I don't know anything about the piano, so I can't replicate the photo exactly."

Jake smiled briefly, like it broke through without his consent, and it took a moment to notice and shove it away. "You only need to look like you're playing. It's just a picture, right?" he said, motioning to the piano.

I nodded and he sat on the bench, spun around, and placed his fingers on the keys. "It's easy to fake it for a photograph. I'll show you."

So, was I supposed to sit next to him? Like, right next to him? Or was I supposed to stand and observe over his shoulders?

Jake twisted his head. "It doesn't bite. I promise."

So I was supposed to sit.

I left a foot of space between us, but the bench was small and I was close enough to smell him—lemon and mint. Fresh. Light. Distracting.

"I've always wanted to play," I said, resting my fingers on the keys. "But growing up, piano lessons never made the cut."

"You can't read sheet music then?"

"Not unless it's all in English." Of course it wasn't, but I didn't remember a thing from my elementary music classes.

His real, unedited smile looked so nice on him. Full lips curved upward, pressing in on his smile lines and creasing around his eyes, which didn't look quite so dark. Could've been the lighting in the room, but I was a firm believer that eyes change colors. Okay, only a little bit.

"You taught your sister," I said.

"She had three lessons."

"But *you* can play." When he nodded, I added, "Will you play something for me?"

Jake blinked. "Like what?"

"Your choice."

"All right." He tapped on his jeans as he thought. Then slowly, he moved his hands into place and started playing.

I recognized the song after six notes. "'Twinkle, Twinkle, Little Star'?"

He grinned, continuing to play. "You said it was my choice, right?"

Sure. But I figured he would play something more... advanced. Something that would've shown off his talent—the talent I assumed he had. "I didn't say I didn't like it."

He finished the short tune, and the last note lingered in the air around us. "Emily knew how to play that song. But it was only because she'd memorized which keys to hit and when."

"Like when you memorize something for a test, but don't really know the material, because you didn't learn it?"

That earned me a laugh. "Just like that."

My chest tightened when he caught me gawking at him. "The only musical talent I have is playing 'Hot Cross Buns' on the recorder." I fiddled my fingers in the air in front of me, pretending to play.

"World's easiest song on the world's easiest instrument. I'm impressed."

My stomach fluttered. "Are you making fun of me now?

Because that wasn't part of the deal."

He returned my smile. "I wouldn't do that."

I didn't believe him.

"How do you like campus?"

He hadn't asked me any personal questions before—other than about the list of done-its. Even though this was a normal thing to ask, I wasn't expecting the shift.

"It's nice," I said. "Nice not being at home. Food on campus isn't great, but whatever."

He nodded, trailing one finger down the length of the piano. His arm brushed against mine, sending tingly waves of heat through my chest.

"Do you live on campus?" I asked, hoping I sounded casual.

"I have an apartment off campus, actually. Got it a few months ago. I lived in the dorms the first two years. They're all right, as far as campus housing goes." He tipped his head, the lines on his forehead deepening with a look I wanted to understand. "If you're interested in piano lessons...I could teach you."

Anticipation bounced around inside me at the thought of spending more time with Jake. "Are you going to let me pay you for those?"

"I told you before, I don't want your money." He pressed down on one of the keys, and a low note echoed and faded. "Besides, Emily always wanted to actually learn. If I teach you…"

I could fill in the blanks of his unfinished sentence. If he taught me to play, the part of Emily that still existed beneath my rib cage could learn to play, too. A done-it she never got to really do. But I thought back to his earlier comment: *let's get this over with.* Was being around me "nice" or not? Maybe he couldn't decide, either…

"You don't need to give me lessons," I said. "You're

already doing enough for me."

He pressed another key. "I want to."

"If you're sure."

"I'm sure."

Rubbing my sweaty palms over my jeans, I nodded. "Piano lessons sound great."

"I'll bring sheet music next time, but you can at least learn the basics now." Jake grinned at the face I made. "It's really simple. The first thing you should know is the pattern," he said, moving his fingers down the line of keys. "Three black. Then two. Then three. And so on."

"Sure." Simple enough so far.

"This direction is down the keyboard." He pressed the keys on the right and moved left, continuing to press in rapid succession. The notes grew progressively lower. "And this is up the keyboard." His left hand stretched out in front of me as he leaned closer, reaching for the other end. He punched the notes from that direction. "With me so far?" I nodded. "Okay. This is where the note middle C is."

I looked at the key. "Okay…"

"We'll get to those. But this is where the first finger position is."

Oh boy.

"Maybe we'll save the basics for next time," he said with a low laugh.

I tried to smile and gave a laugh that sounded like crackling Rice Krispies. Not so cute. "Good idea."

"How about we save this done-it for later then. You can pick out another one since I'm here and I have my camera." His right hand stretched out in front of me, playing a slow rhythm on the keys. He wasn't watching his fingers though. He was watching me, golden locks framing his face, and I wanted to take a picture of *him*.

"You want to save this one for later?" Despite my best

attempts to sound indifferent, uncertainty clouded my voice.

"That way, you won't have to fake it for the photograph."

"Okay. Why don't we…put glow sticks in a pool and go swimming? That done-it sounds ridiculously awesome."

He tipped his head and grinned. "Yeah, that Cheez-It does sound like fun."

"Stop!" I laughed, brushing hair behind my ears. "You can't keep calling it that."

"Guess you need to find a better name then, yeah?"

"Uh-huh. But anyway, what do you mean it sounds like fun? You took the photograph of Emily with the glow-stick-ified pool."

"Right, but I didn't get to go swimming. You know…my apartment complex has a pool. And I've seen glow sticks at the store down the road."

"Oh?" I said it slowly, my chest tightening, lungs working overtime to drag in enough air. Tension wound a giant knot in my gut, and I stared stupidly at him. If I thought getting a tattoo was embarrassing, the glow sticks done-it might be worse.

"Can you not swim?" he said.

I wasn't exactly proud of the sound that came out of my mouth. "I can swim."

Of course *that* made him smile.

"You didn't say anything. Thought maybe I'd hit a sore spot."

"You didn't. I can swim." Sure, it was seventy degrees out—not exactly pool-diving weather. And this meant getting in a swimsuit and jumping into a pool filled with sticks that glow—with Jake—but it was on the list.

He slid off the bench and stood. "You don't want to go swimming?"

"No, it's not that. I'm just…" *Looking for excuses.* "Maybe I don't need to be in the picture," I said, standing and awkwardly moving my legs around the bench. "Emily wasn't in the shot... Never mind. Let's do it."

He grinned. "Good. Besides, if we don't go swimming, how will we get the glow sticks out?"

Oh. Yeah.

This might be ten shades of awkward, but since he seemed genuinely interested in this—*in me?*—it couldn't be that hard.

"I'll have to stop at my dorm. To get something to swim in," I said.

"That's cool. Let's go."

I tried to act nonchalant, like I always had boys I barely knew come back to my place with me. I didn't want him to think I was like that, though—like I did this kind of thing all the time.

Get a grip, Audra.

The walk to my dorm room was spent mostly in silence, but I was okay with the quiet. It didn't feel weird like it did in the coffee shop, and from the way he looked up at the sky, I'd say he was content, too.

Outside my door, I stuck the key in the lock. *Oh man.* He was going to see all of my stuff. Kat and I kept everything clean so it wasn't like he'd see week-old food wrappers and dirty laundry everywhere. No big deal.

I held my breath as I pushed the door and stepped inside, holding it open for him.

"Thanks," he said.

"Uhhh, okay," I mumbled to myself, trying to remember where I put the one swimsuit I looked good in. "You can sit. If you want. Or whatever."

A moment later, my bed creaked and he said, "Nice comforter." Jake ran his hands over it as though it were truly something worth admiring. "Is this a breaking-the-ice tactic for when guys stop by?"

I opened and closed my mouth, then opened it again,

zeroing in on his beautiful lips twisting into a grin. "Um. What?"

"I've never seen anything like it." His tone was half matter-of-fact, half amused. "It's an interesting conversation piece."

My bedspread…as a conversation piece? No. God, no. It was from the third grade and covered in white and pink unicorns. I'd begged and pleaded for it and never once saw the need to get rid of it. Until now. It wasn't quite so cute anymore.

Spreading my arms wide, I smiled, hoping to divert his attention from my reddening cheeks. "Actually, you're the first one I've tested it out on. Looks like it works, huh?"

He laughed, pulling his hands onto his lap. "Guess so."

After searching through the top drawer and then the second, I finally found my swimsuit in the third drawer. When I turned around, Jake stood in front of my short end table, holding a picture frame in his hand.

He set it down when he noticed me watching and said, "Weird."

It was a photo of Mom, Dad, and me. I was twelve and had been in one of those awful hair stages—pigtails and super-short bangs. So maybe he was commenting on my hair. Or maybe it was the bright mint-green shirt I wore.

"No brothers or sisters?" he asked, sticking his hands into his pockets.

"Nope. Only child." Or as Mom liked to say, *her only sweet baby girl.*

Jake scratched his neck, then proceeded to thrust his hand back in his pocket.

I shoved my suit into my purse and sent a quick text to Kat.

Me: *Kind of hanging out with Jake. Getting in his car.*

Going to his place. If you don't hear from me soon, send a search party.

I sent one more text with his address. Just in case.
I looked up. "So, glow sticks?"
"Glow sticks."

Chapter Four

Jake drove an old, beat-up truck, and honestly, he looked good sitting in it. A giant hunk of metal, all rusted and neglected, but he sat comfortably inside the destruction, smelling like mint leaves and freshness.

Thirty minutes later, we were in possession of an absurd number of glow sticks and were headed back to his apartment.

Holy shit. This was really happening.

"What was Emily like?" The words came out of my mouth, and I insta-regretted them.

He met my gaze when he stopped at a red light. "She was your average little sister, I guess. Too full of energy. Annoying and overdramatic at times. But she was smart. Had lots of friends. She was…happy."

"What about your parents?"

I saw the light turn green in my peripheral. He didn't move. Two seconds passed. Then five more.

He pressed down on the gas, looking away. "There's no simple way to sum them up. It's not a story you want to hear anyway. What about your family? Must've been nice being an only child."

I shrugged, gazing through the windshield. "I don't know. Sometimes it was. But other times, I'd wished I had a sibling so my parents didn't spend all of their time and energy worrying about me."

They still would've, though, considering my heart condition, so maybe it was best that they never had another kid.

"Hey, at least they loved you enough to care." His tone was light, but I didn't quite believe the smile he gave me.

The car turned left once, and then again before slowing to a stop. I breathed in, my heart pumping fiercely, fingers twitching.

This was what I wanted. Well, not *this* per se, but the done-it list. Doing some of it with Jake might make it better.

"Let's go," he said, hopping out of the truck.

His apartment and my dorm room were like night and day. Mine was pink and white unicorns, purple photo frames, and quilts with proper names—like Mister Yellow Blanket. His was white walls and black furniture, minimal and modern, tidy but lived-in.

Photos covered some of the blank wall space. Black-and-white photographs in black-and-white frames.

"You know black isn't a color, right?" I said, giving him a half smile.

"No. White isn't a color. Black is all the colors. It's a color."

"Maybe."

He nodded, a hint of satisfaction barely there at the corner of his mouth.

"These photographs," I said, assessing them. "They're pretty incredible."

"Thanks. Most of them are from last year. From an independent study."

"Why all black and white?"

"Because I happen to like the color black."

I looked from the photo I'd been admiring—a close-up shot of a tree branch with a faded background that reminded me of cloudy milk—to a few books lying haphazardly on the coffee table. Some of the titles included *Advanced Photoshop Techniques* and *Ansel Adams: The Camera.*

Most people who took photos like he did would post them all over Instagram. I'd never seen half of these on any of his social media sites. Did he think they weren't good enough to show off? If that was the case, he was so wrong.

I did a slow circle, observing his apartment. There weren't any music or piano books lying around, but he knew how to play. "Are you taking music classes, too?"

"No, piano is just—" His lips froze in place for a moment. "Just a hobby." He turned away, meandering across the room, effectively ending the conversation. Grabbing the bag, he lifted a box of glow sticks, studying it with a mischievous grin. "I hope we bought enough of these."

Oh, there were enough. The entire pool lit up with misdirected lines of light. Blues, greens, yellows, and reds reflected off the water, jumped through the sky, and bounced around the abandoned swimming area.

Staring at the water made me giggle. "But seriously, who would think of this?"

"Emily was random like that," Jake said, staring at the pool, standing next to me. "This was from the Fourth of July three years ago. She didn't get to see any fireworks, so glow sticks were a consolation prize. But it does look pretty awesome."

It sure did. "But what if we get caught?" This was the third time I'd asked since seeing the CLOSED, DO NOT ENTER sign on the fence. Even though the person in charge of locking up the pool at night clearly didn't do a good job, the rules about it being closed after dark were posted in multiple places.

He grinned momentarily. "We're already here, and we've already tossed dozens of glow sticks into the pool. Too late for second-guessing now."

With that, he lifted his T-shirt over his head and threw it on the ground behind us. I tried not to stare at his broad chest or those ab muscles working as he kicked his sandals off, which went *flump* against the pavement.

He glanced at me before diving into the pool, arms outstretched above his head. Cold water sprayed my skin, and he disappeared beneath the pale blue surface.

A few seconds later I still stood at the edge, staring down. Despite the chilly air, my nerve endings were on fire.

Jake popped up on the other side of the pool, shook his head, and wiped his eyes with the back of his palm. "What are you doing still standing there? With your clothes on?"

The fire intensified, making a beeline for my cheeks, and hopefully he was far enough away to miss it. "Um. I didn't know I was supposed to be ready."

"You weren't ready?" He laughed. "What were you waiting for, a bright neon sign that said JUMP?"

"No. I—I don't know."

He swam over to the edge, then gripped it and pulled his body partially out of the water. I got a clear view of his shoulders and the tanned skin covering taut muscles and couldn't look away. My heart thumped so hard, I broke out in a sweat.

Jake chuckled and shook his head. His gaze dropped to my legs and his chest rose with a slow inhale before looking back up. "What are you waiting for now?" His voice was lower this time, and I was almost positive he was smirking at me.

"I…just need to…uh." I backed up, gently kicked my flip-flops onto the pavement, and wiggled out of my jeans. Even though this swimsuit fit perfectly, and the royal-blue material shimmered beautifully against the light, it didn't cover the scar running between my breasts. I'd worn it ten times over the summer, and I'd never been worried about people staring or wondering. But now my fingers hesitated on the bottom of my tank top.

Jake called out, "What are you doing?"

Oh, just stalling. I forced the shirt over my head and tossed it next to my jeans before turning around and heading toward the stairs. "Getting in. What does it look like?"

He shook his head. "You can't use the steps. Dive in."

"What? No way. I'm not diving."

"Come on. Dive in."

"No." I eyed the steps. "The list didn't say anything about diving. So I'm not diving."

"Emily would call you a baby for not doing it."

"She would, or you would?"

He pushed himself off the wall, swimming backward through the water. "She would. I'm not that mean."

I laughed. "*Sure* you're not. I bet she learned it from you."

"That's a secret I'm holding on to."

Jake disappeared beneath the trip-inducing colored water, and I used that as my opportunity to dive. If I looked like an idiot—and I would—I didn't want him to see. The water glided over my body all at once, and the sensation of weightlessness hit me immediately. The entire world fell away and it was only me, the silence, and the nothingness.

I resurfaced, blinking the water out of my eyes, searching for Jake.

"You cheater."

A squeaking noise escaped my lips and I jumped, spinning around. "What?"

"You didn't dive, did you?" He swam closer until he was

only a couple feet away.

"Yes, I did. I dived in while you weren't looking."

"How am I supposed to believe you?" he asked, tipping his head.

I skimmed the top of the water with both hands. "You'll just have to trust me."

With a laugh, Jake shook his head. "That's ridiculous."

"Nuh-uh." I shook my head. "You didn't see me, so you'll never know. *Sooo*…you can either believe me or not. The way I see it, you might as well trust me."

Eerie silence, combined with the cool night air and even cooler water, made my skin prickle. The ice in my veins was just as penetrating as the fire previously coursing through them.

The multicolored lights at the bottom of the pool highlighted his face in a somber orange color, emphasizing the hard line of his lips and the flatness in his eyes. "That's not how trust works."

"That's how it works for me." My voice sounded far away, like I was still underwater. "I'd rather give someone the benefit of the doubt."

"You must not get screwed over a lot."

Before I could respond, he vanished beneath the water's surface. He stayed there long enough for my heart to start racing. I could hold my breath for ten seconds, maybe a little more—but it had been at least thirty.

Jake popped back up at the far end of the pool, where the water was only a few feet deep. I tried to assess his face, but from so far away, all I saw were faded outlines. I considered his statement but didn't like the way it sat in the back of my mind, like a drafty window I couldn't quite fix.

He climbed out of the pool and moseyed to the other end. I probably shouldn't have stared as intently as I did, but oh boy, he was nice to look at. Effortlessly in shape, lean and toned—but there was something off about his stride.

He walked like the weight on his shoulders was too much to carry.

Sad.

I knew what that looked like. I'd seen my parents do it many times—all those days when they thought I would die, *knew* I would die, unless a miracle happened.

And then that miracle did happen.

You're so lucky. That's what they said. My parents and the doctors, the nurses and my friends, and every stranger who ever heard my story. For weeks after my surgery, that's all I thought about. I'd woken up with a brand-new heart. I'd get to go to prom and graduate from high school instead of going in the ground and having a tree planted in my name.

I *was* lucky. So incredibly lucky. To be alive and breathing, to be given a second chance to live life any way I wanted. But looking at Jake, understanding his pain…that wasn't lucky.

His sister was dead and here I was, hanging out with him, using her heart to remind him of her absence.

He must hate me.

"What are you doing?" I asked when Jake had made a full circle around the pool deck, staring at it like a specimen under a microscope.

He headed for the gated fence, and my heart thumped once as if to say *he's leaving you all alone!* But then he said, "I'm going to get my camera from the truck." He shoved his feet into his sandals. "I'll be back."

If I got caught out here, people would assume I was on something—some crazy college girl doing crazy drugs—and then they'd throw me in jail when I tried to explain that no, I was *not* high, I just thought glow sticks in a pool would be awesome.

But this was actually cool—I mean, *so* cool. Emily had been onto something. I decided to float in my personal sea of colors until someone kicked me out. Or tossed me in jail.

I stared up at the endless night sky, and with my ears submerged beneath the water, imagined I was floating in space. After a few minutes of drifting, I swam to the steps, leaned against the railing, and waited, the waterline dipping right below my chest.

Right as I began wondering if Jake had ditched me, I spotted him to my left, gigantic oversize lens in tow.

"That thing is huge," I said.

He lifted it a few inches, adjusting something. "I could make a bad joke out of that, you know."

"Ha. Ha." But my cheeks warmed and I looked away to hide it.

He walked around the deck, lifting and lowering his camera while I watched the muscles in his back flex. And when the light hit them just right, I could see a few faint scars—long lines of lighter skin. A painful childhood bike accident, maybe? A fall from a tree house?

But I couldn't ask something like that, so I kept my mouth shut and watched.

"What are you planning to do with your photography degree?" I asked after the silence began clawing at my brain.

He paused, shrugged one shoulder, and said, "Take photographs."

I pressed my lips together because I couldn't decide if he was being facetious.

He found a seat on the edge of the steps, letting his feet dangle into the water. "It doesn't matter as long as I get to use this." He lifted the camera. "Maybe I'll become a millionaire. Maybe I'll be dead broke the rest of my life and have to live in a cardboard box."

"What will you do when it rains?"

He reached out a hand and moved a piece of wet hair away from my cheek, his warm fingers lingering a heartbeat longer than necessary, then he smiled. "Get soggy, I guess."

My breath caught, and my pulse quickened. I looked away. "Maybe invest in a lot of plastic. It'd be like a raincoat... for your house."

"Look at you, all full of ideas."

"Yeah, yeah." I waved my fingers, sending water droplets flying through the air. "You can thank me later when your cardboard home is safe from the rain."

"Maybe I'll cook you dinner in my rain-free house."

"To be honest, I might pass on that."

He picked up his camera again, still wearing a half grin.

My heart thumped in my ears when he aimed it at me. "Can I be honest? I'm not really a fan of pictures. Not of me, anyway. So this is...a lot harder than I thought it'd be."

"What girl isn't interested in photos of herself?"

The large round lens still pointed directly at my face, but since he never buried his head behind the camera, I couldn't tell when he was actually taking a picture.

"This one," I said, pointing at myself for emphasis. "This girl is not a selfie fan." My face always looked too round, too pale.

Jake's gaze trailed down toward my chest, but his lips pressed together in a way that made me think his focus wasn't on my scar. "You may as well be. You're beautiful."

My cheeks warmed. Something fluttered in my stomach. *He's just a guy. Just an exceptionally attractive guy. Who's also my heart donor's brother.*

I failed to hide my stupid grin. "Thank you, but I'm still not a selfie girl."

"I'll make sure the shot I send you is 'artistic.'" He chuckled softly and set the camera down behind him. With his arms stretched, I spotted the tattoo on his left side, above his ribs. It was dark ink, and the glow sticks only provided so much light, but it was definitely a bird. There were no other details I could make out, and when he turned back, the entire thing faded from view. "So, what're you majoring in?" he asked.

I resisted a snort. "Currently undecided." How the hell was I supposed to know what I wanted to do for the next fifty-plus years?

When I was a sixteen-year-old in heart failure, college was the furthest thing from my mind. I didn't know how long I'd live, and I knew if I made it through high school, there was no way I was going to spend my final month or year— or whatever—in a stuffy classroom. So I never gave much thought to my life's vocation.

"Undecided isn't that uncommon," he said, swishing his feet through the water.

"It feels uncommon."

Jake looked up at the dark sky and tipped his head to the left. "I know what you mean."

I stared at the side of his face, at the straight line of his nose, and when he looked at me, I didn't look away. He leaned closer until his mouth was inches from mine, his lips curving upward. His gaze lowered, and my heart rattled within its cage at the desire overtaking his features.

Or I could've been making that up in my head.

"Maybe we can be cardboard house neighbors. I'll share my plastic with you," I said.

His gaze slowly slid upward, his smile spreading wider. "Sounds like a pretty good plan to me."

Chapter Five

After the night with the glow sticks, Jake didn't talk to me for an entire week. I'd meant to get his number but didn't, so I relied on Facebook, which wasn't working because he'd been a ghost. I thought we had fun, that it ended well.

But I could have been delusional, drunk on the swirling lights—who knew?

My lungs tightened thinking about Jake. Because maybe if I were him, I'd have hated me too.

Emily is dead.

But I wanted and needed these photographs, so I needed Jake.

I rolled over on my bed—where I'd been lying for twenty minutes—and stared at the English textbook I'd left propped open. Homework. That's what I needed to be doing. I was in the middle of reading a short story about a woman who had ten cats that kept slowly disappearing. Super creepy.

With a groan, I shoved the book out of the way and laid my head on the comforter again. Textbooks were boring—except this *one* I'd read once. It had a chapter in it about the heartbeat hypothesis. Anything about hearts caught my attention. The theory basically stated that every living creature had a finite number of heartbeats.

If that was true, then my limit was up long ago. I drew the short straw in life, pulled a low number, and that number—whatever it was—came at age sixteen and it should've been the end to Audra Madison.

But instead, I took someone else's heartbeats, someone else's time. *Emily's* done-its. *Her* could'ves, should'ves, and would'ves.

I lifted myself from my horizontal position and grabbed my phone.

Me: *Hey. When are you free next?*

I sent Jake the Facebook message without thinking twice, but he wasn't online, and I had no idea when he would receive it—or if he'd respond.

Patience was not a virtue I'd mastered yet.

I opened Tumblr and quickly pulled up my own page. Two posts. Fourteen to go.

He kept his promise about making the glow stick picture "artistic." I was in it, yes, but I was underwater, and all you could make out was my giant blob of dark red hair and a faint outline of my legs.

I loved the quote Emily had used, so I used it for my own image, along with her hashtags.

It's okay to be a glow stick; sometimes we need to break beforeweshine.#GlowSticksInThePool#GlowStickParty #NoFireworksForMe #MyFavoritePhotographerJake

I needed to focus on homework and figure out what happened to those cats, but my eyes kept drifting to my phone, waiting for the beep that never came.

• • •

"Audra, we're going to this party." Kat propped her hands on her hips—but her *I mean business* look only made me laugh.

"Why can't we just go get ice cream and watch movies instead? I don't really feel like talking to a bunch of strangers tonight." I sat on the bed and hit the power button on my phone, hoping for new notifications. Nothing. I clicked the phone again and laid it down.

"We're going."

"How about you go to the party, and I'll stay in with the ice cream?"

She shook her head. "No, because I want to go, and I want you to go with me. As my best friend, you're legally bound to come with me as my trusty companion."

I laughed. "How long have you been waiting to use *that* one?"

"You don't want to know. Did it work?" She grinned, wiggling her eyebrows.

"Nope."

"Fine, how about this. You should come with me because I won't have as much fun without you. We can eat our weight in ice cream tomorrow if you want."

I considered for a moment, grinning at her enthusiasm. "Okay, I'll come with you."

Kat always found a way to make me say yes to anything. When we were thirteen, she insisted I wear this bright pink lip gloss to school because it "matched my complexion perfectly." And when we were fifteen, she talked me into spending all my savings on a single red skirt, claiming I looked "stunning" in it. If she wanted me to swim in a shark tank with her, she could've convinced me.

I changed into my favorite pair of skinny jeans, a pink T-shirt, and my supersoft gray sweater. Since the frat house was five blocks away, I opted for ballet flats, and we headed out.

Kat kept a slow pace with me for a while, but once we came within three blocks of the party, we could already hear it. Low thrums of the bass music. Random shouts and laughter. I hurried beside Kat as she hopped and skipped down the sidewalk — probably singing in her head.

The noise level skyrocketed to something like hand grenades and fireworks when we arrived at the front steps. This had to be violating some sort of noise ordinance, but hey, whatever.

We crossed the threshold and within minutes, a couple of guys shoved beers into our hands. The red plastic cup kind that tasted like dirt. I didn't bother mentioning that I rarely drank beer. Alcohol was on my should-be-banned list, both because I was only eighteen, and because my doctor advised against "joining the crowd simply to fit in." She did add that one drink every now and then would be okay, since it'd been two years since the surgery and I was as healthy as could be.

People wandered through the large single-story house, moving from room to room. Some danced to the blaring music, others shot Ping-Pong balls at cups. I was never good at dancing or beer pong, so Kat and I stuck to wandering.

She kept looking left and right as we trailed through the crowd, her hair, perfectly straight tonight, swinging side to side. "Are you looking for someone specific, or another boy toy?"

Kat laughed. "I don't have boy toys."

"Uh-huh."

She glowered for all of five seconds before grinning. "I'm just trying to live up the full college experience before my nursing classes start and I'm stuck in my bed with only an anatomy and physiology textbook to keep me company."

"But you have *two whole years* of gen eds before that happens."

"And I want *all* of those two whole years to be full of

awesomeness." She wrapped her hand around my wrist. "But to answer your question, yes, I am looking for someone specific. A guy I met at the campus coffee shop. Well, two guys technically. They're right over there."

Kat whisked me to the other side of the room, though I didn't know which guys we were headed toward until they stood directly in front of us.

"This is Dillan," Kat said, nodding to a tall guy with sandy-blond hair. "And his friend, Patrick."

"Always nice to meet a fellow ginger," Patrick said, smiling at me.

I laughed awkwardly, touching the side of my hair. "Thanks. I think."

Kat turned away, leaning in toward Dillan, saying something I couldn't hear. That was when Patrick started talking to me. And once he started, I didn't think he knew *how* to stop.

I listened—guess he thought since we were both redheads that made us besties—and someone must have turned up the music, because I said, "What?" every couple of sentences. Eventually I resorted to nodding and smiling. Patrick either didn't care or didn't notice.

He was only an inch or so taller than me, which put him at maybe five foot seven, and I'd be willing to bet our weights were nearly the same. Despite being short and thin, he was actually kind of cute—if I ignored the large gap in his teeth. And he was nice—if I overlooked a few bad jokes.

"Do you want another drink?" he asked, leaning closer.

I shuffled backward and offered him my cup. I'd had nothing else to do besides empty it while Patrick rambled. "Sure."

He grabbed it and disappeared into the crowd of mostly drunk college students. I breathed in, thankful for the break. Kat and Dillan stood closer together now, her hand twisting a lock of hair. Because I couldn't resist anymore, I pulled out my phone to check my messages.

Nothing. But… *Wait.*

Jake read my message. He'd read it and not responded.

What the hell?

I'd been ignored before, but this one, it stung. To know Jake intentionally avoided talking to me—freaking hurt. Even if he was just a guy I barely knew. And yeah, we hadn't spoken since the night in the pool, but I assumed he'd been busy. If he had time to read my message, he surely had time to send a quick reply.

I shut the screen off and tried to ignore the pulsing in my temples and the twisting in my gut.

Fine. Ignore me. Whatever.

But it wasn't fine, and it wasn't whatever.

Patrick came back too soon, holding out the refilled cup.

"Thanks," I said, grabbing it from his fingers and taking a small sip. "I'm going to the bathroom. I'll be back."

Without waiting for his response, I zipped away, between a group of girls and down a hallway. There was a line for the bathroom, of course, so I leaned against a wall, waiting my turn. A girl with nearly nonexistent shorts steadily groped the guy she was with. Their make-out session was an ugly train wreck I shouldn't have watched, but I couldn't help it—I'd never seen anyone fit their whole tongue in a guy's ear.

I finally peeled my gaze away and moved on to something—anything—else. People milled about in various states of drunkenness, and I tried to keep my people-watching as covert as possible. I saw a head of hair that looked strikingly similar to Jake's. The guy was almost the same height, too. Then he turned around and I saw his face, the camera in his hands.

Holy crap.

It was Jake.

No.

Yes.

He stood off to the side, scanning the crowd for something or someone—or maybe nothing at all. Hair fell into his eyes as he looked down at his camera.

When a girl walked out of the bathroom, I eyed the open door and should've been relieved it was finally my turn, but I couldn't resist glancing back at Jake.

His figure slowly melted into the crowd, disappearing near the front door.

I spun in that direction, slinking through the throng, saying "excuse me" and "sorry" again and again. Think I stepped on some feet, too.

I was a few yards away when Jake reached the door, pushing it with his palm.

"Hey," I said, moving faster.

He didn't hear me—or chose to ignore me.

"Jake. *Jake.*"

He halted, halfway down the porch steps.

I planted myself on the top, looking down at him. "What are you doing here?"

"Thought it was an open party?" His voice stayed neutral, but the lines on his forehead deepened.

My spine went rigid. "Why didn't you message me back?"

Silence.

I dropped a few steps until I had to tilt my head back to look at his face. Tapping my fingers against my jeans, I drew in a long breath. "I messaged you." As if he didn't already know. "Uh. I haven't heard from you and…I wanted to set up another time to meet. I don't have your number so…I had to Facebook you and—" The more words I let stumble out, the more I questioned why I'd run after him in the first place.

He tipped his head slightly, his eyes assessing me. "Shit. I…" Digging into his front pocket, he removed his phone and held it out in his palm. "I was in the middle of messaging you back when someone called. I got distracted. Then my phone died and I forgot I'd never finished the message. I'm sorry. I've been distracted a lot lately." Jake's gaze drifted past me. "Busy with classes and work."

"But you're at a party. Life can't be *that* busy."

"I'm not exactly here for the party." He motioned to the camera between his hands, lips tilting into the barest of smiles. "It's not a lie. I'm *not* here for the party."

Where was the art in a party full of drunk, slobbering college students? "Okay." I bit my lower lip and twisted my hands together when his gaze fell on me again.

Jake shoved the phone back into his pocket and stepped closer, reaching his hand out. He hesitated, brows lifting fractionally. Then with a sigh, his fingers curled inward. He dropped his arm and his gaze. "Audra…I'm really sorry."

My mind was stuck on the way my name sounded coming from him in that low, rough voice. I wrapped my arms together, running my hands down them to chase away the line of goose bumps. "It's fine. I understand."

His jaw twitched. Fingers flexed and unflexed. "I've still got more pictures to take," he said, taking a step back. "If you still want a piano lesson, I'll be in the rec center at seven on Monday, okay? Meet me there."

I nodded, offering him the best smile I could manage. But as he turned to go, I whispered, "I'm the one who's sorry."

He flashed me a questioning look. "Sorry for what?"

I lowered my arms and pressed my palms together. "About Emily." *I'm sorry she's dead and I'm not, and that you want her to be standing here and not me. I'm sorry if this isn't what she would've wanted—me living the life she couldn't have.*

I'd never seen anyone stand so still and straight-faced for so long. The only movement was his chest rising and falling with increasing pace.

When he spoke, agony laced every word. "There's nothing

for you to be sorry about."

My whole body trembled, a thousand tiny needles pricked at my skin, and I couldn't keep my voice from wavering. "I think…I feel like—"

"No." He shook his head, inching toward me again. "I don't want your pity. I don't want you apologizing."

Peering across the street at a cluster of trees, I swallowed. The coils in my chest tightened like a winding rubber band until I thought I might snap in two.

Jake said my name again, lower this time, and when I looked at him, he was only inches away. "I have a lot of shit going on. None of it has anything to do with you." Two fingers brushed the edge of my cheek, and he gave me a halfhearted smile. "You just don't know me that well." My skin burned beneath his light caress.

"That's the whole point," I whispered, still shaking. "I don't know anything about you. But I want to."

"I'm not an easy guy to understand." His fingers drifted down my neck, and he took another deep inhale before he pulled his hand away.

I'm beginning to see that. I ran my own hand over the spot where he'd touched me, then rubbed the back of my neck. "Most people aren't."

"I know." His eyes grew unfocused as he lifted the camera up. "I've got to get back to work. See you Monday?"

I nodded and he stepped past me, heading for the back of the house, his shoes crunching over the dry grass.

Flattening my palms against my sides, I looked at the porch steps, wishing I didn't have to go back inside, through the crush of people. Wishing Jake weren't leaving me.

"Hey," he called from yards away, his figure merely a shadow beneath the trees. "I want to know you, too."

Chapter Six

The clock ticked to six fifty, and my muscles tightened as if World War III were about to erupt inside the dorms. I stuck my feet into my gray flats and snatched my keys off the dresser.

Remembering Jake's *rule* about being late — or whatever it was — I made a mad dash for the rec center. By the time I reached the ugly purple-and-gold chair, I was out of breath, tiny hairs sticking to my forehead. Not cute.

In the piano room, Jake sat on the black bench, his back to me, fingers hovering over the keys like he'd been playing something.

I attempted to smooth my wild hair and padded farther into the room.

"Hey there," he said softly, swinging his legs around.

"Hey yourself."

"So, you ready to learn how to read sheet music?"

"Definitely."

I sat next to him on the bench and tried to focus on his hands and not his face, on the notes and not his voice.

That lasted about thirty minutes.

I swallowed and rubbed my palms together. "Who taught you how to play?"

He removed his fingers from the keys and looked at me with stormy eyes. "Ah, I taught myself."

"Really?"

"Yeah. And I haven't played in a long time. It's…kind of weird, I guess."

"Weird that you taught yourself?"

"No, weird because I never figured I'd play again," he said in a soft voice, shrugging a shoulder weighed down with tension.

I swallowed and looked down at my twisting hands. "How come?"

"I told you. Piano is just a hobby. So, you remember where C is?" he asked, closing the door on our brief conversation.

"Um. No."

The lesson continued, and the talk stuck to keys and rhythm and notes, instead of the things that truly mattered.

When we were done for the night, I shifted off the bench and grabbed my purse from the floor.

"Any big plans for tonight?" Jake asked.

I slid the strap over my shoulder. "Oh, uh, not really. I might spend the rest of the evening watching Disney movies." I had no classes on Tuesdays, and I loved Disney, so I figured why not waste the entire night?

He stepped closer, invading my personal space—not that I minded—and dipped his head. "Sounds torturous."

"You don't like Disney? Oh man…we can't be friends."

Placing a hand on my shoulder, he tilted his head, brows raising. "All because of a few animated flicks? That seems mean."

"It's not. They are so much more than animated flicks." They were wonderful and moving and all things fabulous and happy. "All those catchy songs—"

"That's the worst part," he said, moving back, removing his warm touch. "The songs, God, those songs are—"

"They're awesome." My response was loud and shrill and it echoed off the four walls, but I laughed anyway. "That's the best part."

Jake picked his bag up off the floor. "If you say so."

"Oh, I do."

The corners of his mouth moved almost imperceptibly, like he was holding back a laugh. "How about we do lessons on Monday nights? Are you good with that?" His fingers brushed lightly against the back of my hand, but when I looked down, they fell away.

I smiled. "Absolutely."

Disney movie night was an epic failure. Three hours in, I was past the starry-eyed gaze of my seven-year-old self. These movies I'd found so incredible when I was younger were not so awesome.

They were all *lies*.

I drudged through the last movie I'd had lined up because it was my favorite. *Beauty and the Beast*, to my surprise, was still enjoyable despite my jaded Disney's-a-lie mood. But I spent half the time wondering about Jake and Emily and all the things I didn't know. Like how Jake never seemed truly interested in playing the piano but wanted to teach me anyway. How I sometimes thought he enjoyed my company, but then he'd turn around and act so formal, putting space between us. One minute it was *nice* and the next, it felt cold. The questions and unknown answers surrounding Emily's death swirled through my mind.

Whatever happened to her was the thing haunting Jake. Maybe figuring out that piece of the puzzle would help me figure out the puzzle that was Jake.

After the movie, I vowed to not watch any Disney for at least a few weeks. I felt like I had all the emotions sucked out of me and then thrown back in my face as projectile vomit.

But soon that Disney-free week had passed. And then another.

For three weeks, Jake was only available for our Monday night lessons, and we hadn't gotten any further with the done-it list. I'd brought it up a few times and he kept explaining that he had homework and photography and work occupying his time, but also kept promising we'd do one soon.

But I enjoyed our minimal time together in the rec center. Sometimes he'd make me laugh. Sometimes I'd make him laugh. And we'd talk about things that didn't matter, and a few that did, like classes and exams. But there were some days when it seemed the thought of cracking a smile was too much for him to bear, and those were the days we said nothing at all—unless it was about the piano.

And I didn't know what to think, so I tried not thinking at all.

That had to be the one thing humans continually attempted to do—not think at all. It never worked.

I flopped backward on my bed, sighing, glaring at the ceiling.

"We could go get a box of hair dye," Kat said, sticking her hand into the bag of popcorn, which made the whole room smell like burned corn. I never understood how she could eat that stuff every single day.

"Jake isn't here to take the picture."

"So what? You can color your hair, then tell him to bring that camera to your next lesson. He can get the shot then."

I rolled my head to the side, aiming my glare at her. "Does it have to be blue?"

Apparently blue was Emily's favorite color, seeing how she dyed the tips of her hair a bright electric blue. The hashtags she used included #BlueHairDontCare and #MomHatesIt. No quote accompanied that picture.

"As long as it's not red, blond, or brown, I think anything works. How about purple?" Kat offered. "Pink? Orange?"

I rolled over and looked at her. "Am I really supposed to walk around campus with purple hair?"

She chomped on the popcorn, considering. "It doesn't have to be purple *purple*. Just…a kind of purple."

I wasn't buying it. "What kind of purple is that?" Kat might've been dyeing her hair since high school, but I'd never risked it.

"Oh come on." She reached for the bottom of my jeans and pulled. "I'll show you."

Even though it terrified the crap out of me, I let her drag me to the store. I shouldn't have let her convince me no plan was a good plan.

It wasn't. Ever.

Because an hour and a half later, my hair was purple. Not *a kind of purple*, like Kat promised. It was purple, like *holy shit, did you eat too many plums* purple.

"You lied to me!" I pulled at the ends of my hair—once a stunning natural red, now a color reminiscent of Barney. "What the hell am I supposed to do with *this*?"

I whipped around, and her lips twitched—though she did take a step back.

"Purple, Kat. *Purple*."

She threw up her hands in defense. "Look at it this way… your mom would absolutely hate your hair. It's kind of perfect."

"Kind of—no. It's not *kind of* anything except for kind of awful." I twisted back toward the mirror.

"Chill out, girl. It's just hair."

Just hair, she said. Ha. Maybe Kat could pull off bottled purple—in fact, it'd probably make even more guys fall all over her—but me and my ghostly white skin could not. I wanted to break down—cascade into a fountain of snot and salt. It wouldn't have been pretty, but it might have made me feel better.

"We can fix it," Kat said, stepping closer, reaching her hand out to touch my ruined locks.

"But how?" It sounded like a whine.

"We can make it darker."

"Darker? Are you insane?"

Knock-knock.

My heart stuttered. "Oh my God," I whispered. "Someone is here. I can't let anyone see me like this." I could've colored the walls with the shades of my embarrassment. "Shh, shhh. Pretend we're not here."

Kat rolled her big eyes with a snort. "Too late for that. These walls aren't that thick. And the light's on. Pretty much a dead giveaway."

My skin tingled, and I had to resist the urge to rip my hands through my hair to let some of my anxious pressure out. I did a quick scan of our dorm room, trying to think of a solution.

Knock-knock.

Dammit.

"I know!" Kat rushed away from me and slipped inside my bathroom. When she emerged, she tossed a bath towel at me. "Wrap it around your head."

Genius. She was a genius.

Wait. No—Kat was the reason for this mess.

"I'm coming," I said, twisting the towel on the top of my head like I'd just gotten out of the shower. Better than nothing.

I swung the door open too quickly, and like so many times in life, wished I had a superpower, like being able to disappear or melt into the floor. I'd have even accepted one of those *Men in Black* memory-eraser sticks.

I could've been all, *oh hey, Jake, nope, you never saw me like this.*

Because let's face it, a pink towel on the top of my head like a wannabe hat was no sexier than purple hair.

"Hey," I choked out, trying to breathe like a normal person.

He blinked, surprised by my face or hair (or lack thereof) or maybe my extra paleness. "Hey. Sorry if I…" He cleared his throat, looked down the empty hallway. "If I'm interrupting. I thought you were expecting me."

Expecting him? "Huh?"

"You said you'd be here in an hour, and to stop by then."

"I didn't—wait…what?"

Jake's lips twisted, half amused, half uncertain. "Your message? When I asked if you were home?"

I hadn't sent any message…

Turning, I spotted Kat on the edge of her bed, her hand attempting to hide a grin. *Kat.* She'd done it *again.*

"I wanted to give you this."

I returned my attention to Jake and looked at what he held in his hands. "What is it?"

"One of the first piano books I used. It's for beginners. Thought it might help you."

I didn't know what to say, so I simply stood there.

Why did he come all the way over here to give me this? Why not just give it to me when I saw him at our next lesson? Was this his personal book? If so, why did he want me to have it? "Thank you." I hesitated, another question coming to mind. "How come I don't have your number?"

His brows narrowed and then went wide again, a hint of a smile playing on his lips. "I don't have yours."

"You never asked."

"Neither did you."

I stared at him.

"Here's a pen," Kat said, sliding next to me in the doorway. "Write it down in the book?" She sent me a beaming smile and shoved the pen in Jake's direction.

Oh my fucking God, Kat.

But it worked. Maybe that's how she got so many guys to swoon over her—or whatever the guy equivalent of swooning was.

Jake wrote his number on the first page of the book and handed the pen back to her.

"This is Kat, by the way."

She gave a short wave and another smile. "I already know who you are."

My eyes went wide. "Uh, thanks for the book," I said way faster than I meant to. "You didn't have to drop it off, though." I probably wouldn't be able to look at it much for a few days with midterms coming up.

"Sure I did. You need it more than I do."

"I'm not sure insulting my piano skills is a good way to make me play better."

"Who said it was an insult?"

I leaned against the doorframe and gave him a look. "I basically assume that if something you say could be taken as an insult, it should be."

He chuckled. "Thought we agreed I wasn't that mean."

"We agreed on nothing."

He bottled his laughter and shoved his hands deep into the pockets of his jeans. "Everyone has a right to dream, I guess."

"See? Mean. So, anyway. Thanks again. For the book, not the insult."

"Right. Sure thing." He nodded at Kat. "Nice meeting you." And then looked at me. "I'll see you later."

Jake disappeared from the doorway, and I turned to face Kat, who had her arms crossed, grinning wickedly.

"I think I might hate you right now." I shut the door behind me.

"He messaged you while you were in the shower and I figured I'd reply for you. In case you got all worried about your hair."

"You didn't even give me the chance." I would've been worried, but I would've still said yes. "And you couldn't at least give me a heads-up?"

She dropped her arms and shrugged, plopping onto the

bed again. "I meant to. And I thought an hour would be enough time! I'm sorry. Your minor freak-out distracted me."

Uh-huh.

"But now I get it," she said.

"Get what?" I pulled the towel from my head, letting the wet strands fall against my back.

"Piano Boy is hot."

"He—" I paused. "Yeah, he's hot. So what?"

"You've got a thing for Piano Boy." She said it nonchalantly, like it was a fact, not an opinion.

"No one's got a thing for anyone. And can we please, *please* stop giving everyone and everything nicknames?"

She pouted. "Nicknames make everything better."

I rolled my eyes. "Even if I did have a thing for him, Jake certainly doesn't have a thing for me."

"Have you asked him if he does?"

I blanched. "Is that supposed to be funny?"

"If you haven't asked him, then has he told you he doesn't have a thing for you?"

"No," I growled.

"So you can't say he doesn't because you don't know. Same way you can't say you hate shrimp if you've never tried it—you don't know."

"You are not seriously comparing guys and food right now, are you?"

Kat waved a hand, moved over to the Walmart bag, and pulled out another box of hair dye. "Don't you know what a metaphor is?"

"I'm not sure you do."

"Here, we can use this one on you instead of me. I'm not ready to give up my blond hair anyway." She held out the box—a deep mahogany brown.

"What? No way!" I would not introduce more torture to my hair. It might all fall out. I would *not* look good without hair.

"Trust me. This is a dark brown. It'll make your hair darker. Should take away most of the purple. My brother has a friend who's a cosmetologist."

"But you're not."

She shrugged. "I've picked up a few things. It's worth a shot."

So my choices were risk Kat chemically burning my hair off, or go to sociology tomorrow morning looking like a clown.

"But if I lose most of the purple, won't it be defeating the point of the done-it?"

Her lips puckered, and she shook her head. "I said it would take away most of the purple. Trust me, it'll still be purple enough."

"Fine," I said, feeling defeated. "Let's do it."

I put on some music to calm my brain as Kat mixed up the box of dye. Tried to steady my overworked heart. Tried not to worry about my hair.

Even if Kat was right (and maybe she was) that I had a *thing* for Jake, it didn't matter. Sure, we had a few inside jokes and I liked spending time with him, but he and I were only friends.

But we weren't normal friends, like Kat and I were. I knew all about Kat's life—her family, her horrible and awesome dating stories. I knew her past, her present, and her hopes for the future.

Jake let me see what he wanted me to see, and the rest was off-limits.

Maybe it wasn't only me. Maybe he was closed off to everyone.

Chapter Seven

By some miraculous phenomenon, the color of my hair actually looked slightly okay: a dark reddish-brown with only a hint of Barney. A color I could get used to. But still, I vowed never to do it again.

I nudged Kat, who was falling asleep in her seat. Professor Otto's voice was as interesting as a buzzing fly, so I couldn't blame her.

She blinked a few times, remembered where she was, and scowled at me.

I covered my mouth to keep from laughing. The auditorium for our psychology class was huge, but Professor Otto had impeccable vision, and he'd embarrass the hell out of anyone caught sleeping.

"There's only ten minutes left," I whispered.

"That's ten too many."

I offered her a piece of gum. Not much of a consolation, but it was all I had.

Professor Otto finally said, "That's it for today," and Kat popped out of her chair and headed down the aisle. I trailed behind her.

"Do you want to go camping with me?" I asked.

Her head snapped in my direction, and blond bangs flopped into her eyes. "Camping? Like in the woods?"

"Yeah, that's kind of what camping is."

We walked through the glass doors and out into the quad. The late-September sun beat down, warming my face even as a light breeze raised the hair on my exposed arms. I blinked a few times as my eyes adjusted to the light.

Kat made a low noise. "Ahh. I'm not exactly a bug fan…"

"Well, who is?"

She scrunched her nose and shook her head. "Why the hell do you want to go camping?"

"It's on the list."

"Ah. Right."

"But I like camping. And yeah, bugs suck. But campfires are great. S'mores and stars and nature, you know?" Aside from our spending time in my tree house as kids, Kat always vetoed outdoor activities, so asking her to come with me was a long shot.

"I want to say yes, I really do." She gave me big, regretful eyes—which had stopped working on me three years ago. "But camping and I…I don't think we'd get along. Besides, doesn't Jake need to be there to take the photo? What, are the three of us going to share a tent?" She snickered, humor replacing the regret in her eyes.

"You could invite Dillan."

"Oh, he's off my list of date-worthy guys. But really, three is enough of a crowd. You know camping in the woods with Jake alone would be epic, right?"

"No."

"Why not? Because you wouldn't want to do that with him?"

I looked up, squinting at the sky. "That's not the reason."

We crossed the courtyard, where students sat on the grass reading textbooks or writing notes. There were even a couple sleeping.

Kat studied me. "You know, girl, you're going to have to start asking for the things you want. People aren't mind readers. Especially guys."

"I ask for things."

"Like when you asked for Jake's number?"

My stomach toppled over. "I did everything else. I found him on Facebook. Asked him to meet me. Did I want his number before? Yes. But I wanted *him* to ask me. Just one thing. Just that one tiny little thing."

"I know. I know."

"You really won't go camping with me?"

She smiled—one that looked like it belonged in a commercial for gum. "When you're all alone with him in the middle of nowhere, you'll be glad I'm not there wrecking the party."

And two hours later, in the middle of biology, I found myself texting Jake.

Me: *Hey. It's me. Audra. Do you like camping?*

Forty-seven minutes later, after I was back in my dorm, I got a reply.

Jake: *Hey Audra, it's me, Jake.*

I stared at the phone, blinking a few times. "What?" I muttered, fingers poised to type back when another text came through.

Jake: *Yes, I like camping. Why, you want to do that Cheez-It?*

I laughed even though no one but the walls could hear it.

Me: *Yeah, but I can't fend off a bear. Can you?*

Jake: *Of course. But you have to do me a favor.*

Obviously, I asked him what kind of favor.

And he didn't respond before our seven o'clock lesson time. So I showed up in the piano room a full twenty minutes early and literally sat on the edge of my seat.

"Your texting skills are kind of lacking, sir," I said when he walked in. He wore a form-fitting dark green shirt that did his appearance all kinds of favors, and I averted my gaze to keep from ogling.

He raised his eyebrows. "Oh yeah? I use complete words, proper punctuation, and correct grammar."

And it was kind of a dream come true.

"In what way are my skills lacking?"

"You didn't respond to my last text." And the times between his responses were painfully long.

"I knew I'd be seeing you soon."

Touché, Piano Boy.

"All right, so what's this favor?" I asked as he sat on the bench next to me.

"I need a model."

"Like…a model you take pictures of?"

He grinned, pressing a key down with one finger. The high-pitched note rang through the open space, electrifying my nerve endings. "Don't you know what a model is?"

"I know what a model is, but you want *me* to model for you? Aren't you getting enough shots of me with the list?"

"Obviously not."

My cheeks burned, stomach flipped, and my secondhand heart sped up. "What do you need a model for? And why me?"

Jake twisted, inching closer. "I'm working on a

photography project. I don't *need* a model, but I do think your face would be a nice addition to my images."

"My face?"

His expression shifted like he was the keeper of a grand secret. "Yes."

That look and the way he made one simple word sound so warm and smooth lit a lavalike fire in my chest. "What's so special about my face?"

"I thought I told you already."

"Well…you did tell me not to let anything go to my head when you mentioned my face before."

He chuckled, tilting his head. "Yeah, because I didn't want you to think I was some shallow asshole."

"You seem awfully concerned with convincing me you're not an ass."

The laughter faded from his eyes, and his voice dropped low and gravelly. "I know I come across that way sometimes. Can't always help it, but…" Instead of finishing his sentence, he shrugged and looked away.

I licked my lips, fixing my attention on his hand resting against his thigh, so close to my own. Thoughts ran through my mind, and I wanted so badly to say something to wipe away the melancholy aura surrounding him. But my brain failed me, so we sat in silence for half a minute.

"To answer your questions," he said, pressing another key with one finger, "I want to photograph you and your face because you're beautiful." Jake turned his head, a faint smile replacing the flat line of his lips. "And yeah, that isn't doing me any favors in the 'I'm not a shallow jackass' department, but it's the truth."

I swallowed and tried to keep my grin from looking absurd. "Think I can get behind that reasoning."

"Good."

"But what do I have to do? I've never modeled in any

capacity, so you might come to regret this."

"Nah. I definitely won't." His eyes were hooded and dark as he scanned my face. "It'll be easy. But I can't tell you what you have to do. It'll ruin the moment."

"Uh-huh…"

"Come on. You want to go camping. I want you to be my model. It's a fair trade. Plus, I even have camping gear." He wiggled his brows—a little.

And I laughed. "Fine. Fine. Whatever. I'll do it, I guess."

"I have Saturday night off work," he said. "We can go camping then."

That was soon. *Too soon.* "Well…okay."

"There's a place about forty minutes from here. It's nice."

"Okay." I scratched my neck, realized I was doing it, and laced my fingers together in front of me. "We have to make s'mores. And stargaze. That's what Emily did."

He crossed his arms, still wearing the smile I wished to see more often. "I know. I was there."

I laughed, feeling sheepish and ridiculous.

"You ever been camping before?" When I nodded, he licked his lips, assessing me. "Good. Camping with noobs can be pretty rough."

"Oh, I'm no noob."

• • •

Correction: compared to Jake, I was a noob.

I'd come to this conclusion right about the time the tent collapsed in on itself—for the third time—while I tried to put it together.

"You win, stupid tent. *You win*," I muttered, falling back against the ground.

Jake didn't try to hide his laughter. "How about an A for effort?"

"That's like being the prettiest worm."

He held out one hand. "Here, I'll help you."

I placed my palm in his and stood. His fingers stayed there longer than necessary, lightly stroking the back of my hand, but when I looked up, he let go.

He crouched down and started handing me things, giving instructions. I pushed poles together and pulled on tent material, but he did most of the work. In only a few minutes, we had a full-size, non-collapsing tent.

"Awesome." I put my hands on my hips, staring at our handiwork.

Okay, mostly *his*.

I kept staring and as I did, a slow-moving thought wiggled its way into my head.

Oh.

Oh.

We were going to be sleeping in that tent. Together. This seemed so obvious, but it hadn't occurred to me before. What was I doing alone out in the woods with a guy?

I may have made a terrible miscalculation in my plans...

"Did something bite you?" Jake asked, snapping my attention to him.

"Huh?"

"You got really pale. And still. Thought maybe you were going into shock. Bit by a snake or something."

"Snakes?" To my further embarrassment, my voice wavered. "Are there poisonous snakes out here?"

"Technically, they're everywhere in Poudre Canyon—and Fort Collins in general. But don't freak out. It'll be all right."

And it was. I didn't get bitten, and when it got dark, Jake built a fire. I tried to help, but all I did was move a few logs around and hand him the matches.

As I shoved a marshmallow onto a stick, Jake stole the bag from my lap and said, "Nice hair, by the way."

I blinked at him.

"It's different, right?"

"Yeah. It's one of the done-its. Which reminds me, you have to get a shot of my hair."

"I will. The color suits you."

I blinked again, then looked away, feeling dumb. "Thanks."

A few moments went by, and I shoved my stick over the fire, twisting it slowly in my hand. Campfires were one of those weird smells—the ones that smelled awesome right then and there, but afterward? After a fire, my hair and clothes smelled like burned trash. So I always tried extra hard to enjoy the scent while it was still a good one.

"Emily told me one time that you should always compliment a girl's new hair. If you notice," he said. "She also told me that you should definitely notice, because you should be paying attention." Jake paused. Turned his head toward me. "And she was only twelve when she told me that."

"I take it you didn't notice her new hair?"

He laughed. "Yeah. The first time she did it. But she'd done it herself and…well, it looked like shit."

"Did you tell her that?"

"I told her that's why I didn't say anything." Jake picked up a stick from the ground and twirled it between his palms.

"And what did she say?"

"She said *so what*, pretend that you like it. That's what boys are supposed to do." He laughed again.

Did that mean he thought my hair looked terrible and only said "nice hair" because that's what he thought boys were supposed to do?

My heart beat irrationally. *Calm down, it's not that big of a deal.* Just hair. Right?

I sneaked a glance at him, trying to shake away my sudden anxiety.

He smiled, leaned forward, and said, "But apparently if a

girl wants to know if she looks good…she doesn't want you to lie."

I let out my breath, felt the warmth disappearing from my chest, and pulled my burned marshmallow from the stick before popping it into my mouth.

So, he did like my hair?

I was confused.

Reaching down to the marshmallow bag, I pulled out four and shoved them all onto my newly emptied stick, then held the bag out to Jake. "She got it right." I laughed awkwardly and attempted to wipe the sticky goo from my fingers.

Silence surrounded us for the next couple minutes, but then the wind rustled some tree leaves and insects started chirping, or cricking, or whatever it was they did. I scanned the rows of trees and the slopes of the faraway mountains, which in the dark formed one bulky, misshapen shadow. The rustling and chirping died down, and the campground was quiet in that special way only nature can provide. No car engines. No people or technology to disturb the ambiance. We were only miles from the noise of the city, but it felt like we were in a different universe.

"Will you tell me more about Emily?" I asked, then quickly added, "I'm sorry. We probably talk about her enough."

"No. It's all right. I can't remember the last time I really talked about her with anyone. I…miss it." His voice was quiet, but a rough quality tinged his tone.

He hadn't talked about her with anyone? What about his parents? The rest of his family?

I wanted to know, wanted to ask. And I wanted him to tell me that story about his parents he thought I wouldn't want to hear.

But I was afraid those questions would annoy him into silence, so I sat there, chewing the inside of my lip. Guess I'd add them to the list of things I couldn't say.

"She was mean."

I blinked, surprised.

"It's true." Jake laughed, brushing a chunk of hair back from his forehead. "She was a mean little brat, but I still loved her. Aside from the mean streak, she was nice, and sweet, and would offer to help a stranger if given the chance. But she'd tell you when you were wrong, and she'd thank you when no thanks were necessary." He paused, his face growing darker, voice pitching lower. "She was a good person. She deserved much better than what she ended up with."

What could I say to that?

Nothing.

"I'm sorry," I said in a whisper. "I'm so sorry. I know you said you don't want me apologizing, but I can't…I can't help it."

His eyes stayed locked on the fire, the flames flickering orange light across his face. "She would've liked you." He said it so quietly, I thought maybe I'd heard him wrong.

His words ate through my thoughts, leaving only my guilt and regret.

I fidgeted in my seat, tried not to let the crushing silence consume me.

Dozens of heartbeats later, Jake got up from his foldout camping chair. I kept my eyes on the fire to avoid tracking him with my gaze. Watching the way the flames danced in the sky, flickering in and out at the tips, was a decent distraction. Heat found my outstretched feet, wound its way up my ankles, but didn't quite reach the tip of my nose.

"Ready for some stargazing?" he asked from behind me.

I turned my head. "Huh?"

"That was part of the deal, right? Along with you being my model."

Right. I hadn't forgotten that bit.

"Come on."

I stepped through the grass after him until we got to his truck, a few yards away from the fire. Peering closer, I saw all the pillows and blankets he'd thrown in the back.

My cheeks burned even without the heat from the flames. The gesture was sweet and made my chest do a giddy leap—and I had to remind it to calm down, that Jake wasn't doing it because he wanted to make me swoon.

"Smooth thinking," I said, playing it off like I was cool, calm, and collected.

"I've got a few tricks up my sleeve." He grinned.

I hopped into the truck bed, found a seat among the sprawl of blankets and pillows, and remained glad for the dark so he couldn't see my cheeks.

"Are you into the stars at all?" he asked, finding a seat next to me.

"You mean, do I want to be an astronomer? No," I said with a laugh. "But I can appreciate them in all their multitudes or whatever."

I stared up at them, twinkling in the distance. Jake had said on our drive up here that this spot was *the best* for stargazing. Turned out, he was right.

A pitch-black sky was the perfect backdrop for the cluster of flittering white diamonds floating above us. And it reminded me of something I'd read in a textbook once, from some research I did for a report.

Stars not only differed in temperature, but also had entirely different *lifetimes.*

Kind of like people.

They died the same way people did, slowly, by losing energy. Some lived longer, some died young.

Like Emily.

Since stars had a limited amount of hydrogen—and they needed that stuff to exist—they in turn had a finite lifetime of radiance.

The way hearts had a finite number of beats.

It's funny how the universe connected like that. How two things that seemingly had nothing to do with each other both existed in the exact same way. Neither would live forever, and no one knew how long that finite amount of time would be.

Maybe that's why most kids—at least the girls—would choose doodling hearts and stars over 99 percent of everything else. Maybe our souls instinctively *knew*.

Maybe there were no coincidences, never a random luck of the draw.

Guess that was fate.

Chapter Eight

I was lying in the bed of Jake's truck with a blanket pulled up to my chin, my head relaxing on the softest pillow ever. I didn't know what time it was, and it didn't matter. My eyelids dropped closed for a moment, but I could still picture the starry sky in my head, like I hadn't closed my eyes at all.

Emily was into astrology—Jake told me after we'd watched the Big Dipper travel a few degrees across the sky.

"She had an entire shelf full of books on the stuff. Horoscopes. Birth charts. Love in the stars. Anything, you name it," he said.

I opened my eyes, focusing on the twinkling lights in the sky. "Did she believe in that stuff?"

"I don't think she read her daily horoscope and expected it to be true, but the rest? Yeah, probably. She talked about it all the time. *All* the time."

To be honest, it sounded kind of cool. I'd never given it much thought before. I mean, I knew I was a Scorpio. Knew that meant I was supposed to be determined and passionate, compulsive and obstinate. But that sounded like a lot of people.

Jake shifted and laughed softly. "Emily's passions knew no bounds."

"I'm beginning to notice that."

After a few quiet moments of stargazing, he spoke in a voice low and strained, but still gentle somehow. "I'm glad you're here."

I let my head fall to the side and looked up to find him a lot closer than I remembered. "What?"

"I'm glad her death wasn't for *nothing*," he whispered.

Shoving the blanket a few inches down, I pushed back to an almost-sitting position. "I didn't—" The words lodged in my throat, and I stared at his stormy eyes, trying to make sense of what he said.

"I'm glad you're alive. Even if she's not."

A couple seconds passed, my heart thumping all the while. Breathing hadn't been this hard before.

I started crying.

Not the silent tear-rolling-down-my-cheek cry. Nope. Full-on waterworks show, complete with stifled sobs.

Oh my God, stop crying. Why are you crying?!

"Audra, I'm—"

"I'm sorry," I sputtered, wiping at my cheeks, shaking my head. "I didn't mean to... It's not..." I sniffed. "It's just that you don't know...can't know how much...that means to me. I've spent all this time feeling like I shouldn't be here. That— why me? Why me and not her? And I wouldn't blame you for hating me—really, I—"

"Stop," he said softly, pulling my hands away from my face, holding them between his. Trying to wipe away the tears was pointless anyway. "I don't hate you. Okay?"

I nodded slowly, my squeaking noises fading.

And then Jake put his arm around me and pulled me against him.

It made me want to cry all over again, but my head found his chest like a magnet. And in the back of my mind, I knew I'd find this awkward later, but *now*...now it felt right.

He released one hand from mine to brush hair away from my damp cheek. Jake's chest smelled like campfire—the good kind still—and leaves and smoke. All the tension in my body dissolved, his touch replacing it with a comforting warmth.

A few more heartbeats passed, and neither of us said anything. I couldn't concentrate on anything other than the feel of his hand slowly stroking my hair as I leaned against him.

And the fact that I'd just burst into tears.

"I'm still surprised my mom ever wrote you back," Jake said quietly, close to my ear.

"Why? How do you know she's the one who wrote me?" The letter was only signed with *the Cavanaughs*, and I never gave much thought as to who actually penned the words.

"She's the only one who would've. My dad would've tossed your letter in the trash."

My chest tightened with his admission. *Thrown it in the trash?* "He sounds like an ass." I hadn't meant to say it—but the words fell out anyway.

Jake's response was, "Yeah, he is," and he didn't sound the slightest bit offended.

I waited, hoping he'd tell me more.

No such luck.

"Why did it surprise you?" I asked again, slowly, cautiously.

He shifted next to me, alerting all the nerve endings trailing down my arm and into my fingertips. "After Emily died, my mom was...a fucking mess." Another stretch of silence, another tingling of awareness—skin on skin, pulses fluttering close to each other, like off-sync butterflies. "Doubt she even remembers sending it."

"Oh," I said, thankful my face was smashed against his

sweatshirt, hidden from view.

"When Emily died, everything got worse." His voice was scratchier than it had been. Jagged like a broken blade. Rusted and stale.

It slammed into my chest, deep beneath my bones—guilt—and I looked up. His eyebrows were drawn inward. Lips pressed tightly together. Eyes wide and hollow, full of hurt. I couldn't pretend the pain wasn't there, and I couldn't do anything to make it disappear.

"How did she die?" If I knew, maybe then I'd truly understand his pain, and if I understood it...

"Let's talk about something else, okay?" Jake met my unwavering gaze with a haunted expression of his own.

"Why don't you want to tell me?"

"Because it doesn't matter."

"It clearly does." I paused, waiting for words that never came. "I only want to know so I can—"

"*Stop*."

"Jake," I said too quickly.

He dropped his arm and inched away from me. "I don't want to talk about it."

He climbed to his knees, then his feet, and I trailed his figure in the dark, heard the *eerrrr* of the truck bed squealing under his weight.

I squinted my eyes to see him better.

After landing on the ground with a gentle *thunk*, he spun to face me. "She's dead, Audra. Don't get me wrong, okay? I think it's nice that you want to redo her done-it list, but she's not here anymore. She won't get to do *anything* ever again. It doesn't matter how she died, because she's gone. No one can undo that. Not me. And definitely not you."

I blinked once, and he was out of sight, so I stared at the white-spotted sky, replaying the last three minutes over and over in my head.

Should I run after him, throwing out more useless apologies?

Considering I was alive thanks to Emily, I felt desperate to know what he was unwilling to tell me. The truth about what happened to her followed Jake around like an unsettling ghost. It was the reason for the aura of despair that encased him, the cause of his consistent sorrow. And I wanted to change it, take it away, and replace it with something brighter.

But I didn't know how.

A wave of dark clouds inched across the sky, further darkening the surroundings. My gaze found the tips of flames flickering in the blackness. I still couldn't see Jake from my spot in the truck bed, but I'd probably find him near the fire.

What if he wasn't there? The thought attacked my brain and sent a wave of panic through my chest.

Calm down. You're sitting in his truck, where the hell could he have gone?

Okay, he was pissed.

Maybe I was an idiot after all.

Dammit.

I should go say something.

But what? My mouth was what got us into this argument, and anything I said or did wouldn't help.

Maybe you should stop bringing up his sister — you know, the one he is obviously still grieving over.

But he said it was *nice.*

People always said girls were complicated — always sending confusing mixed signals, but in reality, I think that was *all* people.

I didn't understand Jake, and maybe I needed to accept that. But I understood he was angry, and it was absolutely my fault. He didn't owe me an explanation. He didn't owe me anything.

Shoving the blankets out of the way, I got to my feet,

scanning the surrounding area. In every direction—aside from the fire—all I saw was blackness and even darker shadows. I hopped off the bed and shuffled toward the flames, glad for the added warmth as I got closer. Jake sat in one of the two chairs, his back facing me.

"Hey," I said.

He didn't turn around, or look up, or appear to have heard me at all. He was leaning forward, elbows on knees, and his hair was all tufted up from running his hands through it.

Slowly, I moved to the other seat and sat, trying not to stare. But when I finally looked over, I saw the highlighted half of his face, and a glistening streak that looked a lot like a tear.

Jake was crying. Or he had been.

It did something funny to my heartstrings, knowing Jake hurt that much.

I'd never lost anyone close to me. I could only pretend to imagine how losing someone like a sister would hurt. And I could only imagine having a sister in the first place.

Jake glanced my way. "We need to put more wood on the fire to keep it going."

I frowned.

He stood and avoided eye contact as he walked around the campfire, picking up pieces of wood. I tried to read his body language—the way he walked and moved his legs. But it didn't give anything away. He appeared the same as he usually did—casual, calm, relaxed. But knowing there had been tears on his cheeks only moments before, I knew Jake was *not* the same. He was not okay.

And all I wanted to do was fix it, fix him—his pain. But I couldn't because like he said, I couldn't raise the dead, couldn't bring her back, and that was the only thing that might undo his aching.

He tossed a few logs into the fire and poked around with

a stick. Staring at the flames, he reached into his jeans pocket and pulled something out. He took the thin white stick and shoved it between his lips.

"I didn't know you smoked," I said, trying to sound indifferent.

He flicked a lighter that seemed to have appeared out of nowhere, and lit the tip of the cigarette until it burned red. "I've been trying to quit for a few months now. It's not going that well."

As he inhaled his cigarette, I rubbed my palms together and tried not to tap my foot against the ground.

"What do you want from me?" Jake asked after a few minutes of listening to nothing but the crackling flames. He'd said it softly so he didn't sound angry.

But that selection of words didn't sit well in the place between my lungs.

"I don't want anything." My voice sounded weak, strained. "I mean, the photographs, I want those."

He stared at me, not saying anything until he'd hit the last of his cigarette and tossed it into the fire. "You must want something. Everyone wants something."

I almost said that wasn't true but stopped myself, because maybe it was. Aside from the photographs and the piano lessons, I wanted Jake to like me, and not in just a more-than-friends way. I didn't want him to look at me and see only the absence of his sister. I wanted him to say more things like *I'm glad you're here.*

"Seriously, what do you want?" His lips twitched, but any signs of amusement quickly faded.

I licked my lips, swallowed against the lump in my throat. *I want to help you, heal you, fix you.* "I want to know you... want to be your friend."

One of Jake's shoulders lifted in a halfhearted shrug. His hair, tinted orange from the fire, shifted across his forehead.

His lips parted, but he decided against saying whatever was on his mind and looked down at the grass.

"I'm sorry I was an asshat before," I said, standing so I could fend off the chill taking hold of my body. "You don't have to tell me anything. And I already told you, the piano lessons aren't necessary."

"I want to know you, too, like I said before at the party. And I enjoy spending time with you. That's why I offered the lessons. What I don't get"—an uneasy pause—"is why you like hanging out with me?"

So many reasons.

"I don't know what you're talking about," I said, crossing my arms. "That's a question you shouldn't have to ask. Why do you like hanging out with *me*? I'm sure we have the same reasons."

His voice dropped to merely a whisper. "I doubt our reasons are the same."

A shiver raised goose bumps across my neck, even though the heat from the fire burned my cheeks and ears. "If this is about what I said before—for pushing the issue—I really am so, *so* sorry. I shouldn't have done that. I—"

"That's not what this is about."

"Isn't it?"

He shook his head, simultaneously running a hand through his hair, pulling on the golden strands like they were burning his scalp. For a moment, I half expected him to scream. But he didn't. Instead, he relaxed his hands, dropping them to his sides, and let out a slow breath. His voice regained its calm nature when he finally spoke. "Look, I overreacted. There's just some things I don't like talking about."

I couldn't keep pushing him to talk without pushing him away. There was a fine line I needed to learn how to walk. Jake wasn't an open book, no matter how much I wanted him to be.

The two-person tent looked way bigger from the outside. Now, lying next to Jake, wrapped up in my own sleeping bag, it felt ten times too small.

A faint glow from the dying fire acted as a perfect nightlight, but without the additional warmth, one wimpy sleeping bag wasn't enough to fend off the evening chill. And even though it was well past 1:00 a.m., sleep remained out of my reach.

"Are you sleeping?" I whispered into the dark.

"No," he whispered back. "Are you?"

I stifled a laugh and rolled onto my side, sleeping bag crinkling as I did. The firelight allowed me to make out the curve of his jaw and his upturned lips in the dark.

"Can I confess something?" I said.

"Sure."

"I think maybe…I don't like camping."

Jake chuckled, letting his head fall to the side. "What's not to like?"

"For one, it's cold. A lot colder than I expected. And the ground? It's not exactly a great makeshift bed. Oh, and I keep thinking about bugs…and bears."

He sat up, unzipping his sleeping bag and shoving it down. Still chuckling, he reached his arm across me. "Here. Put this on."

I eyed the sweatshirt he pulled from the front of the tent. "Aren't you cold in your T-shirt?"

"Nope."

So I did what he said, unzipping my own bag so I could move my arms, and the material of the dark gray hoodie was soft, warm, and wonderful. "Thank you."

"No thanks necessary." His voice was soft and half a whisper.

Jake leaned back onto his pillow, and I stayed upright, pulling the sleeves of the sweatshirt over my hands, fingering the comfortable material. Glancing up through the skylight, I tried to see the stars, but clouds had rolled in, and there was nothing to see but blacks and grays.

"What's wrong?" he said. "Still thinking about bears?"

I smiled at the darkness before twisting my head. "Uh, yes."

With a gentle laugh, Jake wrapped one arm around my back, guiding me down toward him. My heart skipped around, and I sucked in a breath, holding the air in my lungs—as if that would help. But when my head lay against his firm, warm chest, I breathed out, relaxing my muscles one by one, slowly sinking into him. Forget skipping, my heart was thumping like it had something to prove.

His fingers brushed hair from my cheek and continued down my neck, igniting my skin. Suddenly, it wasn't so cold anymore. The warmth of his hand seeped through the hoodie as he slowly rubbed up and down my arm.

Maybe this meant he'd forgiven me.

Once silence consumed the small space, I was left deciphering our intertwined heartbeats. His thundered beneath my ear, and mine pulsed throughout my entire body. I squeezed my eyes shut. Breathed in slowly. Once. Twice. Five times. "Jake?"

"Hmm?"

"What's your tattoo of?"

His chest rose and fell, but his laugh was soundless. "Ah. It's a hummingbird."

I craned my neck, and in the dark, his eyes were nearly black—and only inches away. "Does it mean anything?"

"Everything means something," he murmured, a faint smile pulling on his lips.

That wasn't much of an answer, so I said nothing and

chose to lay my head back down. Either he would tell me, or he wouldn't. Think I'd learned my lesson about pushing him to talk.

We lay there for what felt like hours, but surely wasn't. I found a perfect spot against Jake's chest, with his arm wrapped around me, his hand still rubbing my arm in a slow rhythm.

"The hummingbird was Emily's spirit animal," he said, breaking the long-standing quiet. "Whatever a spirit animal is... She said something about how those birds can fly backward and that they represent joy and lightness. So, I don't know...the tattoo was my tribute to her, I guess."

"That's...adorable."

He chuckled. "I'll take that as a compliment." And then he kissed the top of my head softly. Quickly. Gently.

My body buzzed with warmth.

"I have a confession to make, too," he said.

"Okay."

Beneath my head, his chest rose with a slow inhale. "When I agreed to do this...I thought it would be really easy, you know? Taking pictures with a pretty girl." He made a sound that wasn't quite a laugh. "You're living proof of something good that came from my sister's death, and I thought *that* would be easy to deal with."

"But...it hasn't been?" I wanted to look at his face, but I didn't want him to see the way my face crumpled in confusion, so I kept my ear against his chest, listening to the *lub-dub* of his heart.

He cleared his throat. "No."

Jake didn't elaborate, but he also didn't let go of me. He didn't push me away. Physically, at least.

Questions burned on the tip of my tongue. I was the living, breathing, in-his-face *thing* that reminded him of Emily, and he didn't have to explain his pain to me.

But God, I wished he would.

Chapter Nine

A week later, I drove home to visit with my mom, and the first thing I did was show her my done-it list. Jake had finally emailed the photograph from our camping trip, and it was my favorite so far. In it, I was pulling a marshmallow off a stick, white goo dripping down my fingers, wearing a silly grin. The sun had fallen, but the sky was still a bright shade of blue with the faintest hints of pink swirling within it, giving it a fantastical feel. Like we truly were in a different universe, and not merely forty miles outside Fort Collins.

He'd also sent me a shot of my not-quite-purple hair. This one was a close-up, the back of my head the only thing in focus. The background was green and blue, but too blurred to decipher. Were those trees in the background, or were they cars? I wasn't sure what day that image was from, but it didn't matter. He could make the ordinary appear magical, and his talent was incredible. No wonder he was Emily's favorite photographer.

"Do you hate it?" I asked Mom, pulling on my hair.

"I think it looks lovely."

I laughed and sat down at the granite breakfast bar, grabbing my phone, scrolling through my Tumblr posts. After staring at the images for far too long, I sighed and set the phone down.

The camping session with Jake had left me questioning everything. Mainly: Were we *more* than friends? We had to be friends in order to be anything more, but what did that even mean—to be someone's friend?

And also—I guess because I was weird—I looked up the definition. As if knowing what Merriam-Webster said would give me a final answer. But the definition was this: one attached to another by affection or esteem. Also: one that is not hostile.

So by Merriam-Webster's definition, Jake Cavanaugh and I, Audra Madison, were *possibly* friends.

"Mom, I still don't like green beans," I said as she tried to spoon some onto my plate next to the fish she'd made for lunch. "Being at college for eight weeks hasn't changed me."

She laughed, shaking her head. "Have you been eating anything decent?"

I took my plate to the table and sat down, pulling one leg up and under the other. "Do Twizzlers count?"

She sent me a look from over her dark-framed glasses, one that used to make me cower. Now it made me laugh.

"I'm only kidding," I said. "I eat just fine. Don't worry."

"I'll see what I can do about that."

I could've been wrong, but I might've seen my mom roll her eyes for the first time in like, well—ever.

"How's Kat?" she asked after sitting next to me.

"Good. Kat being Kat. She's having fun and drinking way too much coffee. Oh, and she's considering going back to using her full name."

Mom brushed loose strands of dark hair back toward her neat bun, tipping her head with interest. "Why is she considering that?"

"I think I gave her the idea that Katarina would be an awesome superhero-esque name to wear on a nursing badge."

She laughed, waving her fork. "That girl is never going to get her parents to start calling her Katarina again."

Mom was right. It took them a whole year before they finally obliged her request.

I went on and on about how great our living together in the dorms was. It was everything I'd imagined it would be, everything we'd envisioned since we started talking about being roommates six months after the transplant. My phone beeped a minute later, and I said, "Speak of the devil. She always knows when I'm talking about her."

But it wasn't Kat who'd texted me.

Jake: *Do you want to hang out tonight?*

Jake wanted to hang out.

Since when did he start texting me saying he wanted to hang out?

"Something wrong?"

I blinked up at Mom. "Oh. No. Nothing's wrong. She wrote a confusing text message. Was trying to decipher it." I added a smile, attempting to cover up my lie. Telling Mom about Jake meant explaining something I wasn't sure I understood myself.

Me: *OK.*

I did want to spend more time with him, even if doing so meant suffering through another Jake puzzle that would never be solved.

But I *could* solve the friends/more than friends dilemma. Maybe.

My phone beeped again, vibrating against the tabletop.

Jake: *My place? I'll make pizza.*

Wait.

I couldn't do that.

"Are you sure nothing's wrong?" Mom asked, concern evident in her tone. "You look a little pale. Are you feeling sick? You have a doctor's appointment tomorrow, but maybe we should—"

"No. No. I'm fine."

You spent an entire night in the woods with the guy. You fell asleep on his chest. How is hanging out at his place any worse?

It wasn't any different—but I felt different and couldn't pinpoint exactly how. The thumping going on in my chest was unnecessary. It was just two friends hanging out, sharing pizza.

After lunch, I drove the forty-minutes back to campus and met Kat for coffee in the rec center. This place was nicer than Pete's Coffee Shop: bright orange walls, glossy flooring, and colorful artwork hanging overtop the line of round tables. But it was simply named the Coffee Place. Now *that* was clichéd.

"It's not a date," I said as we sat down at our favorite spot. Outside was always better—unless it rained. Then we'd stay inside and stare longingly out the window.

"Any guy who invites you over to watch a movie has more than platonic intentions." She said it the way a schoolteacher would. *Thanks for participating, but you're wrong.*

"He didn't say anything about a movie. He said pizza. Those aren't the same."

"Whatever, girl. They may as well be, so keep this in mind when you're there and he's trying to lay the moves on you."

I glared at her. "Maybe I'll be the one laying moves on *him.*"

Her eyes widened briefly—surprised—then she laughed. "I'd pay to see that."

She was right; I didn't have moves. "So how's Matt?" I said, changing the subject, shifting the coffee between my palms.

I only remembered the name of the guy Kat had been seeing lately because of their terrible name combo. I mean... Kat and Matt? How *freaking weird*. But she seemed to be okay with it.

"He's great," she said with a familiar grin, settling into the gray seat. "Actually. For once, I think I really like him."

I laughed. "What, you don't like the other guys you go out with?" I gave it a month until she got bored with this one.

"Well, sure, when I'm actively seeing them I do. But Matt is something else. He's fun. All the time. He's, ugh... I can't explain it."

"Sounds serious."

"I don't think I can do serious." Kat flicked her wrist, and the silver charm bracelet wrapping around her pale skin tinkled, the small stones catching the light, reflecting hints of blue. I'd given that to her for her sixteenth birthday, and she'd worn it most days since.

"Well, if he's fun and nice and not a tool bag, then when can I meet him?"

"Oh! He's having a party next weekend. You should come. It'll be perfect."

"So I can be your third wheel?" I laughed, but when it came to guys and Kat, *he* always ended up as the third wheel.

"You'll have an entire crowd of cute guys to choose from. Or you could ask Jake to come."

I stared out at the students walking through the quad, pretending I didn't hear her.

"Damn, Audra."

"Huh?"

"You'll be happier if you admit it."

"Admit what?"

I kept my eyes on a tree, waiting for Kat to speak. As I thought maybe—just once—she'd let it go, she said, "You have a crush on Piano Boy."

That's all I could think about all day—about how I had a crush on the Piano Boy. And I'd even started referring to him by that nickname in my head.

It had to stop.

Since our camping escapade, I'd tried texting him funny videos or jokes throughout the weeks, or sometimes a *hey, what's up*, but it didn't get me far. Sure, he'd respond, but it always felt one-sided.

Until today.

When Jake opened his door, I hovered a few feet away, afraid to move any farther—not sure why, exactly. A part of me didn't know what to do with myself, and I couldn't stop thinking about what Kat said. The other part said *stop it*, because it was just Jake, and it was definitely *not* a big deal to be here.

"Smells like pepperoni." I commented on the first thing I noticed other than the way his hair looked soft enough to grab and how his lips curved upward as he stared at me.

"Pizza as promised. Do you want a beer?"

"A beer?"

"Yeah." He grinned. "You've had beer before, right?"

"Of course I have."

"Are you allowed to have beer?"

"Legally? Uh, no."

"So?"

My foot went *tap-tap* on the carpet, and I blinked back up at him. "So what?"

"So do you want a beer?" He said it slowly, to be sure I understood.

My cheeks burned, my stomach flip-flopped, and my heart did things I'd rather it not. "Oh. Yeah. Okay." Maybe a beer would help the situation. "I don't want to watch a movie."

Jake halted his retreat to the kitchen and pulled his brows together—and God, *why did I say that*? "That's...fine. I don't remember offering to watch a movie, but okay."

Man, I was an idiot. "I'm good with pizza, though."

An hour later, I'd had one beer and three slices of pizza, and I sat cross-legged on his couch while he sat on the opposite end.

"What've you been doing this past week?" An awkwardness split our silence in two. It wasn't unusual, the weirdness, but asking him about his week felt lame and pitiful. I wanted to ask the questions that meant something, like what kinds of things kept him up at night, and what was keeping him from sharing the thoughts inside his head?

But I was too damn chickenshit.

He chewed some pizza before answering. "Working. Mostly."

I knew he worked a lot of hours at his job in the campus bookstore, and that, combined with classes, kept him busy. But text messages didn't take long. Or a five-minute phone call would've been nice.

"Working on my midterm assignment, too," he added, handing me another beer. "Living the dream, as they say."

When he pulled out a cigarette a moment later, I swallowed my irritation and looked for a distraction. "How many of those do you smoke a day?"

He shrugged. "A couple. Sometimes none. Depends on the day."

"I don't understand how anyone could get past the first hit." I'd tried it one time—with Kat back in eighth grade. It burned my lungs and tasted worse than dirt.

"Once you get past the shitty qualities, cigarettes are a pretty clever little drug."

I eyed the smoke he blew out, trailed the white puffs floating into the air until they dissipated. "It doesn't make sense to me. Why would you go past that first initial crap taste and keep smoking the thing?"

"Guess I thought there was something great waiting for me on the other side of all that shit."

"And was there?"

Jake bowed his head. "Not even close."

I examined his apartment again while he disappeared into the small kitchen. So dark—everything was so black on black on white, I felt like I'd lost all my ability to see colors. *And he likes it this way.*

He thought black was a color—and I still thought he was wrong.

Jake rounded the corner again. "What about whiskey?"

I blinked. "What about it?"

He laughed and sat back down on the couch, this time closer to me. "Do you like it?"

"I only drank it once." About the same time I tried that cigarette with Kat. "It tasted worse than the cigarette, and I think it made me stupid."

Jake shook his head, more laughter echoing in the room. "You probably just felt stupid."

"Isn't that the same thing?"

"I don't think so." He grinned. "We could play a game."

"A drinking game? What, like Never Have I Ever?"

"I was thinking Go Fish."

I snickered, curling my legs beneath me. "You'll never want to talk to me again if we get drunk on your cheap whiskey."

"You're wrong."

My gaze moved away from his hands, took in his eyes and dimpled cheeks. "You promise?"

He tipped his head, laughed again, and said, "Sure. I promise."

For the record, I'd warned him.

Chapter Ten

Jake's whiskey version of Go Fish totally sucked.

But after a couple shots, the game was funny, and as Kat would say, I was wasty-face. This was no good. Somewhere in the back of my head, I knew that. My doctor said a drink every once in a while was okay, and sure, I'd only had two shots of whiskey total—because I was a lightweight—but this was still far past my standard limit.

"Oh my God, is there more pizza?" I said out of nowhere, throwing the cards down. Actually, I think Jake may have been talking.

He raised a brow. "There's a little more, yeah."

"Oh! Do you have cookies?" I stood, planning to head for the kitchen, but didn't move more than a foot. "Or Twizzlers? Dear God, I would marry you right now if you had Twizzlers."

A couple moments passed, and then all I heard was the sound of his deep laughter.

"Why are you laughing at me?" I turned around and stormed toward him, like I was about to beat him up. "You're laughing at me. See, I told you this was a stupid, stupid idea."

Laughing and shaking his head, Jake stood. "Yes, I'm laughing at you. But bad idea? No way."

I laughed—it was contagious. "Whatever. I want pizza. I'm over this stupid game." I made a beeline for the kitchen, and he said something while I stuck my head in the fridge, but I'd stopped listening. The game *was* stupid. He had to know that. "Hey, so…" My hunger forgotten, I shut the fridge door and turned around. "Is this what you do when you're alone? Hang out and get drunk and eat pizza?"

Jake leaned forward on the couch, setting his elbows on his knees. "Sometimes."

I took a step farther into the room. It felt smaller now. "Alone? That sounds dumb. *Super* stupid. Why would you hang out alone when you have me?"

And oh God, I really said that. I laughed so I could focus on something else.

When you have me.

Oh fuck.

But I swore I heard him say, "Good question."

About an hour passed and no matter what I did, I couldn't keep my mouth shut. Also, everything tingled and buzzed from the alcohol burning through my blood—and I was okay with it.

"Can we do something fun, puuh—lease?" I said. "Like, oh! Can we go get Twizzlers?"

He laughed. "Uh. If you really want."

"No. How about skinny-dipping?"

Jake stood and walked toward me. "You want to go skinny-dipping?"

I looked at the ceiling. "No."

When he didn't immediately respond, my heart beat a faster, unpleasant rhythm. *Oh man, he totally thinks I want to get naked with him.*

Wait. Did I?

No. Well, maybe.

I glanced down and saw his smirk—the one he was trying to hide from two feet away.

He's just a guy. You're just a little drunk.

"If you're looking for an excuse to take your clothes off—"

"No!"

Jake pressed his lips firmly together, but if his eyes crinkling were any indication, he was trying hard not to laugh.

"Sometimes I think…" My words were barely audible. "I think I might like it if you kissed me."

No matter what, I couldn't take those words back. They were out there in the world, and it might've been a mistake, but fuck, I hoped not.

We stared at each other silently, and I tried to understand what he was thinking.

I'd *almost* asked him for what I wanted. And if I'd been brave enough, I would've just kissed him.

"I'm not going to kiss you," he said. "Don't—" Head dipped lower. Deep inhale. "Don't get me wrong."

My face fell, my eyes found the ground, and it was all I could do to swallow the giant lump in my throat.

"Hey." He reached for my chin, gently tilting it up so our eyes met again. "I do want to kiss you, Audra. But if I do, it may become a habit…and I can't seem to get rid of habits."

I inhaled the familiar smell of him—lemon mingled with mint—and my blood warmed. He half smiled at me until I felt my lips pull upward despite my disappointment. He wasn't going to kiss me, but he *wanted to.*

"You still haven't held up your end of the bargain," he said.

"What?"

"You were supposed to be my model."

Not now. Was he crazy? "But…that doesn't sound like

fun."

"We had a deal." He tipped his head and edged closer to me on the couch, his thigh pressing against mine.

I fought through the fog in my brain. "I can't be your model. Come on. There's no way."

"How about this. I've got a better deal." He leaned in until the faint hint of whiskey reached my nose, his grin back in place.

"I don't know. I may have gotten myself in over my head with the last one."

Jake laughed. "I think you'll like this. Listen."

I motioned with my hands for him to continue, unconvinced I would like any of it.

"I have an idea. You can fulfill your modeling duties. Then that Cheez-It with the pie in the face you have to replicate? Well, I'll let you obliterate *my* face with a pie."

We stared at each other like we were deciding whether or not to agree to a cease-fire.

"But see, smashing a pie in your face sounds kind of fun and all, but I don't think it will suffice as a reward," I said, my gaze locked onto his full lips.

"Trust me. It'll be a cakewalk. And besides, you technically already owe me. The pie-smashing is simply a bonus."

I scanned the color wheel in his eyes and considered his offer, considered whether trusting him would end in the most embarrassing night of my life.

Okay, maybe that was a *little* dramatic.

"Fine. It's a deal."

He grabbed my outstretched hand and leaned forward, placing a featherlight kiss on my forehead. "Deal." His fingers were warm and rough around my cold ones, but his lips were soft, jolting me with their energy, and it made me feel more alive—even if only for that moment. But then his fingers and lips were gone, and I remembered to smile. "All right. Let's do this."

The grass was a lot colder than I thought it'd be — and prickly.

"I think I'm getting wet," I said, shoving a blade of greenish-brown grass away from my cheek.

Jake laughed — a low, guttural sound that sent a tickle down deep in my chest. "You'll be fine."

But it was weird, our being outside a few hundred yards behind his apartment building. Me on the ground, sprawled out like I'd decided to nap with the bugs and dirt. Him with his camera, standing nearby, laughing at my complaints.

Weird.

"Shut your eyes. Lie however you want. Just keep your eyes closed the whole time, okay?"

I did as he ordered. "Alrighty. You're going to take pictures of me lying here? Isn't that going to look odd? I'll look…" *Dead.*

"Wait."

My eyes popped open — against the rules. Jake pulled his wallet out of his back pocket and opened it up and pulled something out.

"Here," he said, bringing his hand to my face. A pale blue flash of color caught my attention before I saw what it was: a silk flower the size of a quarter. Bold and delicate, fake and stunning.

Jake tucked it behind my ear as I stared at his face, his eyes focusing on where his fingers moved.

"Oh wow," I whispered. "You carry around a flower in your wallet? That's so…"

Adorable.

He grinned, and maybe it was the alcohol, but I swore I saw him blushing in the dark. But that couldn't be right, because the thought of me making *him* blush seemed ludicrous. "It was from Emily," he said. "A gift on my twelfth birthday. Which, by the way, is a terrible birthday gift when you're twelve."

The back of my skull hurt from laughing too hard all night. "Have you always carried it around, then? It didn't get thrown away when she wasn't looking?"

"Don't move," he said when I lifted my head. "Close your eyes again, okay?"

I bit off my response and shut my eyes. "Why do my eyes need to be shut?"

"Just go with it."

"But you didn't answer my—"

"Calm down. You can ask me questions later."

I held my breath for a moment, fought against the urge to open my eyes, peer up at him, and see the look on his face.

"Tell me a story," he said, his voice soft. It reminded me of library story time.

But I totally dug it.

"I caught a frog today and decided to let it go instead of eat it."

The sound of Jake's laughter echoed louder because I couldn't see him. "Not the kind of story I was looking for. But uh, thanks for the best-worst story ever told."

"Well, what kind of story do you want?"

"Tell me a story about when you were happy. Anything. Any day or event you want. Describe it to me."

I stayed quiet as I thought, breathing in the cool night air—still trying to avoid being pricked by blades of grass.

"My birthday," I finally said. "I was, I don't know, maybe nine, maybe younger. But I remember wearing my purple Care Bears shirt—oh man, it was my *favorite*—and it was a super sunny day, and I was *so* excited it was my birthday. You know, my day." Birthdays were always so much bigger when I was younger. "And my dad was cutting the grass on his riding mower. He let me sit on his lap the entire time—even let me drive for a few seconds here and there."

"Care Bears, eh?"

"They were the best thing in the entire world back then."

"Says you."

"Exactly."

"Interesting story choice," he said.

"I think it's because this grass is itching my face." I squirmed, trying to flatten the blades down with my head.

"I was hoping for something juicier, to be honest."

"Uh-huh. Nice try. Can I get up now? Or is it still story time?"

"I got what I need."

With the flower securely between my fingers, I stood, brushing my hair and shirt, attempting to remove all the dirt and grass. "Wait, this flower. It's...the flower Emily got a tattoo of."

"Yeah. They're called forget-me-nots. My mom used to grow them back when she used to garden. Emily was obsessed with them." He looked down at the fake flower. "You should keep it."

"What? No. I can't keep this."

Inclining his head, Jake got a familiar look on his face. "Keep the flower. You have her heart."

A wrenching pain seized my throat. "Exactly why I shouldn't keep it. It's yours. I can't take that from you."

"I'm giving it to you. That's not the same thing."

I frowned, twisted my lips, and looked away, searching for the meaning behind his offer. "All right. I'll keep it."

When I looked back, he smiled. "Good."

We headed for his apartment, and I was still pulling pieces of grass from my skin when we stepped inside. I stared at the flower after setting it down, mesmerized by the bright color and the silkiness of the fake petals.

"So where's my story?" I asked, kicking off my shoes and turning toward him.

"Who said you get a story?" He smirked.

"It's only fair, right?"

"Not a chance. Your story was about Care Bears, cutting grass, and turning nine. I don't think I have an equivalent story to give you—if I were going to give you one." Jake leaned in a little closer—and if I moved my hand a fraction of an inch, we'd be touching. "But you get to smash a pie in my face, remember? That's your reward."

"Can I exchange my reward?" I should've picked a better one—one I truly wanted, needed. Smashing a pie in his face would be all well and good, but I could've paid someone else to be the pie-smashee.

"Nope. Sorry. A deal's a deal."

I glared at him, but it only earned me a wink and a half-assed smile.

"Please?"

He shook his head, faux regret in his eyes.

Shit. "It was worth a try."

"Sure was," he said. "Want another beer?"

"No thanks." *Think I've had enough.*

He indulged in two more beers as we chatted about movies and music and Twizzlers again. I clicked on my phone display. Three in the morning.

"Do you ever sleep?" I asked, my words part slurs, part whispers.

Jake took a sip from his bottle and leaned back, sinking into the couch. "Sure. When I can get my brain to shut off."

"So, I'm pretty freaking drunk. I think. And…" I should've quit while I was ahead—but I didn't listen to the smart little voice whispering sweet nothings in my ear.

My fatal move.

"See, Kat thinks I have a crush on you. I don't. I mean, I *do* wish you'd kiss me, but crush sounds so...know what? Just forget it." I waved my hand. "It's late, I'm drunk, and I'm rambling. I shouldn't be allowed to talk." He smiled, but I was having a hard time keeping my eyes focused. "I should so go home and go to sleep."

"I'll drive you."

"You can't drive."

"I'll walk you, then."

"No, no." I waved my hands some more. "I'll sleep right here." My hand found the armrest, and my head followed. Since Jake sat on the carpet and not actually *on* the couch, there was plenty of room to stretch my feet out.

"You can sleep wherever you want," he said, getting up from the floor.

"Mm." I shut my eyes, predicting I would pass out in less than thirty seconds—a new record.

A few moments passed, and Jake's voice came from above me. "Here's a blanket. Sorry, but it's black."

I couldn't manage to open my eyes again, but I could handle a smile. "Good thing you're adorable," I mumbled.

He laughed—I think—and then said, "Good night, angel." But maybe I was already dreaming.

Chapter Eleven

I awoke on Jake's couch, his black blanket wrapped around me, and blinked through the haze of the early-morning light. My head pounded like a band had taken up residence in my head and wouldn't shut up. I swallowed, my mouth sticky and sandpaper dry, stomach churning with the remnants of last night's alcohol. My body reminded me of how drinking that much had been a bad idea.

But...what was I supposed to do now?

I'd never ended up in this situation before. I had no idea if he was still sleeping, and if so, whether I should wake him or let him sleep while I sneaked out.

A couple minutes later, I discovered those things didn't matter—considering Jake wasn't even *there*.

Great. I'd scared him out of his own apartment.

I assumed he'd be back soon. Geez, I hoped so.

At least I had some time to put my hair in order, and since Jake kept a superclean bathroom, I spent extra time in front of the mirror pinching color into my cheeks. I even did the whole "use your finger as a toothbrush" thing, but still had a mouthful of cotton—minty cotton, though.

Minutes passed and Jake hadn't come home, so I sent him a text.

Me: *Should I be expecting a ransom call later? Or maybe you're faking your death and framing me?*

No response.

My only company was an impossibly loud clock.

Tick. Tick.

I couldn't believe he owned such an annoying thing, and as I imagined throwing it out the window, there came a *click* at the door.

Jake walked inside, and I stood awkwardly in the center of his living room. He paused, as if the picture wasn't quite right.

"Morning," he said with a smile, his hair falling into his eyes as he messed with the door and the items in his hands.

I fiddled with the bottom of my T-shirt. "I feel like my brain exploded. Did that happen?"

Jake laughed. "I'll get you some Tylenol. It'll help with the brain explosion."

Probably about time to get out of here. "So, thanks for letting me crash on your couch."

"Don't mention it." He held up a bag. "I got McDonald's. Didn't know what you liked though, so I got one of…almost everything."

"Breakfast?"

"Don't tell me you're against breakfast. Unless it's a religious thing. Then I guess I could let it slide."

I laughed. "No. I love breakfast. Like, would marry it if I could, or like a fat kid loves—okay, you get it."

He handed me the bag. "Got it."

After consuming two thousand calories of McGoodness, Jake sat on the couch with me.

"I bought a pie, too," he said.

My head whipped around. "Oh! Can we do that now?"

Jake chuckled, shaking his head. "How about after I finish my coffee?"

"I guess that sounds fair," I said after a moment of debating.

A buzzing noise sounded through the air, and it took a while for me to recognize it. My phone.

Oh crap.

I scrambled to pick it up. "Mom." I cleared my throat, tried out a happier tone. "What's up?"

"Where are you?" she said. "I've been knocking on your door for five minutes."

What?

Oh no.

"What time is it?" I croaked.

"After eight, Audra. What are you doing? Are you not here?" I could tell by her voice she was growing impatient. Guess that's where I got it from.

I mashed my palm into my forehead and wished I had a moment to feel sorry for myself. "I'll be there in a few, Mom. I'm sorry. See you soon."

I hung up because she would only keep talking, asking why I wasn't at my dorm and how could I forget my appointment this morning—because it wasn't like me to flake out.

"I've gotta go," I said, popping off the couch and shuffling around, looking for my shoes. "I was supposed to meet my mom, and I completely, utterly fucking forgot."

• • •

When I saw Jake in the piano room two days later, I turned bright red—I knew it because my face was so hot, I thought it may burst at any moment.

I'd spent the past few days rethinking the night I passed out on his couch.

At least the parts I remembered clearly.

A few minutes into our lesson, I noticed a slow-forming grin Jake kept trying to hide, but every time he didn't think I was looking, it was there. This was basically the opposite of how things typically went—he usually looked sadder when he thought I wasn't looking.

So, needless to say, my reddening cheeks were only getting worse.

"All right, do I have spinach in my teeth or something?" I asked, sliding an inch away from him on the piano bench.

"Did you eat spinach today?" He made a face as if spinach were code for dirt.

"Well, no."

Grinning, Jake said, "Who's Mister Yellow?"

Oh. My. God.

The blood trickled away from my face, and my stomach lurched. "What?" I said, knowing he would never let me play dumb about this.

"You talk in your sleep. The other night..."

I resisted the urge to slam my head against the piano keys. *Oh shit.* "Mister Yellow Blanket is my blanket from when I was a kid. I, uh, named it."

He wasn't laughing, but I could see it on his face, hear it in his voice. "So kids really do name their shit? It must be a girl thing."

"Hey, that's sexist." One of my hands flew up—without my permission—and made a *stop* motion.

One side of his mouth climbed higher.

"Boys name their blankets and toys, too." I yanked my hand down. They did, didn't they?

"Nah. *I* never did."

"Maybe you're weird."

"You named your blanket, and I'm weird?"

I paused, fighting back a grin. "Uh-huh, that's what I'm going with."

He gave me a crooked smile, his hand reaching out to push hair behind my ear. "I think someone's having delusions of grandeur."

"Don't be a dick," I murmured, fixing my gaze on the sheet music, though my brain was still focused on the warmth of his fingers trailing down the side of my neck.

"You're cute when you're angry."

Sheet music forgotten, I glared at him, my cheeks blazing again. "When am I going to get to smash that pie in your face, huh?"

He lowered his hand. "When you stop calling me names."

That might never happen.

When our lesson was over, we headed out of the piano room, and I spotted Jake's camera bag slung over his shoulder, along with his messenger bag.

"Taking pictures today?" I asked, and when he nodded I said, "Isn't it going to be dark in like thirty minutes?"

"Night photography is a thing."

I frowned, feeling stupid. "What are you taking pictures of?"

We walked down the steps of the rec center, toward the front doors. Passing the gym, which had glass walls, I peered in at the students running on the treadmill, lifting weights, and the few who looked as if they didn't know what a weight was.

He moved to the right to give a group of students enough space to walk past us. Our shoulders bumped, and even after the oncoming students cleared, Jake stayed within inches of me. The back of his hand brushed against mine—it might've been an accident, but I chose to believe it was on purpose. "Haven't decided. The mountains maybe," he said. "I finished shooting for my midterm assignment, so I'm starting on the final."

A thought shocked my blood with a cool rush of panic. "Those photos you took of me… Are other people going to see them?"

Turning his head to stare at me, he lifted one brow, only increasing my feeling of stupidity. "What good would the photos be if no one saw them?"

Right. "But I haven't even seen them." I didn't get to approve. Maybe I looked stupid, or weird, or not so hot. "*Do* I get to see them ever?"

Jake shrugged, looking away from me. "It's not like I'm keeping them from you. It's not a big secret."

I gripped my bag tighter and smashed my lips to keep from pressing the issue because his body screamed *subject closed.*

Finally out in the night air, Jake slowed his step and nodded out in the distance. "I'm parked over there. You want a ride back to the dorms?"

I breathed slowly, trying to capture the thoughts swimming in my head, trying to decide if they should be heard. Because all the things I wanted from Jake were things I shouldn't want. Things he didn't want to give me.

"Yeah," I said. "That'd be great."

Neither of us said a word while he drove me to the parking lot. His car idled as I sat still, my fingers twitching over my bag.

"Do you want company?" I finally asked.

He remained motionless, blinking a few times. Then he angled his head, the parking lot lamps casting a glow against one side of his face and that crooked smile. "You want to come with me?"

"If you want company."

He laughed—barely—and looked away, like he was laughing at some personal joke, and maybe he was slightly offended by it. "You're not wearing heels, are you?"

"Have you ever seen me wear heels?"

He looked down at my feet—even though they couldn't be seen in the dark truck. "Guess not. All right. You might get bored, though."

"Doubt it."

His smile grew. "If you say so."

"I don't mean to sound concerned but…where the hell are we?" I had lost track of all the turns through the woods, trees, and prickly bushes.

We'd only gone a few miles outside of campus, but I was certain I'd starve to death if he abandoned me there.

"Don't worry. I come here all the time."

"Sounds like some famous last words."

Jake laughed. "Seriously. I do come here all the time. I could do this blindfolded."

"No one could do this blindfolded."

The moon provided little in the way of light, so I could only see a few feet in front of me. Since Jake was wearing black—*surprise*—I watched his hair as a guide for where to go.

He hopped down a hill that looked intimidating in the dark, but he made it to the bottom like he had military-grade night vision.

"Uh." I hesitated. "I can't afford to break a leg."

He made a snorting sound, and I could picture him grinning. "You won't break a leg." Within moments he stood in front of me. "Here."

Now close enough to see his outstretched hand, I slowly wrapped my fingers around his. We stumbled down the hill— thanks to me—as I squeezed his hand too tightly. At the bottom, my upper body collided into his.

He ran both hands up my arms, steadying me. "Almost there," he whispered near my ear. "Just up this hill."

Up the hill?

Jake gently squeezed my shoulders and pulled his hands back. I balled my fingers together and followed him, trying to steady my breathing.

After my physical therapy ended a year and a half ago, I only did minor exercises. Mostly yoga and walking to keep my body and health intact. Exercising to lose weight or gain muscles had never been a concern. Maybe it was time I paid more visits to the free gym facilities.

But the view—oh, this view. It was so worth all the scratches across my arms from the wild tree branches.

I'd thought our camping night was beautiful. But this was better. *Way* better.

The moon glowed orange, huge overhead, turning the clouds a deep purple. And from where we stood, I could see the silhouette of the quiet mountains in the distance. Giant trees missing half their leaves surrounded us. The other half of the dying leaves lay beneath our feet, crackling as we walked over them.

"Whoa," I murmured, taking it all in.

Jake already had his camera out. He fiddled with it on his tripod.

I found a spot on the grass while he worked silently. Blades between my fingers made me think of our photo session—and then I was thinking about the ridiculous things I'd said. A warm blush crept up my neck. One that tickled and made my skin itchy.

"How'd you find this place?" I asked, running my hands along the ground.

Judging by the crease in his forehead and the taut line of his jaw, he was thinking hard about his answer. But he wasn't trying to remember.

He was deciding how much he wanted to share.

"I was looking for a beautiful place one time," he said softly, putting his head near the back of the camera and turning a knob. "And then I found this hill. Stopped looking after that."

"A beautiful place to photograph?"

His hands stopped moving. He pulled his head back, angling it toward the ground. "In a way."

"That's very vague of you."

Jake fiddled with the camera—which looked like it cost more than a mediocre car—and backed away. His laugh was a soft, vibrating sound. "You just ask weird questions." Shoes crunched over rocks and leaves as he inched closer to where I sat.

"What? Weird how?"

"How do you think I found this place?" He lowered himself beside me, gave me a grin I'd buy if I didn't know him at all. "How does anyone find anything?"

A fountain of puzzle pieces spewing from his mouth. "By...looking for it?"

"Yes."

"You're completely insane." I laughed, shaking my head. "So I'm not sure what that makes me."

"Isn't it obvious?"

His eyes reflected the starlight, which got me thinking about stars again. And other finite things.

I said, "I like you. And that maybe makes me nuts."

"Are you trying to offend me, angel?" His voice was deep, full of an emotion I couldn't pin down.

My heart, that stupid thing—*just kidding, I love you, stupid heart*—adored hearing him speak that way. "Are you offended?"

"Mm. Maybe."

"Why did you call me that?" It came out low, quivering like it made me nervous. And maybe it did.

His grin faded. He dipped his head, shifted his torso until his lips were inches from mine. Close enough to—

Not close enough.

"It suits you." Simple. Solid. Sincere.

It squeezed my heart, made it sing and cry all at once.

Our breaths mingled together in the air between our mouths—still so close. A clicking sound came from the camera, oddly loud when surrounded by so much quiet.

Inhale. Exhale. Again. Again.

"Jake…"

And then he pressed his lips against mine, and it took too many frantic heartbeats to realize he was kissing me.

My mouth opened to his. There was fire, urgency, and need burning between us. Hot, yet tame. Slow, but intense. His hands grazed my face and neck, then wound around my back. He pulled me closer, and my own hands found his chest, fisted against his sweatshirt as I fell into him. I forgot to breathe, because who needed to breathe when there was *this*.

When our lips broke apart, his hands moved to cup my face. He slowly caressed my cheeks and placed a kiss against my forehead.

Surely this was a dream.

I blinked, steadied my heart rate as best I could, and finally got my voice to work. "Thought you said you weren't going to do that? You know…the habit thing."

He could've lit fires with the smile he gave. "I have enough bad habits, might as well have a good one, too."

Chapter Twelve

I was having more fun coming up with Kat/Matt jokes in my head than I was at this party. Maybe parties weren't my thing.

That couldn't be right.

"You could at least try to look like you don't want to stab your eyes out." Kat, suddenly in front of me, crossed her arms and gave me her practiced death glare.

"I wasn't thinking about stabbing my own eyes." *Actually, I was making fun of your choice in boy.*

Worse—that was worse.

Kat scowled, assessing me. Her mouth pulled into a thin line, the way it always did when she attempted to—as she called it—read my wordy face.

"I like him, Audra. Pretend to care." She bumped her hip into mine, a wicked grin playing on her lips.

"Uh-huh. The same way you liked Brent? And Dillan? And— *Ow.*" My fingers flew to my arm. "You pinched me," I said with a laugh.

"You bet your ass I did. Now cheer the fuck up. Would it make any difference if I told you Piano Boy is here?"

"What? Jake's here?"

She exaggerated an eye roll. "Damn. If I'd known it would cheer you up that much I would've told you before."

"Before? You saw him here earlier and didn't tell me?"

She sent me a look usually reserved for boyfriends. "Because I knew this would happen. I'd tell you and then you'd spend the rest of the night looking for him."

"That doesn't seem very fair."

"I know. I'm sorry."

My eyes scanned the crowd for Jake, but it was pointless. He wouldn't draw attention to himself, so it was harder than those Where's Waldo? books. I hadn't seen him in days, since our impromptu kiss in the middle of beautiful nowhere.

"See? This. This is what I didn't want." Kat grabbed my hand and hauled me through the throng of students. "If you like Piano Boy, you can't go looking for him like this."

"Can we please stop calling him that?" I allowed her to pull me along until some girl almost ran right into me.

Kat paused and turned around. "Audra, it doesn't matter what we call him. The rules are still the same."

"You mean your dating rules?" She'd tried explaining them to me a few times. But I was never overly interested in dating, so it seemed like too much work: don't be clingy, don't be overly available but also don't be *too* hard to get, only say yes to a date *if* the right criteria were there, and so on and so on.

It was ridiculous.

"Come on. Let's go outside. Forget about Piano Boy. I'll forget about Matt—for a little while, anyway. Let's have some fun. Pretty fucking please?" She grinned, gesturing toward the back door.

We passed a group of girls all wearing short skirts or short shorts, all wearing the same bored-to-death expression. Another cluster of students hooted and laughed at who knew what. Once outside, we refilled our drinks from the keg on the patio. Kat dragged me to the wide open space behind the house where a bonfire raged, sending puffs of dark smoke into the night air. It reminded me of camping with Jake.

I stood next to Kat as she talked animatedly about something that happened in her statistics class. She stopped midsentence when the group of people behind us began shouting. We both turned to see what everyone was freaking out about, and a loud *crack* caught my attention. Once I realized what was going on, I almost scurried back inside. Being near two dudes going at each other wasn't smart. But among the swinging fists and swarming crowd, I spotted a head of hair I knew well.

No.

Lots of people had dirty-blond hair; that couldn't be him.

The two guys crashed to the ground a couple feet in front of me. They rolled violently, and I had to skip backward, out of their way.

Oh God. It was him.

"Jake." My voice couldn't be heard. I'd whispered his name so softly, I wondered if I'd actually said it out loud. "*Jake.*"

My back hit a brick wall, sending a chill up my spine, and I watched the scene I couldn't stop, couldn't change, couldn't fix.

Some people cheered. Everyone moved closer. Why would they want to be closer? No one tried to stop the two brawling guys. The sound of bone meeting flesh and bone cracking against bone echoed in the night air.

As my heart thudded inside my chest, something changed. The chaos of the crowd raged in my ears. Everything got louder, louder, *louder*.

Jake hovered over the unknown guy, who'd stopped moving, and his hands neared his throat. Too many seconds passed and a dark, terrible burning twisted through my veins with every too-quick pump of my heart.

"Jake!" My feet moved, and I put up no resistance, even though my brain didn't completely agree with what I was doing. "Jake." Inches away—too close. All he had to do was twist his shoulders and I would've been behind the wrong side of an elbow.

But his arms slackened, his body becoming immovable—except for his eyes. They found me, recognition flared, and something cold and slimy slid down my chest.

Jake pushed off the guy and was on his feet in seconds. The one on the ground rolled over, gripping his face with one hand, coughing and spewing spit and blood. But then I wasn't paying attention to him anymore.

I followed Jake, yelling his name as he pushed through the thickening crowd. He could hear me, but he wouldn't stop.

"Stop running away," I shouted. "It's just me, Jake. Please."

He halted so quickly, I almost slammed into his solid back.

Tipping my chin up, I said his name again and examined his face. Blood trickled from the corner of his mouth. He promptly wiped the back of his hand across it, looking away.

"Leave me alone, Audra," he said in a strangled voice, whipping around once more and stomping through the grass.

I was going to do anything *but* leave him alone.

Trotting behind him, I caught his sleeve and tried again. "Jake. Talk to me. What happened?"

He pulled his arm free of my loose grasp. "Nothing happened. It's fine. *I'm* fine. But you should stay away from me right now. Okay?"

I shook my head, but he wasn't looking. "Because you'll hit me?"

His chest heaved as he came to a hasty stop, raking an angry hand through his hair. "No, of course not."

Taking a step closer, I hoped I'd broken through whatever

wall he'd constructed.

"I don't have to hit you to hurt you." His voice shook, like gravel spewing from the back of his throat. "But I will hurt you."

I drifted backward, blinking in surprise and confusion. "That's stupid. You're not going to hurt me."

"It's not *stupid*."

We were far enough away from the party noise to feel isolated in the dark. Too loud to be hanging out on a public street.

Jake clenched his fists, sucked in air, then unclenched them. Again and again and again. His breathing slowed, but it didn't appear to be helping—his jaw was tight, brows pinched together, shoulders rigid as stone.

"I'll take the rest of your photos, and I'll give you piano lessons because I'm not one to go back on my word, but I'm no good for anything else," he said, lowering his voice like we'd suddenly fallen into a library. "I can't be your friend—I can't be anyone's friend."

"What are you saying?" I whispered. I was confused about the details, but I knew that feeling in my gut—the one buzzing down my nerves, sending electric shocks through my limbs, straight to my heart.

"I'm sorry, Audra."

He took a few more breaths as my heart spun itself into a giant tangle of pulses.

"So, what?" I threw up my hands to conceal their shaking. "You're going to give me piano lessons, but nothing else is okay? I'm supposed to act like it's cool to be your friend two hours a week, but be okay with you shunning me the rest of the time?"

"It's not like tha—"

"Yes, it is!"

Jake dipped his head, shifting his weight from foot to foot.

"You'll thank me later."

He spun and strode through the grass, leaving me stuck to the ground with the words he'd said—and the ones I hadn't.

I'd wanted to say *don't go. You're wrong.* So wrong. *About me and about you—everyone can be a friend.* I wanted to be his friend—more than his friend—someone he could confide in, share his secrets with.

I wanted to tell him that no matter what was going on, it would be okay.

My eyes stung as I stood alone in the dark, watching his silhouette fade into nothing. It wasn't fair—the way he could walk away so easily, and there wasn't a thing in this world I could do to stop him.

Chapter Thirteen

Jake wasn't at the piano room on Monday.

Honestly, I hadn't expected that—or the repeated punch in the gut I suffered.

I spent the first thirty minutes staring down the hall, down at my phone, at the hall, then back at my phone. I sat in the hideous purple chair, clutching my bag against my chest.

It took me an hour to truly believe he wasn't coming.

It shouldn't have taken so long, but I was never any good at giving up.

His words echoed in my head: *I'm no good for anything else.*

He was wrong. I wished—more than I wished to have been born with a healthy heart—that he could know that.

I sent him a text, but didn't expect a response.

Me: *I waited for you. Hope you're okay.*

Constant pressure found a home in my chest, followed me around campus while I studied and while I lay in bed at night trying not to think. It didn't make sense. One day he was kissing me. Days later he was blowing me off.

The more I tried not to think about Jake, the more his face popped into my brain. Things always worked out that way.

The following Monday, I sat at the piano bench while I stared at the walls and waited for a boy who never came.

• • •

"Come out with me," Kat pleaded for the fifth time in ten minutes. "Put on some, you know, clothes, and do something with your hair. We'll go out, have some fun."

I glared. "I'm wearing, you know, clothes. And what's wrong with my hair? It's in a ponytail."

"Exactly."

"Whatever." I fell back against my pillows and shut my eyes. "I don't feel like doing anything to my hair, or putting on Kat-approved clothing. Not tonight."

"Why not tonight?"

"I don't feel like it."

I could sense her glaring at me, so I sat up and stared back—a stare-down—something we did that accomplished absolutely nada. She'd try not to blink. I'd try not to blink. It would last a few seconds and then we'd both laugh.

"I mean this in the nicest way possible, but you're the lamest college freshman I've ever met," she said, shaking her head and pushing herself off the floor.

Everything felt like total ass, so maybe she had a point.

"I'll get Matt to come with me." Kat picked her purse up off the floor and stuck her feet into her shoes. "If you wanna mope, you can sit around and mope by yourself. I still love the shit out of you, even if you are being lame."

"How does that saying go? *Boo, you whore.*"

She laughed. "The phrase you are looking for is 'tough love.'"

"Blah, blah. Yeah, yeah. Whatever." I pulled Mister Yellow Blanket over my legs. "For the record, I'm not moping. I just don't want to go out."

"I'll allow you to indulge your delusions this one time. M'kay?"

I tossed a pillow at her head, missing by a foot. "I'd like an exchange on my clearly broken friend. I've got a lifetime warranty, right?"

"Oh no. Returns are not accepted. All sales are final, remember?" She twisted the door handle with a giggle. "Sorry. You can't get rid of me."

"Should've read the fine print."

"Eh. You live and you learn, right?"

I grinned. "Obviously."

"Sure you don't want to go?" she asked, hesitating with one foot out the door.

"Yeah, I'm sure. And I'm good. Promise."

Kat arched an eyebrow, saying she didn't believe me. And okay, I *was* lying—just a little. "Fine. Don't come. But remember." She pointed a finger, made a serious face, and I tried not to laugh. "Don't fall in love with maybe and supposed to. They'll never love you back."

It took twenty minutes from the time Kat shut the door to the time I made sense of the unsettling feeling zipping through me like a homicidal Ping-Pong ball. I was bored. And angry. And annoyed.

Twenty more minutes passed. I did a little screaming into my pillow. Freaking out alone was okay, right? Then I threw on some real clothes—my favorite pair of jeans and a light sweater—and stuffed my feet into my shoes. But I left my hair the way it was.

I needed out of this tiny box.

I spent time wandering around campus. The latest classes ended hours ago, so not many students lingered around. And it was Friday night. Most people had things to do, friends to see, beer to drink. Whatever. Not me. And even though I'd chosen this fate, it didn't make me happy.

That was probably some type of metaphor.

The pathways were dark, lit only by the blue security lamps. I approached the rec center, and the closer I got, the brighter it became. Light poured from the windows, cascaded down the brick walls, and fell across the pavement for yards.

I wasn't surprised when I found myself at the piano room.

All the lights were off. Turning them on felt like disturbing something peaceful, so I walked inside, ignoring the switch on the wall. It wasn't pitch-black, and I easily found my way to the piano bench. When I sat, it was a tiny bit harder to breathe.

My fingers ran across the keys without pressing them, so the room stayed silent.

Too long I sat there, until the quiet got to me. This was no better than my room.

I was about to stand when I remembered what I had in my purse: the sheet music for "Twinkle, Twinkle, Little Star." I'd folded it and stuck it in there so I could look at it often, try to keep the notes fresh in my mind. I hadn't managed to play the entire song yet. Not without getting frustrated and giving up.

I pulled out the sheet music from under my antirejection meds. My heart beat harder, like it was screaming at me, trying to tell me something.

Sorry, heart, I don't understand you.

But my heart wasn't mine anymore, so maybe there was a true disconnect. Maybe it wasn't something I made up in my head. It was a heart just like the one I'd had, only this one never belonged to me, never *would* belong to me.

They say every cell in the body is capable of retaining memories. I'd read stories about transplant patients who claimed to become a completely different person afterward —

angry, violent, depressed. Some have even claimed to fall in love with a near stranger because of their new heart. I didn't feel like a different person, and I didn't suddenly love someone new.

I unfolded the sheet music, tried smoothing out the wrinkles, and then set it above the keys. I placed my hands in their proper spots to begin the familiar melody. After a few slow breaths, I hit the first note.

And kept going. And going.

My fingers hit the right keys (okay, mostly the right keys), and there weren't long pauses between notes because I didn't have to think too hard about where to move my hands. And I realized while I moved my fingers, pressed them down, shifted, pressed, again and again, it actually sounded like "Twinkle, Twinkle." It sounded like real music.

The song was nothing close to piano mastery, but I'd done it. I played the entire song.

Jake taught me how to play the piano. And no one was there to see it—to hear it.

My heart picked up its screaming again, and pain stung the backs of my eyes. I squeezed them shut, blacked out the piano keys and sheet music. Tried to be happy—only happy—that I'd done it.

But it didn't matter how hard I squeezed, I couldn't be only happy. The empty spaces in my chest filled with poisoned air that burned straight down to my soul.

I wish you were here.

I did *not* cry at the piano bench, thank you very much. But fuck, I wanted to.

When I walked out of the room, most of my sadness stayed behind. I passed the glass walls and hideous purple chair, and then trudged up a short staircase, my sneakers squeaking against the tile. Reaching the exit, I shoved through the doors, an unfamiliar feeling raging in my head and just below my rib cage.

I stood in front of Jake's apartment door, staring at its plainness, unable to remember when I decided to come here. He'd made it clear he wanted me to stay away. Then he bailed on the lessons.

He bailed.

But maybe if I knocked, we could talk, and then—I don't know, maybe we could fix whatever broke. Maybe if I knocked, it would fix everything.

But maybe not.

I shouldn't have been here, but my stupid feet didn't obey, so what the hell was I supposed to do?

Don't fall in love with maybe and supposed to. They'll never love you back.

Leave. I needed to leave.

I backed up, still staring at the door, rubbing my sweaty, shaky palms down my jeans. *But what if—*

I pulled out my phone, sent Kat an SOS text. Maybe if she told me I should leave, my feet would finally listen. She could be my voice of reason. I paced, waiting. Up and down the hall, staring at the cracks in the corners.

When ten minutes went by, I pulled out my phone again and dialed her number.

"Hello?"

But the voice on the other end wasn't Kat.

"Mrs. Werner?" I recognized her mom's Russian accent.

"Kat—she…she's been in an accident," she said between controlled sobs.

Pain seared through my chest as Mrs. Werner gushed bits of information. Kat's car was hit from the side on the corner of West Laurel and South Shields Streets. An ambulance rushed her and the boy she was with to the ER. Both were in critical condition, both were in surgery right now. But that was all they knew.

Every nerve ending in my body sizzled, cracked, and then exploded, like I'd gone up in flames. I couldn't breathe—something that once seemed so easy. I hung up the phone and held it limply in my hand until it finally fell and smashed against the floor.

Seconds passed, maybe minutes. I remembered how to breathe at some point, but when I did, it allowed the silent sobs to escape.

Then I heard a voice. My name. Remembered I was in front of Jake's door. Remembered what I'd been doing and thinking before that phone call.

And now he stood a few feet away, holding the door with one hand, a pinched-up expression on his gorgeous face.

"Audra?" he said again, looking at me like maybe I *was* on fire.

But I couldn't think of a thing to do other than grab my phone, turn around, and sprint away.

I had a love/hate relationship with hospitals.

Guess I had them to thank for my life—but how many people died inside these walls? Every day. Every hour. Every minute.

As a patient, you either came to live or you came to die.

I stumbled through the doors of the emergency room wing, drunk off my despair. The girl at the desk—with the pretty red hair—looked up and smiled. *How could anyone smile right now?*

"Katarina Werner," I said. "Where is she?"

The girl tapped at her keyboard, frowned at the screen,

and took too long to tell me where my best friend was. "She's in surgery right now. The waiting room is right through those doors." She nodded. "It might be a few hours, though."

I'd never been the one in the waiting room before.

Kat's parents were there, and after an hour, her brother was, too. So it was the four of us sitting, then standing, pacing, and sitting again. The three of them had matching faces. Wide eyes that weren't actually looking at anything. Tight lips and even tighter jaws. I wondered if mine matched theirs, too.

Fiddling with my phone, I considered calling my parents, but I could barely speak without my voice breaking, so I decided to wait until Kat was out of surgery and I had good news to tell them.

"They were T-boned," Kat's dad said at one point. "Out of nowhere."

But can anything actually come out of nowhere? A giant, hulking car doesn't simply appear out of thin air. Matt was driving, so he wasn't looking. Or he didn't look properly. Or maybe it was the other driver's fault—maybe he was speeding or ran a red light. Or maybe Matt was drunk.

It didn't matter.

Matt's small four-door car was smashed by a massive truck, and that was the only fact that did matter. Kat's side took most of the damage, but they were both in critical condition, so who cared whose fault it was.

I only wanted Kat to be okay, to be *alive*.

The TV in the corner played a cartoon I didn't recognize. I watched the screen but didn't pay any real attention. My phone vibrated in my pocket. Probably another text from Jake, but since I didn't have a response for him, I ignored it.

Mrs. Werner sat next to me, put her hand on mine, and squeezed. She left her fingers on top of mine, and we waited.

I tapped my foot against the tile. Was this how my parents felt when I was in surgery getting a new heart? I'd always known it was hard for them—thought I knew—but I hadn't given them nearly enough credit.

Waiting to hear if someone you love is still alive was an excruciating task.

Midnight came and passed.

So did 1:00 a.m.

I was about to pull out my phone when a doctor with salt-and-pepper hair stepped through a set of double doors. Mrs. Werner stood, but I couldn't get my feet to move. I couldn't even keep my eyes on the doctor's face. This was it—what we'd been waiting for.

The moment violent sobs filled the mostly empty waiting room, I knew.

My chest collapsed in on itself, crumbling, breaking apart. Hearing the words out loud would destroy me—it would make it real. It couldn't be real.

But it was.

Kat was dead.

Chapter Fourteen

They say the first stage of grief is denial.

They were so fucking wrong.

The moment I found out Kat was dead, the foundation of my life crumbled, and my heart might as well have been failing. She'd never breathe again, never smile again. I'd never see her again. That wasn't denial.

It was complete truth. Complete understanding. But humans, well, I don't think we were built to handle that. So denial took over, covered the wound, and masked the pain. But there was that moment in the beginning—a lightning strike of feeling, mercifully quick, when I heard the news and stared into the blackness, and horrible as it was, understood everything.

It was three fifteen in the morning, and I'd stumbled my way back to Jake's apartment. My parents were out of state for the weekend, and I had no other friends, so where else could I go? There was no way I was going back to the dorm room Kat and I shared. No way I'd spend the night staring at her things, thinking of how only a few hours ago, she was alive, and now she wasn't.

Down the hall from Jake's, I leaned against the wall and called my mom. She didn't answer, as expected, but I left a short message so she wouldn't see a late-night missed phone call and worry something happened to me. "I'm okay" were the first words out of my mouth, but it was a complete lie. I wasn't okay, and something *did* happen to me.

I'd lost my best friend.

Ambling slowly down the hall, I wiped under my eyes and tried to breathe. Through Jake's door, I listened to his clock *tick, tick, tick*ing as I stood, numb, on his doorstep. Finally I knocked.

He opened his door like he'd been expecting me. "Are you okay?"

I stared, and the words I couldn't say formed a lump in my throat. I shook my head, tears darting down my cheeks.

When Jake wrapped his arms around me, ran his hand over my hair, and whispered something meant to be soothing, I only cried harder.

I wiped my eyes and blinked at the walls around me—the ones covered in black-and-white photographs. I'd been preoccupied enough to not realize Jake had maneuvered me inside his apartment.

A crying girl in the middle of the night was likely *not* something he wanted to deal with.

"I'm sorry," I blurted out, wiping at my eyes again.

"Sorry for what?" He sat on the couch, guiding me down next to him.

"For being here. I'm sorry. I was leaving—dammit, I was *leaving*." I said it more to myself, pressing the heels of my palms against my swollen eyes.

The world wasn't right. *Not right. Not right.*

It would never be right again.

"Audra." His soft and gentle voice started a fresh batch of

tears. "Tell me what happened."

Remembering to breathe, I nodded and tried to put the details together in my brain. "I should've gone with her. Maybe then—" My eyes burned, and my throat felt like someone had raked down all the walls. "Oh my God, it's my fault, isn't it?"

Jake placed his warm hands on my shoulders, gripping tightly enough to grab my attention. "I don't know what you're talking about, but I know it's not your fault. It's not, okay?"

"Kat is dead." The words came out like a plea.

I'd had other things I planned to say—details about the wreck and the hospital—but the strangled sobs took over. Jake's hands moved from my shoulders, pulling me against him. His embrace was warm, solid, and strong. Once I'd gained control of my crying, I managed to explain what happened— at least enough for him to understand.

I shook my head, his features blurred by my tears. "What if…what if—I should've gone with her. I should've—" Blinking, I tried to find his eyes, tried to focus on them. "Maybe I could've saved her."

His forehead pinched together, and his gaze dipped down. "Yeah. Or maybe you'd both be dead." Jake's voice wasn't so soft anymore. "But you're not dead. And it's not your fault."

I heard his voice, but his words didn't register. All I could think was *this can't be real.* Over and over. *This can't be real!* Everything hurt—my heart especially. The last time it had hurt this way was when Scott Lancaster broke up with me in the middle of senior year.

But this was worse.

Kat was like my *girl* boyfriend. My forever friend. Whatever. I loved her. We might as well have been sisters.

And now she was dead.

"It'll be okay." Jake's soft voice was back.

"No. No, I don't think so."

He ran his hands down my arms—I'd forgotten he was still touching me. "You're right."

"What?" I croaked, watching him as his fingers moved along my skin.

"It's all bullshit. People tell you how pain fades. Hurt and regret disappear. Missing someone ends. Everything will be okay. Things will get better." He drew his hands back, shoving them into the pockets of his lounge pants. "But it's not always true. People say those things because we all want to believe those lies. It makes us feel better...you don't deserve the lies."

I wiped my cheeks and something like a laugh escaped my throat. "I did it. I played the song. I finally played that damn song all by myself, and you know who was there to hear it? No one. Not even Kat. Especially not you." My heart pumped harder, angrier, but on the plus side, the tears stopped. "You didn't show up for our lessons. You bailed on me after that line about not being one to break your word. You cut me out. Just like that. And now—"

Worried I might detonate at any moment, I snapped my mouth shut, scanning his pinched face, the sadness in his steely eyes.

"Audra," he said slowly, cautiously. "Do you want to talk about your friend or do you want to talk about...us?"

Us? Ha! "Does it matter? My best friend is dead, and whatever we talk about isn't going to change that."

Don't fall in love with maybe and supposed to.

"And I shouldn't be here," I said. "I shouldn't have come back."

"Don't do that. Don't go."

"Why not?" I shoved off the couch, moving away from him and toward the door. "You *left* me."

He didn't move, didn't try to stop me, but he said, "I know I'm an asshole. I'm sorry for that. I also know sorry is useless. And yeah, you can leave if you want. I deserve that. But I *want* you to stay."

It was a miracle I hadn't exploded and blown this building to smithereens.

I whirled around. "Why weren't you there? Why weren't you in the piano room?" It didn't make sense to shoot my anger at Jake, but dammit, I wanted to blame someone for something. And if he hadn't left me, maybe I would've felt like going to that stupid party, and maybe Kat would still be alive.

My chin quivered, and I sniffled. Jake's mouth fell open, but then he pressed his lips together and bowed his head.

"You were right when you said it wasn't fair. For it to only be on my terms, what I wanted. You...you don't deserve that. I meant it when I said I'm no good for anything else. I want to be good enough to be your friend." He swallowed, looking away, pulling his hands free from his pockets. "I want to be good enough to be more than your friend, but I can't. I thought it would be easier this way—to give you an out."

The breath I took in tore at my lungs, ripped at my sore throat. "I didn't want an out, Jake."

It took him a full minute to respond. "Maybe not then. Maybe not now. But one day, you'll be glad to have taken it."

"What, you can see the future now?" I eyed the door again. "You're not a fucking Magic 8 Ball. You can't assume things like that."

"I kind of can."

Fine. "I'm leaving."

I stood, spun for the door, and marched three steps, reached for the handle, and tripped over a shoe lying haphazardly on the floor. I stumbled forward, my hands outstretched to brace my fall.

Holding back a scream, I twisted onto my butt and leaned against the wall. I hugged my elbows, feeling like a giant popped balloon. My grand exit had been destroyed—completely and utterly. How unfair.

As if that mattered.

As if *any* of this mattered. Kat went somewhere without me and was never coming back.

If I'd convinced her to stay in, watch a few movies, and eat too much popcorn and ice cream... Maybe I could've done something different.

I should've.

The ache crept back into my chest, seeping heartache and sorrow through my pores. God, would this awful feeling ever go away?

My cheeks were wet again. They hadn't been a second ago, when I'd been heading for the door. *Fuck*, I was so done with the crying.

"Audra?"

And Jake was there, and I still hadn't *left*. Everything was wrong.

"I can't believe she's—" The word lodged in my throat, choking me like a violent, angry hand.

He slid down the wall beside me and spread out his arms, inviting me in, and my first thought was how I didn't want that.

But I did.

So I collided into his chest, let him rub his hand up and down my back, and I cried, convinced it would never stop.

"I know it hurts," he whispered into my ear. "I'm sorry for that. But I'm here and—and I'm sorry I wasn't before."

I meant to move my head, or say something, but I couldn't without restarting the waterworks. Any other night, I would've tried to decipher exactly what he meant. I could've and would've spent hours on it. But this wasn't any other night.

It was the night the world broke my heart.

Chapter Fifteen

For ten glorious seconds, I was unaware of anything but the feel of a down pillow and cool air. But then my eyes fluttered open and I remembered. The pain returned slowly, aching through every part of my body and soul until everything went numb.

I rolled over, focused on the walls that were white like mine, but *not* mine. Jake's room. Jake's bed. Alone.

Guess I thought I'd only dreamed he carried me. I wanted to smile, but my numbness prevented the action.

I found my phone on the pillow next to me. Picking it up, I scrolled through my missed calls and missed texts. I also noted the time. Two thirty? In the afternoon?

With the curtains drawn, the room remained mostly dark. The bed cradled me, tempting me to stay cloaked in its warm embrace. But as much as I wanted to hide, I didn't, and instead found my way to the living room, wishing I could teleport out of the apartment and not face Jake. Not after all the crying.

He sat on the couch, staring at his laptop, but when I walked in, he shoved it aside.

"Don't ask me if I'm all right," I whispered.

He averted his gaze. "Are you hungry?"

"I don't think so."

"You should probably eat something."

I stared, but he still wasn't looking. "Thank you."

That got him to look. "For what?"

For listening to me cry for hours on end. For holding me when I really needed it. For carrying me to bed. "For being here."

With an almost imperceptible shake of his head, Jake looked like I'd insulted him, rather than thanked him. "Is it really enough?"

I took in a breath and was properly reminded of the beating my lungs took last night. "I don't know...I should probably go. My mom's been calling...and Kat's mom—"

Jake moved off the couch, and I noticed the T-shirt he wore—the same one he had on the day we met.

Feeling the pressure start between my ribs, I darted for my purse, shoved my phone inside, and slipped on my shoes. My head couldn't handle any more. Neither could my heart.

He rubbed the side of his jaw, nodding. "All right."

I hesitated on my way to the door as I tried to keep my shit together. I could break down later.

Jake pushed aside the hair falling onto his forehead and looked up, met my gaze—that was all it took. Tears pricked at my eyes, and a slow burning began at the back of my throat.

"Bye," I said, trying not to choke.

I headed for the door and didn't look back, didn't pause to see what his face looked like, see if the space between his eyes crinkled with sadness or regret.

My confusion and feelings for Jake would have to wait for another day—a less shit-filled one.

• • •

Almost twenty-four hours passed, and the crying became tiring and annoying, making my eyes puffy and red. I sat on my bed, leaning against the wall, Mister Yellow Blanket wrapped over my legs. The phone went off a few times, but I ignored it, choosing instead to sit like a statue and stare at nothing.

Her name would never show up on my caller ID.

I'd never get to talk to her again. Never get to see her again—not alive, anyway.

She'd never laugh, or roll her eyes, or get to do any of the things she might have put on a done-it list.

I shut my eyes, wishing I could sleep, just to get a break.

Someone knocked on my door, and I almost threw a pillow at it. When whoever it was knocked again, I crawled off the bed and padded toward the door.

I honestly hadn't expected to see Jake on the other side, standing a foot away from the door, hands in his pockets.

"Are you busy?" he asked.

"Depends on your definition, I guess."

"You're not busy. Come on."

I raised a brow, watching his hand as he motioned with it. "Come on, what?"

He stepped closer, licking his lips and tilting his head. "Come with me. Please?"

"Where are we going?"

He almost smiled, doing that tiny quirk thing of his. And damn, I didn't realize how much I'd missed it.

"All right," I said. "It's not like I'm sleeping anyway."

Thirty minutes later, we were at an isolated spot in the middle of nowhere that resembled where he'd taken pictures before. This place had an equally awesome view but required less of a hike—and fewer hills—to reach it.

"If you take pictures of me like this, I'll hurt you," I said, staring up into the dark.

"Don't worry. I didn't bring my camera. Tonight, I have a different idea." He stepped in front of me and reached into his bag, producing a bottle of liquor and a two-liter of Coke. "I think I know a thing or two. And one of those things is the appropriate time to get shit-faced."

I choked out a laugh. "You brought me out here to get shit-faced?"

"And to talk."

It wasn't exactly romantic, but it was good enough for me. "Is this another one of your beautiful places?"

"Sort of. It's peaceful out here. Don't you think?"

I nodded—not that there was an inkling of peace within me.

When he offered the bottle, I took it and slammed back a small shot. It burned my throat, traveled down to the pit of my empty stomach, instantly warming me from the inside. Good thing Kat had taught me how to take a shot—even if my glass was usually filled with OJ instead of alcohol. *Like a guy,* she'd said. Which I altered to be *like a queen.* Whenever we were doing shots, that was our toast.

"Thanks," I said when he handed me the Coke bottle. Taking another sip, I wondered how long it would take to kick in. Straight rum tasted as bad as straight whiskey, so I decided right then and there that all liquor was terrible.

But the terrible liquor didn't bother me as much as my terrible thoughts did.

I turned away. The sky was dark, but covered in clouds. I squinted, trying to spot the patches of starlight, but found only a few.

"Is it always going to feel this way?" I asked.

"Like what?"

"Like…the whole world will never be right again."

He didn't answer for a long time. I wrapped my arms around my waist and turned. He'd spread out a square blanket on the leaf-covered ground. "You really thought of everything," I said.

"The world will never be right again." Jake took one step forward. He paused before adding, "But it will get easier, I think. Especially for you."

"What the hell does *that* mean?"

He dropped his voice, though there was no one remotely nearby. "I mean, you have other people. You've still got everything else. You'll recover. If I can recover, so can you."

"You think you've recovered?"

He paused, shoulders hunching, and searched my face. "No."

I wanted to roll my eyes, attempt some lame joke, or punch him in the arm playfully—like I might've done a few weeks ago. But I couldn't do anything but stare at the blanket on the ground. "I don't think I'm following you," I said, still not looking at him. "Are you trying to make me feel better or…?"

He sighed, shuffled toward the blanket, and sat. "I'm not good at this. I'm sorry. I wasn't trying to make you feel worse."

Picking up the liquor bottle, he nodded at the spot beside him.

I sat. Maybe a little too quickly. I chugged another small shot, followed by a sip of Coke. Jake did the same, then shoved the bottle back to me. "No way." I waved my hand.

"Come on. It's the right thing to do."

Something about the way he looked at me turned my insides warm and fuzzy. Or maybe that was the alcohol. His grin lit up his entire face, the lines around his eyes and mouth becoming distinct. Jake was not one to offer many genuine smiles. Not even to me. And the way he could alternate between looks of agony and smiles baffled me.

"I really shouldn't drink anymore."

"I understand."

But I eyed the clear bottle, appreciating the way my pain dulled as the alcohol swirled in my stomach. So I took another swig. "Yuck. Just make sure I don't pass out here tonight, okay?"

"That should be a given by now, don't you think?"

"I don't know. I'm not so sure of anything anymore."

His smile disappeared.

Damn. *Way to go, mouth.*

I looked away, picking at the frayed ends of the blanket. "Who were you beating up at that party?"

He shifted, pulling his knees up to rest his arms against them. With a heavy exhale, he said, "Ah. A guy I know."

I waited, images my brain stored from that night flashing in my head — swinging fists, body parts tumbling toward the ground, Jake walking away from me.

And him telling me we couldn't be friends.

"Why does it matter?" he asked, gravel threading through his tone.

"Because I care. And it obviously matters to you if you put forth the effort to swing on some guy. So…it matters to me."

His face remained calm and collected as he stared out into the nothingness in front of us. "A guy I know from back home. We were talking. He said some bullshit about my sister. Guess I kind of lost it."

I paused, letting his words settle in. "Oh."

When he turned his head, I met his stare, my brain slightly foggy from the rum. I flicked a mosquito off my arm and prayed I got it before it started itching. *Bugs.*

"Okay, so you were beating this guy up." I tried to keep my voice casual, like we were friends.

Because we were. I was almost positive.

"It was stupid," Jake said softly.

I thought about asking for more details, but decided

I probably didn't want to know. "What about after, when I stopped you outside the party?"

His jaw shifted. So did his gaze. "What about it?"

"Why did you…say those things?"

"I don't have the answers you're looking for… I thought I was doing you a favor. Thought it was for the best."

He kissed me, then claimed I was better off without him. That's what he thought was best? "You were wrong."

He ground his jaw, his fingers clenching around his knees. "Maybe."

I stretched my legs out farther and shifted so my ass wouldn't go numb. "You really don't have any friends?" It felt safer somehow to whisper it.

The noise he made was akin to a laugh, but it wasn't *really* a laugh. "We're friends, aren't we?"

Despite his insistence that we couldn't be friends, I nodded. Fire burned in my stomach, but my legs and feet, fingers and nose stung like ice.

"There's one other person I'd call a friend. But he stayed back home in Platteville. Went to a community college. I couldn't stay there." Jake flattened his legs and twisted until he faced me. "I spend a lot of time alone. Most of my time. I kind of…forgot how to be a friend. Micah and I were friends in middle school and most of high school, but I couldn't tell you why—or how—you become friends with someone anymore."

Yeah, I knew the feeling. Maybe it was a talent you only possessed when you were young, and adults had no clue how to make friends.

"I need to know…" *Do you have feelings for me?* A question I should've asked, because like Kat said, I needed to start asking for the things I wanted, but I couldn't force the words to leave my lips. "Are you still going to teach me piano and finish the photographs? After you didn't show up, I figured…"

A few moments passed, and the taciturn cold stung my skin and gnawed at my nose. Silence.

If he said no, I'd shatter into a million pieces. I was already a ticking time bomb, and I had no idea if he knew how precarious this moment was.

"I'm kind of a mess inside," he said. "I'll disappoint you. And you don't deserve that."

I bit my lip and looked away. "So you're done. Fine."

I reached for the bottle, but he grabbed my arm.

"I didn't say that."

"Well, what then? I can't decipher a Jake puzzle right now."

"Look, Audra, I'm just…" Then *he* grabbed the bottle and downed three loud gulps before shaking his head. "I'm no good at this."

I was sinking. My best friend was gone. And now Jake was all but saying good-bye.

"Do you think pain is finite?" I heard myself say.

Another change of topic. Another distraction. Another moment to remember to breathe.

And Jake said nothing.

"I've been thinking about finite things a lot lately. Like stars." My voice wavered, but I didn't care. "And heartbeats. Our lives are finite, like the life of a star is finite. Do you think…?" I stared until he met my gaze. "Is there a limit to pain?"

Jake tipped his head. "There has to be."

"Does there?" I wanted to believe it.

His gaze moved downward, away from my eyes, and stopped at my lips. I was hyperaware of him looking at me, of him being this close to me. My nerves electrified with the thought of shifting closer, annihilating the gap between us.

"Everything is finite, isn't it?" he said. "Nothing lasts forever."

"What about love? They say that's supposed to last forever. You don't think it's true?" My cheeks still burned, and I bit my lip to keep my facial expressions in check.

His brow furrowed. "Pain can't last forever."

"Just a long, long time, right?"

"I wish I could tell you no."

I ran my hands over the ground, picked at a blade of grass. "And love?"

A low, strangled sound came from his throat. "Your guess is probably better than mine."

"You've never been in love?"

The question hung heavy in the air, and I tore apart the blade of grass between my fingernails. Silence continued.

I should learn when to keep my mouth shut.

Jake finally said, "I'm not sure I understand the concept."

I let the shredded grass flutter to the ground, choosing to gape at him instead.

"Don't look at me like that."

"Like what?"

"Like I belong on a different planet."

"Well…it would explain a lot."

It was supposed to be a joke, to lighten the mood, to keep my heart from cracking further. But he didn't respond.

Through my tightening throat, I whispered, "You loved your sister, right?"

Jake dragged a hand through his hair, breaking eye contact. "Sure. So I know how to love one person."

"I thought I was in love once." I picked at another piece of grass between my fingers. "But he turned out to be a jerk."

"Isn't that what always happens?"

"I guess so."

I squirmed and cleared my throat before pulling my iPhone from my pocket. "We need music. Don't you think?"

"Sure. Why not?"

We didn't need music. I needed a distraction from thoughts of Jake, love, and jerks.

I scrolled through my music, trying to decide on something that would change the mood. Like Lady Gaga? Or something mellow, like Coldplay? Maybe Coldplay was too…sad.

"You pick first." I handed the phone over to him.

"What do you want to listen to?"

"I don't know. That's why I'm making you pick first."

He tapped the screen. "But we always listen to my music. In my car. At my apartment."

"So what? Just pick one for me."

While Jake scrolled through the songs, tapping on the screen, I appraised the dark night sky. But looking at the stars led my thoughts to places I didn't want to go.

The notes from a moderately slow song drifted through the air. Not anything like the rock music he usually played.

I can't say the words, but I need you in my life.

Did he really pick this song for *me*? Or did he pick one he thought I'd like? Guess I should've been more specific. Or I shouldn't have put so much thought into it.

Time goes by and I can't lie, I wish you'd stay awhile.

I shifted when a tingle ran down my spine. "I expected something else."

A faint smile played on his lips. "What did you expect?"

"Just…not this."

He turned his head, but not before I saw the smile deepen. "Good."

I picked up the phone and told my brain to shut up. Overanalyzing everything wasn't going to help.

"Are you going to play a song for me now?" When I eyed him, he added, "It's only fair."

"Okay." I made it look like I had to think about it for a while, but I didn't. Lots of songs made me think of Jake. But I couldn't play *any* of those for him—no freaking way.

"I can't," I finally said.

"You know that's unacceptable, right?"

I choked on a laugh. "You pick another. I, uh, can't think of one right now."

His brows pitched upward, then slowly lowered. "It's all right. We don't need the music anyway."

"Sure." I nodded, twisting my fingers.

We sat together, not saying a word, and it was anything but comfortable.

But the silence Jake and I shared wasn't always like that. There were times we didn't need words. That was part of why I liked hanging out with him so much. On good days, it felt like our souls had been friends for a very long time, like we knew *exactly* how to be around each other. Then I'd always go and ruin it, bringing up topics like Emily. Or love. And on bad days, when his aura of sadness blazed like an alarm he couldn't turn off, I felt like I was doing everything all wrong.

Our hearts have been friends for a very long time.

I glanced over, caught him already staring at me, and wondered if my recycled heart was the reason Jake and I couldn't be more than friends.

Chapter Sixteen

I stared at Kat's empty bed, thinking about *maybe* and *supposed to*.

What if she was wrong? She didn't know Jake like I did. It wasn't that simple. Maybe you couldn't define everyone with a single true statement.

I hadn't seen Jake in two days, but we'd had a running text conversation going, talking about nothing in particular — classes, homework, TV shows, music. Neither of us mentioned the big issues at hand.

Our undemanding ramblings gave my mind something to do besides think and worry and hurt. We never finished our conversation about being friends, or the one about continued piano lessons.

I shoved a pillow behind my back as my phone beeped. With a grumble, I edged my torso off the bed and snatched the phone from the dresser.

Jake: *You want to get out of your dorm room?*

I almost asked him how he knew where I was, but then

I remembered: Where else would a brokenhearted girl be at eight o'clock on a Thursday night, right?

Me: *Definitely.*

There were worse things I could do.

Jake: *I'll pick you up in 15.*

As I waited, I slipped on my shoes and threw on a zip-up jacket. I swiped Chapstick onto my lips with a single quick glance in the mirror. Looking at myself—at my swollen red eyes, and the fluff my hair had become because I couldn't be bothered with a blow-dryer—was to be avoided at all costs.

On my way out the door, I halted, my gaze landing on a framed photo of Kat and me. It was purple and pink with "Best Friends" written across the bottom in cute script. I mean, sure, it was super girlie and belonged in a teenager's bedroom—not a college freshman's—but I wasn't embarrassed by it the way I was with my bedspread.

Photographs were all I had left of her.

A memory in a purple-and-pink frame. A massive hole in my heart.

I told myself I'd have one shot and be done. "I don't want you to think I'm using you for your alcohol," I told Jake after handing him the bottle of rum.

He set it down on the floor beside the couch. "Aren't you though?"

"No." My cheeks blushed anyway. "Sure, the alcohol is nice." For dulling my pain, not for my health. "But that's not what I'm using you for."

"Oh?" He leaned forward, tipped his head. "What are you using me for?"

Pulling my legs up underneath me, I giggled. (Since when did rum make me giggly?) "Your good looks. You know, eye candy."

A grin broke through, spreading wider until he was holding back a laugh. "We spend most of our time together… alone. I don't think you're getting very good use out of me."

When Jake said things like that, sometimes I wondered if he was flirting with me. Of course he was flirting, right?

"I'll use you however I choose, thank you very much," I said.

Ohhh, that came out so wrong.

But he laughed. "Guess I don't really get a say in it, do I?"

"Nope." I eyed the TV, which was set to a muted comedy show.

I wasn't using him. I *wanted* him. Wanted to see and touch him. For us to hang out. For him to smile and laugh with me. And I wanted him to kiss me again.

"Do you think I have to go to the funeral?" I asked, watching Jake in my peripheral.

He cleared his throat, hesitating before answering. "Why wouldn't you want to go?"

"Funerals are for the living, right? Well, what if I don't think I want to go? I don't need a funeral to feel better about things. Going isn't going to make Kat any less *dead.*"

My breath became the loudest sound in the room for several long moments. Bitterness hung heavy in the air, like my own personal cloud of misery.

Jake angled his body toward me and lowered his voice, taut and brittle. "You didn't answer my question."

I pressed my back into the couch cushion. "I hate them. I—I don't want to go, be around all those people, sit there and cry and…" *See her.*

A funeral was the final good-bye, and I wasn't ready for that.

"So don't go."

I stared at his straight face, breathing slowly, attempting to calm my nerves. "You don't think I should go?"

He shook his head. "I didn't say that. But if you don't want to go, then don't."

"I told Kat's parents I'd give her eulogy." Based on a promise I'd made to her when we were fourteen. "I can't just...not go."

"But you said—"

"I know. I know. But I figured you'd tell me how I'm supposed to go, how it's the right thing to do, how—actually...I don't know why I thought that at all."

He rubbed his knuckles along his jaw. "It would make me a hypocrite to say you should go. I didn't go to Emily's."

"You didn't?"

He stood, walked around the couch, and disappeared from sight. "No. Made it to the church parking lot. I sat there for a while but didn't end up going in."

Twisting my fingers together, I stared at an insignificant spot on the floor. "Do you regret it?"

"I would've only made things worse." Jake's voice came from behind me. Leaning over the couch, he set something down in my lap. "Here. I thought this might help."

"Oh my God." I unfurled my fingers. "A *pie*."

He came back around and stood in front of me. "Yeah. I owe you, right?"

I laughed. "I kind of want to eat it."

"That is the only pie I'm buying for face-smashing purposes. If you want to eat it, you'll have to provide your own next time."

I stood, holding the pie as though it were pure gold. "Holy crap, this is awesome." I removed the plastic lid and tossed it on the couch. "I'm so smashing this pie in your face."

He grinned, annihilating all of my anxiety. "Should I be

worried?"

"A little pie never hurt anyone. Does this mean I can snap a picture of you covered in pie and post it for the done-it?"

"Whatever you want, Cheez-It."

And *bam*. I smashed that thing right at his face. Not too hard—but little globs of yellow goo went flying past him, landing on the wall and falling onto the floor. Pieces of pie covered his face and dripped onto his shirt.

I bent forward laughing. "That was *so* much fun."

He laughed, too, crinkling his pie-covered face and bringing his hands up to wipe it off. "It's...colder than I expected."

Through my fading giggles, I twisted to set the pan down and said, "That was kinda epic, don't you think?"

"Hey, look."

I turned back to see one pie-covered hand zooming toward my face. Before I could lunge out of the way, his fingers smeared banana cream across my nose and cheek.

"I can't believe you fell for that. But I had to see how it looked from the other side."

For the briefest moment, I thought I'd start crying—a mixture of sadness and hysterical pie-induced laughter. But I didn't. I was proud of that.

He wiped more globs of crust and whipped cream from his chin and lips, chuckling to himself. "Eating it might not have been so bad. It's damn good pie."

I mimicked his actions, wiping the dessert from my cheek. Something about eating the pie straight from my face didn't seem right. But whatever. I smiled and licked my fingers. "Oh damn, that is good."

Jake chuckled again. "Take a picture so I can get this pie out of my hair. And the floor."

Oops. "Okay, okay." I dug through my purse sitting on the edge of the couch until I located my phone. "Say cheese."

And he actually did, drawing the word out. I snapped a photo, then we both fell into obnoxious laughter.

Tossing my phone aside, I pressed one hand to my chest, trying to catch my breath. "I'm never going to be able to look at cheese the same way. You know that, right?"

He wiped pie from his forehead with a short chuckle. "That might've been my intention all along."

"Such a jerk." But I grinned.

"I'm going to hop in the shower. I'll be quick."

I nodded and when he disappeared, I went to the kitchen to rinse my hands. After wetting a paper towel, I wiped it across my face. I considered looking in the mirror to double-check that I'd gotten it all. But a part of me didn't care.

Water fell from the shower, muffled through the closed bathroom door. The comedy show still played silently on TV, but I had no interest in it. I wiped most of the pie from the floor, but paper towels only did so much—and they tore apart when I scrubbed the carpet. When I'd done all I could, I sat on the couch and resorted to looking around—something I'd done inside Jake's apartment so many times.

White walls surrounding a simple black couch and black-framed photos. Even a black rug. I wanted to buy him a red throw pillow to add some color.

The only thing that wasn't overwhelmingly black was a box beneath the coffee table. It was a royal blue—slightly better. It was tattered around the corners, maybe from being opened over and over, but I imagined it was dusty on top like its days of being overused were done.

I sank to the floor, reached out my hand to touch it—because I had to know. Was it something Jake found important, something he used a lot? Or was it that lost box of "things" I suspected it to be?

The mystery box wasn't heavy. It slid out from underneath the table with ease.

No dust.

I frowned, examining it closer.

So what was in the box?

Put it back.

That was the right thing to do. Pulling it to check for dust was violating his privacy enough. Shit, that made me weird.

But I had to know what was inside.

Maybe it was where he kept his photographs. Maybe the ones of me were in there.

Ask him.

What if it was something else and he didn't want to tell me?

This internal debate continued. Frantic, scattered thoughts buzzed, and I turned the box around, and played with the corner, testing how easily the lid would slip off.

I removed the lid, instantly regretting it. No matter what the box contained, it wasn't worth the ache in my chest or the way my head pounded.

But I reached inside anyway, as if my fingers had a mind of their own. The contents were mostly papers. A small notebook stuck out. A few envelopes. Folded notes—some carefully, some haphazardly. Something yellow caught my eye. A thick notebook, worn down over time.

I gaped, my hands frozen above the pile of miscellaneous things.

My eyes darted to the bathroom door. Water still rumbled through the pipes so I pulled the notebook from the box, thumbing the pages quickly.

It was page after page of scribbled writing. Sometimes only a few words, sometimes a few lines. There were even drawings on some of the pages. Landscapes mostly. Trees. Bushes. Mountains. Flowers.

The images were beautiful, while the words were sad.

I tried to steady my shaking hands as I flipped through the

pages, through mentions of Emily and of his parents. Words of hopelessness and despair. Words meant for Jake's eyes only.

One line appeared on multiple pages, over and over again until it was burned into the back of my skull. *What's the point?*

The point of what?

I had a bone-deep feeling I already knew the answer and simply refused to acknowledge it. So I shoved Jake's journal back into the box, trying to make all the contents appear untouched. Placing the lid back on, I blew out a breath.

The water shut off.

A heavy weight sat on my chest, smothering me in guilt.

What had I done?

Chapter Seventeen

I sat completely still on the couch, watching the muted TV, but paying no real attention. If I could help it, I'd never look at that box again.

"Are you hungry?" Jake asked, stepping into the living room, freshly showered and pie-free.

"Nope. I've got this." Lifting the bottle of rum, I wiggled it in the air and forced my lips into a smile. There was no room in my stomach for food *and* guilt.

"Planning on drinking until you can't see straight?"

"You know what they say. Don't knock it till you try it."

He closed the distance between us. The smell of soap and something spicy wafted in the air as he pulled the bottle from my grasp.

"Hey."

"Seriously," he said, brows pulling together. "That's not a good life plan. Don't try it."

"How would you know?"

"Trust me. I know."

My chest pounded, swift waves of electricity pulsing

through my veins. I'd gone through Jake's stuff. I'd violated his things. And now I only wanted to forget what I'd seen. "You never tell me anything."

Jake moved in front of me, a serious edge to his expression, and as if I were a skittish schoolgirl, my cheeks burned, and I looked away from his face.

"Some things you don't want to know."

I glanced up for a moment, wanting to protest, but the room blurred, so I put my head into my palms and groaned. "I'm sorry. *I'm sorry.*"

"Whatever you're sorry about, don't be."

I shook my head, still buried in my hands. Last month, I'd told Jake *you'll just have to trust me.* He'd said that wasn't how trust worked. And now what was I doing?

Ruining everything.

The couch dipped beside me. "You really played the whole song?"

"What?" I mumbled through my fingers.

"'Twinkle, Twinkle Little Star'? You played it all the way through?" When I nodded, he said, "Think you can do it again?"

I lifted my head and gave him a sideways glance. "I hope so."

His hand dropped to my shoulder, and he gave a light squeeze. "Let's go."

"Huh? Go where?"

"The piano room."

"Right now?"

"I want to hear you play it. I'll bring my camera." He stood again and held out his hand.

"How come you're always taking pictures of me when I've been drinking?" I ask, staring and considering his outstretched hand.

He laughed. "It's not intentional. Come on. We'll find

something to eat first."

Forty-five minutes later, I no longer felt the effects from the single shot I'd taken. I'd destroyed two double cheeseburgers and an entire container of fries. Funny, I didn't feel guilty for that.

We sat at the piano bench, and I pulled out the folded sheet of music. I didn't look at him as I opened it and flattened the creases.

"You keep that in your purse?"

"I look at it a lot when I get bored in class or whatever. I like having it on me."

He smiled—a huge, stupid one that made my stomach turn over.

"What?" I blinked, trying not to look nervous. "It's not that weird." I set the sheet music in its place above the keys. "Girls keep all kinds of things in their purses."

"It's not weird," he agreed.

"Then what's with the psycho killer grin?"

That erased it. "What?"

I laughed—more of a half-assed giggle. "I'm kidding. But you're making me kind of nervous."

"I know."

"I don't like it."

"Smiling makes you nervous. Got it," he said. "I'll try not to smile anymore."

"Jake." I eyed him. "You know exactly what I'm talking about."

"I do know exactly what you're talking about." He inclined his head, lifting one eyebrow. "And sorry."

"What are you sorry for?"

Wordlessly, his gaze dropped to my lips. My heart sped up, aware of how he was looking at me—confused by it. His eyes trailed back up my face before I looked away.

"Sorry for making you nervous," he murmured.

I laughed, but it was still full of nervous jitters.

"I *am* nervous," I said, staring at the sheet music. "What if I can't do it again? What if that one time I played—that time I was alone—what if it was a fluke?"

"I don't believe that." Jake's hand covered mine, squeezing lightly. "You've got this. I know you do."

A slow burn wound its way from my fingertips to my heart, sending it into overdrive. "What if you're wrong?"

"What if I'm right?"

I looked over his shoulder, and then I shook my head. "So it's a shot in the dark."

"I'm right." He leaned in closer, squeezed my hand a little tighter. "I know you can do this, angel. You don't have to trust me. Just trust you."

His words splintered my soul, and I felt a hysterical crying fit coming on. "I don't think I know how to do that anymore... trust anyone. Or anything. Not even myself."

His fingers moved and threaded through my hair. He pushed strands away from my eyes, tucking stray pieces behind my ear as I stared at the keys and tried not to cry.

"I know how you feel." His fingers caressed my cheek, then lower, against my neck.

My skin tingled, and I wanted to bury my face against his chest, for him to wrap his arms around me until all my pain melted away. But I was afraid I would crumble into tiny, unrecognizable pieces of despair, so I didn't move an inch. "I wish you didn't. It's a terrible feeling."

He offered a small smile, and I was heartsick when his warm fingers no longer pressed against me. I should've leaned into him, asking him for the things I wanted, like Kat insisted I start doing.

But I couldn't—I should've been apologizing. Asking him to forgive the fact that I riffled through his stuff. That I saw what I saw.

That I know what I know.

And I couldn't do that, either.

But what did I know?

Jake had private thoughts—secrets—he shared with no one. So what?

The sound of electronic notes broke up the silence. It was the first time I'd ever heard Jake's phone ring. He glanced down, pulling it from his pocket. Two seconds later, the phone rested on his lap, silenced.

I didn't realize I was staring until he looked at me and said, "It was my mom."

"Oh. Why didn't you answer?"

"She wants me to come home and visit. She knows I won't, but she keeps calling anyway."

"Why won't you go?"

He didn't respond. Instead, he stared at the sheet music in front of us, his hands visibly tightening over his knees.

"I'm sorry," I said, shaking my head. "It's none of my business."

I didn't want a repeat of our camping trip. And I'd been wrong before—for trying to push. For invading his privacy. Everyone had a right to their secrets.

"I haven't seen them in two years," Jake said. "My parents. My mom calls me sometimes. Asks me to drive down there to visit. She wants me to come over for my birthday. I've told her no three times already."

With all the Facebook stalking I'd done, I should have remembered his birthday was coming up.

"But the truth is, I don't want to see them." He paused, glancing sideways. "My dad is always drunk, and my mom is usually passed out from her meds—or not taking them. And the latter is much worse. It's always a shit show every time I see them. What's the point?"

What's the point?

I took a few breaths, rubbed my palms together, and tried to keep my face neutral. But I'd heard the bitterness laced over every word, heard the anger and resentment in his quiet explanation of the two people who should've meant more to him.

I thought of my mom and dad, of how much I simply *adored* them as parents. Sure, they'd grounded me more times than I could count. They'd punished me for sneaking out of the house, and taken away my cell phone. They'd done all the appropriate *mean parents* things. But they weren't mean. They were great. And I loved them.

Jake didn't have to say it—he didn't love his parents.

Sure, maybe some biological part of him loved them because he was supposed to love them—they were his parents, after all. But then, was that love? If you only love a thing because you're supposed to, is it worth anything?

That didn't sound like the kind of love I'd want to have.

"I'm sorry," I finally said.

"It's not your fault my deal of the cards was shittier than most. And I thought I told you I didn't want you apologizing to me for anything."

Because I wanted to change the subject—because I knew *he* wanted me to—I said, "So what are you doing for your birthday?" And yes, I was stalling, too.

"I'm not into the whole celebration thing."

"That's super lame, you know."

His eyebrows shifted upward. "You're not plotting out a surprise party for me, are you? Because you should know, I disapprove."

I cracked a smile. "How would I throw you a party? Who would I invite? Neither of us has any friends."

It was supposed to be a joke—until I'd said it and felt the truth behind it. My words fell flat, a complete merrymaking buzzkill.

"We're friends…" he said after a long stretch of silence. "But you're basically the only one because I'm not sure I know how to be a good one."

I inhaled slowly, wiping my palms against my jeans. "Just don't shut me out again." *Please.*

"I shouldn't be making those kinds of promises," he said, not looking at me, his hands in tight balls. "Given my track record." He paused. "But I'll try."

My lips parted, about to tell Jake I didn't get it. There were lots of things he didn't want to tell me—so, okay. Fine. That at least made sense. But what didn't make any freaking sense was all the back-and-forth. First he said he wouldn't kiss me, then he did…then he said he couldn't be my friend, and now he could? To put it simply, I was confused.

But I didn't say any of that. Desperation looked good on no one.

"You want to give the song a shot?" he asked, oblivious to the torment inside my head.

Since I had nothing left to say, I nodded.

I shoved all thoughts of Kat and Emily—and her enigmatic brother—to a dark place in the back of my mind, and focused on the black-and-white sheet music.

The song is all that matters.

That's what I told myself, over and over until I believed it. And after two false starts, I played through the song. As it turned out, Jake had been right.

"See," he said once I'd finished. "Knew you could do it."

Chapter Eighteen

Kat and I discussed our funerals once. How we envisioned them. What music we wanted. Who we thought would show up. We laughed about it, eating popcorn on her bed. She declared that "Satisfied Mind" by Jeff Buckley would be her funeral song. "It's a happy sad," is what she'd said.

And she wanted people at her funeral to be happy sad.

I sat hunched over in the pew when her song came on, and I couldn't find the happiness anywhere in me. It made me even sadder—that I couldn't give her what she'd wanted.

I would never be able to listen to that song again.

She was only eighteen. Emily was only seventeen. Not nearly enough time for either of them. It wasn't fair, and I didn't fucking care that life wasn't supposed to be fair.

I pressed a hand over my mouth to keep from making noise as the pressure in my chest increased.

They were both dead, and they shouldn't be.

But maybe I should.

Mom came back to the aisle where I sat. She shifted past me and took a seat. "Honey, how are you doing?"

I shook my head. *Not good.* But I couldn't speak.

She handed me a tissue, which I balled inside my fist.

I started thinking about what Emily's funeral might've been like. If there was music or a slideshow, and what kind of flowers surrounded her. Did she ever have a conversation with her best friend about her one-day funeral? Did she have a song picked out?

Thoughts of Emily led to thoughts of Jake.

And the most awful thing was...I wanted so badly to talk to Kat about him.

God, I fucking missed her. And a part of me still hoped this was one big joke, one long nightmare I could wake up from. Kat would be there, sitting on her bed, and I would tell her all about it. We'd make jokes, and she'd say something like *you can't get rid of me that easily.* She would laugh and tell me how stupid I was being.

But those thoughts were only delusions in my head.

In a parallel universe, another Kat was alive. Maybe parallel-Audra stopped her from going to the party. Maybe *that* version of myself demanded Kat was required to stay in and mope with me, as per our friendship agreement.

This possibility tore through my chest like a rocket, sending waves of pain that hurt so much, I wanted to pass out just to feel relief.

Mom wrapped her arm around my shoulder and rubbed it, making me feel ten years old, but I didn't mind because I was too sad to care.

Kat had said she expected dozens of people to show up to her funeral—she'd been right. The seats were filling up, and there had to be at least fifty people in attendance. She'd always been popular. Everyone liked her—okay, not entirely true. She knew how to be a bitch, and she pissed a few people off along the way. But all in all, Kat was a good person. Easy to like. Easy to miss.

"Honey," Mom whispered, moving her arm.

"Hmm?" I blinked at her through the fog in my vision.

She nodded behind me. I swiveled in the seat, expecting to see someone I knew—a high school friend maybe. But when I looked up, it wasn't someone I'd shared a lunch period with or gone to a volleyball game with.

"Jake." It was the first real word I'd spoken in over an hour.

He wore a pair of simple black pants with a button-up black shirt. Hands stuck into his pockets, he pulled his lips upward halfheartedly. "Hey. Is this seat open?"

I looked at the empty seat beside me and nodded.

Without saying anything else, Jake sat and gave me a sideways glance.

"What are you doing here?" I whispered, trying to keep my voice steady.

"I thought you might need a friend."

I clasped the unused tissue tighter. "I really hate funerals."

His lopsided smile sent shivers through my deadened heart.

Jake leaned closer. "I like the music. Those funerals where they opt not to play anything over the speaker system? They're so quiet. It's like you have to tiptoe around, making sure you don't wake the dead."

If it were a different day, I would've agreed.

"I can't go back in time and go to Emily's, but…if I can be here for you and for your friend, maybe I can somehow… redeem myself for not being there when I should've been."

"You drove forty-five minutes to attend the funeral of a girl you met once. In a doorway."

His hand found mine, warm and so much bigger. Interlocking our fingers, he said, "I hope it's coming across as sweet, rather than stalkerish."

I wanted to laugh for the first time that day, but I wasn't

quite there yet. "The former."

Squeezing my hand, he leaned over and kissed my forehead. I sucked in air and turned to look at him, but his gaze shifted to the pew in front of us. His presence settled the part of me that had vibrated around all day like a shrieking alarm clock unwilling to shut up, and I could finally breathe again.

The preacher or priest — or whichever — started talking. I never could keep them straight. "The life of the dead is placed in the memory of the living."

I tried not to listen to everything he said. Sometimes it got to be too much, and I wanted to scream from all the bottled sobs. Jake's hand never left mine as the service continued.

"The truth is," the man addressing the crowd said, "you will grieve forever."

Maybe he could've lied to us instead?

"You will never be able to replace what your heart lost. You will be broken, but you will mend. You'll never recover from your loss, but your heart will be repaired. You'll never be the same afterward. But why would you want to be?"

He continued with a quote by Epicurus, an ancient Greek philosopher. "'Why should I fear death? If I am, death is not. If death is, I am not. Why should I fear that which can only exist when I do not?'"

I was never afraid of death — of dying.

I was never afraid of *my* death.

That day, when Kat and I talked about our funerals, she'd said, "If I die first, you're going to give my eulogy, right?"

"No way," I'd said immediately. "I'd burst into tears. It would be awful to watch. You wouldn't want me defiling your memory like that."

"Oh please. Who else is going to stand up there and tell everyone how awesome I was?"

"Your future husband?" I'd suggested, throwing popcorn

at her head. "Your son or daughter? Someone who has better public speaking skills than me?"

That had earned me an eye roll. "I don't care who else is in my future. They won't be able to say they knew me when. Not like you. You have to promise you'll give my eulogy if I die first. And make it epic. I don't care if you cry. In fact, I *hope* you cry."

I'd made her a promise. I had no choice but to stand in front of all these people—most of whom I knew—and give them the eulogy Kat would've wanted.

"Kat and I met in the fourth grade," I said, after giving myself instructions on how to breathe. *In. Out. Slower. In. Out. In. Out.* "We were making turkeys out of construction paper for a project and while I wasn't looking, she glued all of my pieces together in the wrong spots. She'd pretty much ruined it. And when I asked her why she did it...she looked at me with the biggest, saddest eyes and said, 'Your pieces were better than mine.' And then she started crying." *In. Out.* "I can't tell you why I bought that line of crap, but I did." I laughed hoarsely to myself, looking at the wooden beams running across the ceiling. Kat had always been good at using the puppy dog look to get out of things, even back then.

"From that moment on, we were inseparable," I said, still looking up, still trying to keep my shit together. "It was almost like we had ESP, the way we understood each other, the way we were always connected. And I..." I lowered my chin. Squeezed my eyes shut. Ignored the pounding of my heart.

I was supposed to die first—before everyone I knew, everyone I loved. Those were the cards life had given me. Then fate was altered, leaving an invisible hole in my heart more catastrophic than the one I'd been born with.

I opened my eyes and looked out at the people, over the tops of their heads. "And...she would be *really* pissed off if she knew I said this but...there's not a thing in this world I wouldn't give to trade places with her."

My gaze found Jake, but when it did, he dropped his head, lowered his eyes, despair crumpling his beautiful features.

And I cried.

Chapter Nineteen

"Do you want to get a coffee or something?" Jake asked after the funeral was over.

Despite everything, the thought of something as simple as coffee with Jake still did stupid things to my heart. "I would, but I'm going over to my parents' for dinner."

Mom's voice interrupted from behind us. "You're more than welcome to invite him, honey."

I fixed my face into flat lines as soon as she said it, hoping I wouldn't blush like a ten-year-old caught playing with her mother's makeup. "Uh," I sputtered, watching Jake's lips curve into a smile. I understood that particular smile—he was laughing *at* me. Oh man. "Yeah, I mean, you could come over—if you wanted, but it's totally cool if you don't."

Mom, what the hell are you doing? God, I hoped my mental signals were getting through. *Jake and I aren't even dating. He does* not *want to come over for dinner.*

But my ESP only ever worked with Kat.

"Would you like to come over, Jake?" Mom asked him directly this time, bypassing me.

He'd lost most of his smile. *Ha! See how that spotlight feels? Not so good.*

"Well, if no one is going to object, let's get going," she said with a wave of her hand. "I'll see you both there." And she disappeared into the thinning crowd.

"What did you do?" I asked him.

"Me?" His brows pulled together. "You're related to her. It was your responsibility to tell her no."

"Did you just make that up?"

"'Course not."

I eyed him. "Uh-huh. You're wrong, though. You were supposed to say you were busy. Thanks, but I have to go feed my bunny. You know, something like that."

"How is that better?" Jake asked.

"Or, *ooh*, you have pet snails. You have to feed your pet snails."

"How is *that* better?"

I shrugged. "Snails are low maintenance. They fit you."

"I'm going to take that as a compliment."

I nodded and broke away to say my good-byes. I kept it to Kat's immediate family. Five minutes to say good-bye and try not to cry anymore. Smile. Try to be happy. It was hard enough not to run from the room, knowing fresh air and relief were on the other side of that door.

Jake and I didn't talk as we climbed into his truck and headed to my parents' house. The ride was short, and when we were coming up on their street I said, "Most dudes would've bailed. Like, immediately." Maybe even boyfriends. "You *want* to have dinner with my parents, don't you?" I shifted my body sideways, pinning him with a look.

"I wouldn't go that far." He glanced away from the road.

"Turn right up here. Why else would you agree to this?"

"Maybe I'm hoping your mom will pull out the baby pictures."

Oh, she wouldn't do that, she —

She would.

I untied my hair and retied it, just for something to do with my hands as we pulled into the driveway. My parents had never met any of my boyfriends—although I only had one that counted.

But Jake wasn't my boyfriend.

"Am I smiling too much again?"

"Huh?" I turned at Jake's question.

"You look nervous. Is it my smiling?" There was no trace of a smile to be found.

I stared, confused for a few beats—and then began laughing—a frenzied sound that was thick with sadness.

His lips strained to one side, considering. He said, "Better," and climbed out of the truck.

I'd sat at this dinner table so many times, but never with a guy who I wished more than anything would kiss me again. Adding in the fact that we just returned from my best friend's funeral—it was awkward, to say the least.

Dinner with the parents always sounded terrible to me. All that small talk? All those interview-type questions? No, thank you. I'd rather drive a drill through my eye.

But Jake responded to every one of Mom's and Dad's questions like it didn't bother him. Granted, they kept their questions to school and work and campus—but how did it not bother him that this was *so* weird?

Jake didn't like talking to people. Sometimes he didn't even like talking to me.

"Honey, is something wrong?" Mom asked.

I blinked up from my vacant stare at the peas on my plate. "What? No." I glanced at Jake, who smirked.

This made no sense.

"I'm good," I said, putting on a smile.

After dinner, Mom insisted Jake and I didn't need to help clean up, so we went out to the back porch.

"Are you enjoying yourself?" I asked him after shutting the sliding glass door.

"The food was good." He smiled.

I buttoned my coat and stuck my hands into my pockets to protect them from the wind. "I don't get it."

"Get what?"

"Family dinners don't seem like your kind of thing."

He chuckled and dragged one foot against the wood. "You remember my theory about people showing up late?"

"I don't know if I'd call that a theory, but I remember."

"I have another theory."

"Oh?" I stepped off the patio onto the grass, motioning for him to follow.

"I think people have no choice but to be themselves when they're around their parents," he said, catching up to me. "You can't hide who you are."

I eyed him. "So you thought I was lying to you about who I am?"

"I didn't say that."

"Okay. Say I believe you. Did your theory prove anything?"

Jake turned away from me, but not before I saw his smile. "It did."

I stopped walking, unwilling to go farther until he spit it out already. "What did it prove?"

Dead leaves crackled beneath his feet when he turned back to me. "Smiling isn't the only thing that makes you nervous."

"Uh-huh. Glad your experiment worked out for you."

"So am I."

What would meeting his parents prove? Anything?

I continued toward the tree house at the back of the property. Jake kept pace beside me.

I shoved the old tree house door open. The wood creaked, showing its old age, and I stepped inside. "My dad was disappointed they never had a boy, I think. He built me this tree house when I was eight. But it was originally up in the air. You had to walk up a few steps to get to it, and I was scared of heights. I may have cried once or twice. So he ended up taking it down and rebuilding it directly on the grass."

Jake trailed me inside the small structure. Two wooden stools sat inside next to the simple square window.

"Kat and I practically lived in here," I said, running my hand over the roughened wood. It was our live-in Barbie Dreamhouse, minus the dream. The dreams only existed in our heads.

"Are you still afraid of heights?" he asked, leaning against the planks that formed the walls.

I shrugged, biting on my lower lip. The only reason I got over most of that fear was because Kat never had it, and I thought she was brave. I'd wanted to be brave, too. "Maybe a little."

I stared out the window at the thinning trees, thinking of the days Kat and I spent in the tree house until Jake spoke, interrupting my reminiscing.

"What's this?"

He pointed at an engraving of the letters KAAA in one of the wood planks. Kat and I did that one night when we were fifteen, right after Billy Jacobson broke up with her and we decided we didn't need boys. "K, triple A," I said. "Kat and Audra Always. It was our thing." BFF was too common, too boring. "K, triple A" had a nice ring to it.

"Creative." Jake smiled, but after another moment it disappeared as if it hadn't existed at all. "I can't imagine what that must've been like."

"What?"

"Having a childhood where a tree house was a possibility."

I stared at him, but he kept watching the chair like it might do a trick. My fingers itched to reach out to him again, but I couldn't. And that didn't make me brave. It made me a coward.

"You were lucky," he said, taking a seat.

"Maybe," I whispered.

He finally looked up, his eyes wide but dark, lips stretched but open. "All I ever wanted to do was run away. Did you ever feel like that?"

My pounding heart pumped cold blood through my veins.

"I thought about it all the time. Dreamed about it. Almost did it, even." His gaze dropped, and he shook his head. Maybe he was wondering if he should take down the invisible wall he kept between us. "I wanted to run away and then be able to come back…come back and save them."

I sucked in the stale, frigid oxygen, but there wasn't enough air in the tiny tree house anymore.

Jake stood, his voice almost inaudible now. "I wanted to save them. My sister and my mom. But I didn't."

I took a step forward, still trying to breathe. "You can't save everyone."

"I didn't want to save everyone."

I tried not to be hurt by the anger in his words, but I stopped moving forward, still inches away.

"I only wanted to save *them*."

Long moments went by. My frantic heartbeat had become a typical thing for me, and soon enough, not being able to breathe would be a typical thing, too.

"If you're to blame," I said. "If it's your fault she's dead… then it's my fault Kat is dead. So unless you're going to tell me that's true—"

"It's not the same thing, Audra."

"Yes, it is. If you don't want me blaming myself for something I couldn't have prevented, then you'd better not do the same thing."

He twisted his jaw, eyed me, and stayed silent.

"You know I'm right," I said, whispering now. "It's not your fault. It's not...not my fault either." Saying the words out loud didn't make me believe them. My voice cracked with the lie, and my heart pulsed with the longing to trust my own words.

Jake's chest rose and fell quickly. Guess I wasn't the only one not getting enough oxygen. "I want to believe that."

Ignoring the pounding in my head and the enormous urge to break down and cry, I hugged him, wrapping my arms tightly around his back. Breathing in his clean, fresh scent, I memorized the way it felt to be in his arms, because I always had this aching feeling it would be the *last* time. I whispered against the soft material of his shirt, "Me, too."

With his arms still wrapped around my waist, I looked up. His face was haloed by the porch lights streaming through the tree house window. I started to inch back, but his hands pressed against my hips, urging me to stay.

Our mouths collided, and the air between us hummed electric. This kiss was slower than our first. Different somehow. My pulse jumped, a brightness flashed behind my eyes, and my beloved tree house fell away. Everything fell away. It was just me and Jake. His lips and mine. And for a moment, while his tongue explored my mouth and his fingers grazed my lower back, my pain ceased to matter. Nothing mattered aside from the warmth buzzing through my veins and the quick beating of my heart.

I never knew a kiss could do that—make your heart sing. But then, I never knew a heart could sing, either.

Chapter Twenty

One week.

That's how long Kat had been dead.

I stared at my phone once or twice daily, expecting to see her name on my caller ID. See a text from her. Hear her tell me how she was completely in love with my new shoes and would do *anything* if she could borrow them.

Seven days.

How many until I'd stop hurting?

I wanted to drop out of my classes, but Jake talked me out of it. Still not sure how he managed that.

Laying my cheek against my palm, I shut my eyes, wishing class would end already. I liked psychology before. But Kat had been in this class with me. And the material we were learning made me want to hide in my room and never come out.

I was depressed enough as it was—on the verge of tears at any given moment.

"Anger," Professor Otto said, "is a natural defense against pain."

I pried my eyes open, blinked up at the clock.

"If someone is expressing anger it is more likely than not caused by an underlying pain. This is especially true in clinically depressed patients."

Depression was the chapter we were on. Fucking perfect.

I blocked out the rest of the lecture. I couldn't listen anymore and still keep my sanity.

When class finally ended, I headed for the auditorium doors, and my phone vibrated in my hand.

Jake: *If you come to the piano room, I'll play something for you.*

Distracted by his text, I nearly ran into a girl turning the corner. I mumbled my apologies, adjusting the strap on my bag.

It was a strange request from Jake. His lessons always focused on me hitting the keys, creating the music. Not the other way around. And he'd never offered to play anything for me before.

When I got to the piano room, Jake was alone. As usual.

Every time I saw him, I thought of what Kat said to me. And then I'd think of our kiss the other night, and I'd *know* she was wrong. Or that she could've been wrong. Jake was capable of more than *maybe* and *supposed to.*

"Hey." I inched toward the piano and lowered my bag to the floor. "Since when do you come here during the day?"

He shifted, making room for me on the bench. "I normally don't. But I've been working on something. So. All right, ready to hear this?"

I nodded.

He lifted his arms and inhaled a steadying breath. He pressed down on the black and white keys, filling the quiet room with music. His fingers glided across the piano seamlessly until the song lilted to an end.

All I could do was stare at his hands, unmoving now.

"So it was terrible," he said matter-of-factly. "It's okay. I can take it."

"No. No." I laughed. "*No*. It was great. Jake, it was beautiful."

His smile took on a weird shift, part of his mouth crunching together, his eyebrows following suit. "It's no Bach or 'Clair de Lune' but…I haven't written a whole lot of songs."

"Wait. You wrote that?"

His brows relaxed, but his mouth kept the jagged shape. "Yep."

Now that I knew, I wanted to hear it again. "Seriously?"

"I guess you inspired me."

I swallowed thickly, the cadence of my heart picking up. "Oh—you. You what, wrote that…for me?"

He didn't.

Jake laughed—a low, warm sound. "Yes."

Sure, there were no words to the song, so it was no confession of undying love or anything. But it was beautiful and unique and—holy *shit*. "You—" My throat constricted, causing my voice to squeak. "But why?"

He shrugged like it was really no big deal. "Why not?"

"I don't know what to say. I…thank you."

"Giving you these lessons has reminded me of why I liked playing in the first place. So it's the least I could do."

I bit on my lower lip, trying not to blush. "Definitely not the least you could do. Seriously. It's great. You're great."

His lips moved, but not into a smile—and it was all I could pay attention to. He was so close. Mere inches away. "Thank you."

"I'm the one thanking you, remember?" I said, looking away from his lips.

Jake stayed silent, placing his hands atop the keys. He made a few notes, slowly, carefully. Even those sounded beautiful. But then he stopped and twisted toward me.

He kissed me. Gently. Deeply. Fiercely. Like he was trying to tell me something he couldn't put into words.

Fireworks ricocheted in my chest as he pulled away, and even still when he returned to slowly pressing the piano keys. He glanced over, and a subtle smile brightened his face. When he looked at me like that, I wondered if maybe, just maybe, he felt the electricity, too.

After a few minutes of listening to him play, my stomach turned and toppled around, stabbing me with invisible needles instead of thrilling fireworks—just like that. No warning. That's the way it always happened when I thought about Kat. Sometimes I'd get distracted enough to truly *not* be thinking about her. Like before. And then *wham*—all the agony would return. How long could a person survive with that kind of pain?

"It never stops hurting," I whispered.

Jake stilled his fingers, turning the room silent. "Nothing lasts forever, angel."

I turned to him. "Why do you call me that?"

"You can keep asking me, and I will keep telling you the same reason."

I wanted to laugh—but the pain in my chest insisted I cry.

"I think this pain might last forever," I said. "Maybe you were wrong."

"You'd doubt me?"

"You're the one who hasn't seen your parents in two years because of what happened, so if you're trying to tell me you're not still in any pain, I call bullshit."

I wasn't looking at him while I spoke, so when I turned and took in his expression, something new twisted in my gut.

"You're right," he said slowly, controlling his voice and steadying it out. "I haven't seen them. And yes, I still feel pain over what happened." His face lost all its happiness, all its clarity. Now it was empty, and if there was a fraction of emotion left, it was only agony. "But I hope that one day I won't have to feel that way anymore. Am I not allowed to do that?"

His voice hardened as he spoke, increasing the storm in my chest exponentially.

I'm such an asshole.

No wonder I never had real friends other than Kat.

"I shouldn't have said that. I'm sorry." I smashed my hands together instead of pounding them against my forehead. "I'm just so—I feel so *awful* all the time, and I didn't mean to be rude. I don't know anything about your family. I have no right to say any of that."

Jake's face didn't relax as much as I'd hoped. "I don't like talking about them. I honestly don't like remembering they exist."

"That's why I'm trying to apologize."

My heart ticked off the time as it passed in silence. I'd done it again. Pushed too far. But I tried to stop myself, I tried—

"Do you still want to know how she died?"

The air turned colder, and the room felt smaller now, emphasizing the closeness of Jake and me. "You don't have to tell me."

He opened his mouth, staring hard at my face, but he didn't make a sound. One second passed. Two seconds. Three. And then I stopped counting.

"When we were little," he said, breaking the silence that was constricting my heart, "my dad always beat on me. Sometimes he beat my mom, but mostly me. *Definitely* never Emily. I would have never…let that happen. And I don't mean he smacked me around when he got pissed off. He beat me until I thought I might pass out and not wake up, until I thought, this time might be the last. And if not this time, maybe the next…"

I stared at his furrowed brow and hard, angry jaw. At his clenched fists sitting side by side on his lap. His chest rising. Falling.

What did his heart sound like—how fast was it beating?

It was a nice diversion from thinking about Jake's father beating the living hell out of him.

After hushed moments of imagined heartbeats, Jake continued. "I moved out the day I turned eighteen and I thought—" His words turned to murmurs. "I don't know what happened after I left. Emily was seventeen. She only had a year before she could move away to school. She was okay. She was happy. *She was okay.* There's no way she killed herself."

Oh God.

"Jake," I said, staggered by the jagged sound of my voice.

He looked at me for the first time since he'd started talking. "She didn't kill herself."

I swallowed. Remembered to breathe.

He shook his head, running a hand through his hair roughly. "My parents told me there were drugs in her system when she died. But they didn't tell me which ones. And it's not like I ever got to see a medical examiner's report. So it doesn't prove a thing. Not to me. My parents could've easily lied."

"What do you mean? Why…why would they do that?"

He stared silently at the piano. Maybe he didn't want to say it as much as I didn't want to think it.

A noise behind us shattered the illusion that we were alone. I swiveled my shoulders and spotted a janitor pushing a cart. He stopped by the trash can inside the room and shoved the lid off. When I turned back to Jake, his gaze locked with mine.

"I don't know what happened," he said in a whisper. "But my parents are to blame. Emily didn't end her life with a handful of pills. I know she didn't."

I watched the janitor again as he slowly padded out of the room, pushing the cart in front of him. Once he was gone, I scooted off the bench. I felt like I'd been let out of a small box. Relieved. But not completely.

Because Jake thought his parents were to blame for Emily's death.

"That's why you don't talk to them," I said. "But…what about your mom? I mean, was it just your dad who…"

"My mom couldn't stop him, even if she'd wanted to. Sometimes I don't know if she did want to."

Because if she'd wanted to stop him, wouldn't she have left? For her own sake? To save her children?

"She's mentally ill," he said, sliding off the bench. "But it's never been a good enough excuse for me."

I followed him away from the piano and toward the door.

"You want to get something to eat before your next class?" he asked—he'd decided he was done sharing. I wouldn't get to ask any more questions about his mom or her illness or why his parents would lie.

I nodded, but food sounded terrible. I was still trying to stop my stomach from flipping around; how was I supposed to put food in it?

But I wanted to spend more time with Jake. I always did. Especially now—now that without him, I was all alone.

We walked past the cafeteria area where students sat around the scattered tables. Some talking, some eating, and some staring at their laptop screens, chewing. I looked over and up, wishing I could ask all of the questions on my mind.

"I've got a gallery exhibition opening on Friday," Jake said, and I grabbed his arm, pulling him to a stop.

"Seriously? Why didn't you say anything before? That sounds like a big deal."

He shrugged. "It is, I guess. I don't know why…it's not like I'm used to having people to invite."

He gave a smile I didn't believe, and it hurt in places I didn't even know could hurt. I thought of my parents and all the things we'd done together. Spelling bees. School plays. Even dance recitals and volleyball games I couldn't participate in. If I had my photographs on display, they'd absolutely be there.

"Is my picture going to be in the exhibition?" I asked, to steer my thoughts in a different direction.

"That photograph may have made the cut."

I smiled. I'd been counting them lately—my smiles—since Kat's funeral. The numbers weren't great, but they were bigger around Jake.

"So you'll be there?" he asked.

"Of course. I've been impatiently waiting to see what you did with my face."

He laughed. "It's in the art gallery on the first floor of the fine arts building. Opens at five. Closes at eight. So whenever you want to come."

I kept the smile on my face even when a thousand new thoughts poured into my brain. Ones like *everyone will be staring at my face*. But who the hell cared? Things like that weren't important. Things like honesty and bravery—those were important.

Honesty like Jake telling me about Emily. And bravery like I didn't have—to tell Jake how I really felt.

He held the main exit door open for me. The October air chilled my fingers, the same way thoughts of Emily chilled my heart.

As we neared my dorm, Jake said, "Are you free tomorrow afternoon?"

"Yeah, my last class is over at one. Why?"

"Let's go somewhere. I have this idea, and I know the perfect place." He sent me my favorite crooked smile. "I'll pick you up at two, okay? Dress warmly."

I didn't sleep that night. Staring at the swirls of plaster on the ceiling, I wondered what really happened, if Emily did kill herself.

Jake lived with that question for two years. No wonder he had demons nipping at his soul, knocking on his door, and threatening everything he sought to have.

I wanted—*needed*—to help him. If I could only figure out how.

Chapter Twenty-One

I wore a dark brown sweater and my favorite pair of boots. The air was brisk, but not intolerable, so I wasn't too worried — until Jake parked his truck in front of what appeared to be nothing more than a nondescript dirt road.

He reached into the backseat and pulled out two bags. One I recognized as his camera bag, and the other was a medium-sized duffel.

"Pictures?" I asked.

"Not exactly." His face gave nothing away, and while I sat there trying to figure it out, he opened the door.

I frowned, but followed suit, climbing out of my seat and walking around the front of the truck. "You get a kick out of it, don't you?"

"Kick out of what?"

"Confusing people. Being cryptic and mysterious and all that jazz."

He laughed, spreading his free arm out to the side as if to say *you caught me*. "The look you get on your face makes it all worth it."

"For real?"

Setting the bags on the ground, Jake smirked. "Have I ever lied to you before?"

The question invaded my mind, spreading a fresh wave of guilt throughout my body. *No. I'm the only one who's lied.* "But you—"

"Come on." He stepped forward, laying his hand against my shoulder and squeezing. "It's a surprise. Most people like surprises."

I shook my head. "I'm not most people."

"I know. That's why I like you." Jake moved his hand to my face, cupping my cheek, and kissed me lightly on the forehead. "So come on." His fingers lingered against my skin, brushing hair away from my face. He smiled, then turned away, swiping his bags from the gravel and dirt.

I caught up to him, and we walked down the overgrown path. It was eerily quiet, with only the occasional chirping of a bird breaking up the silence. That and our footsteps crunching over gravel and fallen leaves.

Five minutes later, we stepped into a wide-open field. Dull green grass and multicolored leaves covered the space, and aside from the trees, there wasn't much to see. It was no extravagant garden, but it was secluded and something about that was tranquil. Comforting.

"Is this the part where you tell me what we're doing here?" I asked.

"It's the perfect spot for a picnic, don't you think?"

I eyed him. He just smiled and walked out to the middle of the field. I followed, and he set his bags down, then unzipped the duffel. He pulled out a few plastic bags and a dark blue blanket.

"I've never had a picnic before." Not like this.

"I was hoping you'd say that."

"You were?"

Without looking at me, Jake spread the blanket out across the grass. "It's a new one for your list."

Oh. "A picnic wasn't on Emily's Tumblr though."

Jake motioned for me to sit, so I did. He knelt on the blanket and opened up the grocery bags, pulling the contents out. "No. That's why I said it's a new one."

"But…" I curled my legs to the side and accepted the sandwich he handed me, as well as a can of Coke. "We didn't finish Emily's done-its yet."

He tossed a bag of pretzels my way, followed by a bag of Oreos. "I know. But who says you can't do one of your own before you finish the list?"

Guess he had a point.

Jake lifted a bag of Twizzlers, red and glorious, waving them in the air. "Thought you might appreciate these."

"You sure do know the way to my heart," I said, reaching for them.

He laughed and handed them over. "One more thing. Our picnic wouldn't be complete without some of these." With a sly grin, he revealed a box, displaying it like a prize on some lame game show.

I covered my mouth with my hand, and laughed. "You didn't."

"What, you think your eyes are deceiving you?"

"Cheez-Its?"

He set the box down. "Appropriate, right? Bonus: they're actually pretty good."

"Totally appropriate," I agreed.

"Sorry it's nothing gourmet. No cheese, grapes, and wine. I guess peanut butter and jelly is far from romantic, but it was the best I could do."

"You're trying to be romantic?"

His gaze slid sideways, looking out at the thick lining of trees. "Ah, romance isn't exactly my thing. In theory, it sounds good. Sounds easy. But I always seem to fuck it up." He smiled, finally settling his eyes on me again. "I wanted to do something nice."

It was nice, and I told him so.

By the time we finished our picnic lunch, a soft breeze had picked up, scattering leaves throughout the vacant field and onto our blanket. We talked about everything and nothing all at the same time, and I decided this *was* romantic. Not in the way flowers, or gifts, or expensive dates are romantic—those things are easy. Besides, I favored the quiet conversations with Jake in desolate places, sharing inside jokes, eating Cheez-Its and Twizzlers.

After everything was put away aside from the blanket, Jake and I ended up lying on our backs, staring up at the clouds rolling by slowly overhead. I spent the entire time smiling, because this was the happiest I'd been since Kat died.

Jake grew quiet, and the silence was comfortable, until it wasn't. Until thoughts of my best friend led to thoughts of his sister and a vise squeezed my heart, reminding me of my never-ending pain.

I rolled onto my side, propping my head on my hand. "Can I ask you something?"

He slid his gaze my way, and his gray eyes almost looked green in the sunlight. "Obviously."

I'd planned to ask him what he thought his parents actually did—would they really have hurt their own daughter? But Jake looked so content, happy even, and I couldn't bring myself to ruin it. So instead, I picked a different question. "Will you be in the picture with me? The one for my list?"

His brows pulled together slightly, but he was grinning. "Only if I get to choose the caption."

"And I get to choose the hashtags?"

"Sure."

I sat up, a giddy, childlike feeling swelling in my chest.

Jake agreeing to a photo felt like some kind of victory. Lying back down, I held my phone out and laughed. "Say cheese."

And he did.

. . .

I uploaded the best shot of Jake and me to Tumblr, added his chosen Ansel Adams quote, and included my selection of hashtags.

Not everybody trusts paintings, but people believe photographs.

#PicnicInTheMiddleOfNowhere   #Twizzlers4Life
#PhotoSaysItAll #MyFavoritePhotographerJake

The photo of us was silly, but admittedly adorable. I'd never seen a picture where Jake looked so...carefree. I sent him the link, because he needed to see it, too.

Smiling stupidly at my phone, I scrolled through my Facebook feed because I had nothing better to do for the next hour until class. And when boredom got the better of me, I searched for Emily's page.

It was like a living, breathing memorial site. Friends still commented every once in a while, even though she'd been gone for two years. It occurred mostly on her birthday and on the anniversary of her death.

Kat's page was already transforming into a digital memorial. Two years from now, her page would be identical to Emily's. I didn't know if I wanted my Facebook page to exist after I was dead and gone, but I bet Kat would've.

I stared at the screen like I'd done so many times before when I'd searched Emily's name, scrolling through her wall, finding notes like *I miss you.* Or *I'm still thinking about you, Emily!*

Jake's confession about her death and his parents tumbled around in my head while I perused her page. Didn't he want to know what happened? Had he ever considered coming right out and asking his parents?

I answered my own questions as soon as I thought them. Surely he wanted to know the truth, but there was no way in hell he'd ever *ask*.

My eyes scanned over the latest post on Emily's wall. *Memorial service this Sunday at two o'clock.*

This Sunday would be two years since my heart transplant. Two years since she died. I didn't think people actually held anniversary-of-death memorials.

I clicked on the girl who commented. Dana Brixton. I'd deduced—with my awesomely creepy detective skills—that she was one of Emily's best friends. At least that's what it looked like based on their photos together and comments to each other in the past.

Tapping my fingers against my black leggings, I considered what I was about to do. Creepy? Or justified? Maybe creepy-justified?

With my heart booming against my rib cage, I decided.

Me: *I'm a friend of Emily's. (Something like a second cousin twice removed or whatever.) I'd like to come to the memorial this weekend. Can you give me more details? Thank you.*

I hit send and let out a long, slow breath. My Facebook messages had become so serious, so life-or-death. Social media used to be pointless fun. Now it housed all the answers I'd grown desperate for. And it was freaking weird.

A new message.

She'd responded—holy crap that was quick.

Dana: *Yeah! Logan Hills Church. 453 Gibraltar Rd.*

At 2 p.m. Glad to hear you're coming. Do you want to speak during the service?

Uh. Oh no. I quickly sent a thanks, but no thanks reply. I wanted to be as invisible as possible.

When Jake texted me moments after closing the stupid app, guilt pricked at my spine.

Jake: *It's cheesy, but I like it. Speaking of cheese... Pizza?*

Me: *Only if we can get a Hawaiian this time.*

I smiled to myself after hitting send, but it faded when the guilt stabbed harder.

I didn't want to tell Jake I was going to the memorial, but keeping it from him felt like a lie.

Jake: *Gross.*

I stared at his response and wanted to laugh. I was trying to help him, not hide things from him — not any *more* things.

Me: *Fine. Pepperoni and mushrooms.*

We finalized our plans for pizza, and I changed into jeans, pulled on a sweater, and stared at my reflection. Not my face, but the color of my hair. The kind-of-purple that never was.

Kat.

I searched for a tie and threw my hair on top of my head — so there was less of it to stare at — and left my dorm room.

After we finished our pizza, Jake said he wanted to get some photos before the sun went down. I offered to go with him, and twenty minutes later, I hopped out of his truck, throwing on my gray zip-up hoodie.

"More hiking through hills?" I asked.

"Just one hill." Jake smiled, slinging the camera bag over his shoulder.

I didn't actually mind the hiking—kind of liked it, even. Exercise was never big on my list of fun activities, but I'd always loved being outside.

"So you're doing more landscape photos?" I asked as he set up his equipment.

"Not exactly." He fiddled with the camera for a moment. "I'm taking pictures of the clouds while the sun is setting."

I leaned against a nearby tree, wrapping my arms around my waist. "Why clouds?"

"I wanted to do something I haven't done yet. It'll be more abstract than my normal stuff." Jake crouched, digging through his camera bag.

"But...why clouds?"

"What color is the sky right now? What color are the clouds?"

I looked out in the distance, even though I already knew. "Bright orange with some pink streaks. Some light blues and whites, too. Maybe a little red."

Jake rose from his crouched position. Looked at the sky. Looked at me. He chuckled softly, then went back to messing with his equipment.

I waited, but he didn't say anything. "Is this a riddle?"

His feet crunched over the multitude of broken twigs, heading my way. "I don't see the same sky."

Was he trying to go all Psych 101 on me? *Everyone sees a different sky because everyone is different.* Or something like that? Yeah right, that was so not Jake. "What do you mean?"

He stood in front of me, the wind blowing golden pieces of hair across his forehead. I pressed my back against the rough tree bark harder, although I would've rather used it as a springboard to propel myself into his arms.

I laughed at my own thoughts. The sound was one part giddy and two parts nervous.

Inclining his head, Jake said, "I'm color-blind."

My laughter died a quick, squeaky death. I stepped forward, one palm flattening against the tree. "What?"

"Yeah." He shrugged like it was no big thing.

"You never told me that before." Unless we were drunk — which, come to think of it, was a possibility.

"Back in elementary school, kids used to make fun of me for it." He looked out at the color-wheel sky instead of my face. "My dad suggested beating them up. He said if I did it right, they would never make fun of me again."

I forced my lungs to expand, take in much-needed air, but all I could notice was the way his scent electrified me. Too bad *not* breathing wasn't an option. "So did you? Beat them up?"

He surveyed me, all traces of laughter disappearing from his face. Flat lines. Hardened jaw. "They never made fun of me again."

So many heartbeats passed while everything in my chest seized. I smiled—because I had to do something with my mouth other than let it hang open.

Thinking about his dad led to thinking about my plans for Emily's memorial service. I reconsidered telling Jake about it, and guilt nudged me when I didn't because it was lying by omission, and he didn't deserve any more of that from me. But he might've told me not to go, and I was definitely going. If I wanted to find the answers he needed—but wouldn't admit to needing—I had to go.

I moved closer to him. Hoping to derail the guilty path my thoughts were taking, I said, "So…what colors can't you see?"

"It's not that I can't see them, but I have a hard time distinguishing between red and green. Mostly. The sky, to me, doesn't have much red or pink in it." He stepped backward, turning toward his camera. "The final collection of photos will look entirely different to everyone else."

"Isn't that how everything always is for you?"

He almost smiled. "Yes, but this is intentional. And it's art. As long as you call it art, you can justify it pretty much however you want."

"That's kind of genius."

His chuckle carried with the wind, faintly echoing through the trees. "Glad we agree."

"Wait, these pictures will be in color? No more black and white?"

"Hey, don't be so quick to judge," he said with another laugh. "I'm only doing it for this assignment."

"Well, okay, but I think I'm confused. Doesn't your color blindness keep you from getting a good picture?"

He gave me a look as if to say *it's a secret.* "It gets in the way sometimes. And I always have my final prints viewed by someone else, just to be sure."

I almost asked him why he'd pick a major—and a career—that was automatically more difficult because of his color blindness. But then I thought about it more, and decided that nothing else would've made sense.

I watched him set up his camera for a few more pictures. "Do you photograph the same places more than once?"

He kept messing with the camera, adjusting the tripod. "Sometimes."

"Like all these beautiful places you keep bringing me to?"

Jake turned. He smiled, but a wistful expression overtook the rest of his features. "Yes."

Quietness fell around us again while he took a few more shots, me standing by watching with interest. "So your birthday is in two days. Are you doing anything?" He hadn't mentioned it since he told me how his mom wanted him to come visit.

"No. Birthdays aren't really my thing."

"I never understood that," I said, hugging my elbows. "You're celebrating the day of your birth. You only get one. Why not make a party out of it?"

He shrugged, staring out at the clouds, maybe searching for a hidden message. "But everyone has a birthday. How many people share your birthday with you? I don't think it's a big deal, and I've never understood why people like to make it one."

I took a few steps sideways, turned my head to better hide the disappointment. "It's a reason to be happy. A reason to celebrate. You know, celebrating having made it out alive for one more year."

After a moment, Jake's feet crunched across the grass, and then I heard his voice whispering, just inches from my ear. "I'm sorry."

I peeked at him, watched a muscle tic along his jaw. "Sorry for what?"

He raked a hand through his hair, and I imagined him fumbling over the words in his head like I often did. "You've spent your life looking at birthdays that way. And for good reason. I think that what I said…might have been a bit inconsiderate. And I'm sorry."

I stared at his pinched eyes and worried lips. "I think you got it wrong." When he gave me a confused look, I continued. "Most people under the age of twenty — or even forty or fifty — don't live with the question, *Will I live to see my next birthday?* I get that. I don't expect people to treat me differently or act differently or even look at the world differently because I was born with a hole in my heart. But I wish—" I wished he wasn't so cavalier about his own life — about his own birthday, because it meant something to me, because *he* meant a whole lot to me.

"You wish what?" he said, stepping closer, the pained look still on his face.

I shook my head, kept my mouth clamped together because I felt one of my hysteria fits burning through my lungs and stinging the backs of my eyes. *I'm ridiculous.*

"Hey," he whispered, putting his hands on the sides of my shoulders, dipping his head lower, so close to mine. "Tell me what's wrong."

"It's nothing," I choked out, attempting to hold my tears back.

Jake didn't speak for a while. He ran his hands up and down my arms, and the movement kept me grounded, kept me focused on the here and now. Me and him. Here and now.

I wanted to bury my face against his chest, lean into him, and feel his warm body press against mine.

So I did.

With his heartbeat echoing in my ear and his fingers running through my hair, he said, "You want to hear a story?"

"What kind of story?" I asked with a sniffle, peering up.

"The one you asked for after we took the photos in the grass."

"You're going to tell me a time you were really happy?"

"If you want." When I nodded, he grazed his hands down to my wrists, slowly wrapped his fingers around mine, and said, "My mom used to play the piano when I was little. She was really good at it. I remember listening to her play. Some nights she'd play for hours. I used to fall asleep to it. But when I was nine—or ten maybe—she stopped playing. After that was when things got worse. And on the nights when things would get really bad…Emily would come into my room and beg me to play the piano for her. Apparently, she fell asleep to the music, too. But I told her I couldn't, because I didn't know how to play." Jake paused, breaking away from me. "She kept asking me, kept begging me to learn so I could play for her, because Mom wouldn't. So a few years later, I bought that beginners book—the one I gave you—and I taught myself.

"I wasn't all that good, but it was something. Then one night, Emily came into my room crying, begging me to play, just like all the nights before. But that time…that time I could do it. I could finally play for her. I don't think I ever saw her as happy as she looked that night."

I thought I understood the ways in which a heart could break. But Jake's story formed epic craters in my chest. That's why he was so weird about the piano sometimes, why he sometimes stared at it with a far-away look, why he didn't think he'd ever play again.

There were no words good enough for me to say.

He looked down, long eyelashes fanning his face, and I latched onto his fingers tighter. A cool gust of air blew my hair up and over my shoulders. I shivered from the chill, and Jake raised his chin, met my appraising gaze. He leaned in and kissed me softly. It was the simplest thing in the world, but it felt bigger than that inside my chest. When he pulled back, his lips lifted into a smile. I couldn't help but smile back.

Still, my heart continued to ache as I switched between watching the sky and watching him take pictures, swiveling the camera to get the right angle. I tried to imagine the sky from his point of view—without the red or pink. Was it still beautiful? I'd bet so. Just a different kind of beautiful.

"I should take up photography as a hobby," I said after a while. "Maybe you could give me photo lessons next."

He sent me a sideways glance. "Sure. Your first lesson is this: not all things can be fixed with an Instagram filter."

"I'm only kidding. You already gave me piano lessons for nothing."

"Company's not nothing."

A warm tingling spread throughout my chest, and I

beamed, wondering if being around me made *him* warm and tingly inside. But…

What if Kat was right and my feelings for Jake would only end in pain? Maybe he could never give me what I wanted. Never love me. Not that I loved him…

But I could.

Chapter Twenty-Two

I'd never been inside the art gallery until now. I'd never had a reason to go there before. I wasn't against art, but I wasn't particularly seeking it out. Especially not in the form of a student exhibition.

But Jake's work would be there. And that included the portrait of me I was itching to see.

And Jake would be there. There was always that.

The way the crowd murmured made the place feel like a library with extra rules. And there were a lot of people. More than I expected. I continued glancing around, glad I decided on wearing my knee-length black-and-white skirt instead of a pair of jeans. The last thing I wanted was to show up dressed inappropriately.

I spotted Jake on the other side of the gallery, past the table of finger foods and other items you could eat off a stick. His arms hung casually by his sides, shoved into the pockets of his dark gray dress pants. A light yellow button-down shirt complemented his skin tone perfectly. Girls would've literally murdered for that slightly tanned complexion.

Carefully weaving through the crowd, I attempted to take in everything as I grew closer to Jake. But like a magnet, my gaze was only drawn to him. He was all I *wanted* to look at. Even if that meant ignoring the entire exhibit or missing my portrait.

My barely-heeled shoes clicked out the steps it took to reach Jake, creating an eccentric cadence to go along with my heartbeat.

Now only a few feet away, his head lifted, and the slight knit to his brows disappeared.

"I must say, you dress up quite well," I said.

"No mismatching colors. I'm impressed."

"Because I'm color-blind, you mean?"

"Of course not." I laughed. "The tie is a nice touch."

He fingered the dark gray material. "This is my one and only tie."

"You only have one?"

Jake tipped his head with a conspiratorial grin. "Do I look like the kind of guy who owns a lot of ties?"

"Now that you mention it, no."

His gray eyes appraised me from head to toe, and I resisted the urge to fiddle with my skirt or to make sure the long-sleeved shirt hung just right. A smile pulled on one side of his mouth, highlighting the dimple pressing into his cheek.

"You...look perfect," he whispered.

A low hum buzzed in my head, stripping my brain of a proper response. How did so few words from him affect me so much?

"Thank you," I finally managed.

Jake held my gaze for another moment and then turned, nodding toward a corner section of the gallery. "My work is over there."

"All the way in the back?"

"I asked for it to be put there."

"Oh? That's…very *Jake* of you."

"Yeah, but do you know why?"

No clue. But I knew he had a reason for everything. "Because you like being in the corner?"

Jake moved a hand from his pocket, scratched under his chin, and said, "By the time people get to the back, they've seen pretty much everything. And in the art world, you'd better go first or you'd better go last. No one will remember what came in the middle."

He turned slightly and started walking. I followed, stealing glances at his profile as often as possible.

"So what's the point of the middle then?" I asked. "If everyone only remembers the beginning and the end?"

"Without the middle, being *first* or *last* means nothing."

The middle gave the rest its meaning.

Like life, maybe. People were born and then they died. Everyone remembered those events. But without the life in between… "You're right. But why pick last instead of first?"

He grinned. "Why not?"

The sound of my shoes clicking on the linoleum paled in comparison to the booming in my chest. We neared his art, and I spotted his name on a tiny removable plaque on the wall. I read the Artist's Note underneath:

JAKE CAVANAUGH – DIGITAL SILVER PRINTS

A collection of black-and-white prints, because I prefer to view the world in colors that don't exist. Also, I really like the color black.

A grin tugged at my cheeks, and I looked up at the photos. Two rows of framed prints hung side by side. I started at the lower right-hand corner—closest to where I was standing. Scanning the images, I moved slightly as I took one in and then moved on to the next.

"Jake, these are great." I didn't know *why* they were great, technically speaking. I looked from photo to photo, trying to find the common element that made them all so poignant. Whether it was the fancy camera or the lighting he'd employed, or the focus or simply the subject—something about his shots captured each subject in that perfect moment of natural, heartfelt expression.

And then I saw my face.

I was laughing, my eyes shut, hair spilling around me on the grass, and holy crap, I couldn't stop staring. It wasn't an expression I recognized on myself. He'd managed to take an awesome, genuine photo, and I almost didn't believe it was me. My hair no longer radiated purple, and my eyes were no longer bright green. Instead, they were faded shades of gray. Seeing this, I could understand why Jake liked black-and-white photography so much.

But the forget-me-not flower in the image wasn't black and white like everything else. It still held its blue, white and yellow tones, though the colors were subdued, like he'd washed away half the saturation.

"The flower," I whispered. "It's not black."

"I thought you'd like it."

I stepped back, taking in all the images as a collection. "You did that for me?"

Jake rubbed the side of his jaw and looked to be fighting off embarrassment. "I don't remember the last time I had color in my final photographs. My professor was surprised, but she said it added 'emotion' and 'honesty.'" He made air quotes with his fingers. "But whatever it adds, it works. I would've never considered it if not for you."

I turned sideways, unsure of the right words. His expression conveyed an emotion I couldn't quite pin down. Likely because of that stupid wall he always kept up. *Tear it down already—here, use my hammer.*

Jake twisted, stretching out his arm. "You see this guy here?"

I looked at the photograph. It was a guy with a tuft of messy hair, wearing an expression that reminded me of a game show contestant—super stoked to be there.

"I took this one at the party. That night I saw you…and told you I wasn't there for the beer."

"Really? I wouldn't think a picture like this could come from a frat party."

"No, you wouldn't think so. But the idea behind this collection was to capture human facial expressions—the different emotions everyone experiences."

"You're pretty incredible." My body shifted closer to him without my permission. The fresh scent of lemon and mint burned my senses. "And I think you downplay your skills too often."

"You think I should brag about my photography skills? To whom?"

"All of your friends."

His lips quirked. "Right. They'd enjoy that."

I gazed at the pictures more, at the colors—or lack thereof.

"There's a lot of great artwork in this exhibition," Jake said, gesturing with his hand. "I was never into painting as a medium, but the work up by the entrance is incredible. If you want to take a look around?"

A part of me only wanted to stand there and stare at Jake's photographs, because I was still in awe of what he'd done. But if I did that, I'd end up looking like a human statue posing as a work of art. So we meandered through the wide two-story gallery, stopping to look at sculptures and paintings and drawings. They were *all* incredible—especially the paintings by the front.

"I wish I'd been born with a talent like this," I said as we walked up to a large landscape painting. An abstract forest—

fiery reds and burning golds were used instead of the typical browns and greens.

If I were an amazing painter or photographer or sculptor, I'd *know* what I wanted to do with my life, right? If I had that kind of talent, I'd be compelled to use it. I'd even take a talent in mathematics, or being a chemistry whiz kid. Then I'd know what I had to offer the world.

"Talent's only part of it," Jake said as we moved down the wall, on to the next painting. "If you don't have any determination or desire, it's pretty useless."

"But if you don't have any talent, what are you supposed to do with your determination and desire?"

He gave me half a grin. "Then you have to find the determination and desire to work really, *really* hard to get good at something. You can train yourself to do a lot of things you'd never expect." I agreed with him. But as we continued walking through the gallery, I started thinking about all the things you *couldn't* train yourself to do. You couldn't teach your hair to grow a different color, or train your bones to grow longer.

You couldn't make yourself love another person, or make yourself forget someone.

By the time we'd wandered through the entire exhibition, it was near closing time, so I waited for Jake as he went to get his bag from a room in the back. When he reappeared, instead of carrying a bag, he held something rectangular wrapped in brown paper.

In a Jake-like manner, he headed toward the gallery doors without another word.

Once I caught up to him, he tilted his head, a curious smile playing on his lips. I raised my brows, watching and waiting. He definitely got a kick out of my impatience.

He held the main door to the art building open, the package — or whatever it was — tucked under the other arm.

The night air was cooler than I expected it to be, sending shivers down my shoulders. But the sky was cloudless, allowing a grand display of constellations to light up the darkness.

"I have something for you." Jake let the door shut behind us. The brown paper crackled while he unwrapped the mystery item. "I didn't end up using this shot for my exhibition. For a few different reasons. But I want you to have it."

I took the framed photo when he offered it to me. This one would have fit in perfectly with the rest—the girl's expression was stunning. Wide smile and equally wide eyes. Blond hair framing a pale heart-shaped face. Pure happiness.

"It's Kat," I said, a maniacal rhythm to my heart. "You took a picture of Kat… When?"

"At that party." His voice grew softer. "I saw you two there, before you saw me."

"That sounds a little creepy," I whispered.

"Photographers have to be a little creepy. Or it just wouldn't work."

I laughed and stared at the photo again, my fingers tightening over the edge of the frame. "This is perfect." Kat would have loved, loved, *loved* it. She looked so pretty, it almost made me jealous. "You didn't take stalkerish photos of me that night, did you?"

"I didn't take any pictures of you that night. You looked annoyed—which would've made for an interesting photo." He grinned. "But the one in the grass turned out perfect."

"So that's why you had me tell you that stupid story while I lay in the grass?"

He wedged his hands into his pockets, body shaking with a laugh. "If you thought it was stupid, why did you pick it?"

"I don't know…it made me happy. You said to pick a happy story. So I did."

But my story was *nothing* compared to the one he'd shared with me. Mine was cotton candy and rainbows, while his was sledgehammers and heartbreak.

He shook his head. "Your story wasn't stupid."

Maybe. "This really is the best," I said, wanting to forget about feeling stupid. I held the frame a few inches higher. "I don't know how to thank you."

"You don't have to." He stepped closer, leaned over, and dropped his voice. "I'm glad I could make you smile."

"Look at you, getting all cheesy and stuff."

"Ah, a little cheese never hurt anyone, right?" Jake laughed—which I'd decided was my favorite sound because it was something I had to earn, and because it did something warm and fuzzy to my insides. "Come on. I'll walk you to your dorm."

He started down the steps. I followed, and when I caught up to him, his fingers laced through mine. We walked like that—hand in hand—until we arrived at my dorm. Time with Jake was always too short.

And then I had a thought that made the back of my neck tingle.

I looked up at him, keys dangling between my fingers. "Do you want to come in? Hang out? I can probably find a Disney movie I don't know all the words to."

He leaned closer, lowering his voice like we were talking about bank robbing instead of animated fairy tales. "Is there an option where dancing silverware and magic carpets aren't a thing?"

"That'll always be a thing. Sorry."

He laughed, looking down the hallway and back. "If we skip the Disney, I'm all in."

I pretended to consider for a moment. "All right, fine. No Disney. But we're getting a Hawaiian pizza."

More laughter floated through the hall as I unlocked the door and shoved it forward. Once inside, I set the photo of Kat on my dresser, my gaze lingering on it.

"Pineapple on a pizza should be a crime," Jake said, stepping farther into my room.

"I think pineapple haters should be stoned."

"Stoned? That's a bit harsh, don't you think?"

I laughed, turning away from the dresser. "I *really* like pineapples."

A smile lit up Jake's face, and I eyed my bedspread, once again wishing it didn't make me look like a twelve-year-old.

"Maybe we should get two pizzas," he said.

"Oh, you're not getting out of this. You got out of Disney."

His lips twitched, and he was closer now. My heart stuttered when his hand found the side of my face. His fingers left a tingling trail blazing across my cheek and down my neck as his warm lips fit perfectly against my own, opening just enough to keep it sweet, but still intoxicating. My hands found his solid chest, felt the rapid thrumming beneath.

And if heartbeats were currency, *this* was the best way to spend them.

He pulled back an inch, rubbing his thumb down the side of my jaw. "You do make me cheesy."

I smiled, breathing in. His scent was forever etched into my memory. "You'd better not be blaming *me* for any of your cheesiness."

He chuckled softly, pulling my head against his chest. I shut my eyes, smiling into the blackness, happy for the rapid beating of my perfect, borrowed heart.

I only wished I could tell Kat how happy I was.

Chapter Twenty-Three

Kissing Jake would never get old, but when he opened the door on Saturday afternoon, I had to tell my brain to shut up about the kissing. There were more important things going on—like confetti.

I tossed the glittering yellow dust into the air above Jake's head. "Happy birthday," I said between my fits of giggling.

His eyes went wide with horror, mouth hanging open like I'd set fire to his bed. After a moment (and more giggles), he brushed confetti off his arm. "You got me glitter for my birthday?" He stepped back from the doorway looking like he might start yelling.

"It's not glitter, it's confetti. And it's yellow. Not pink. It *could've* been pink. Be happy."

His lips finally turned upward. "Guess it could've been worse."

"Could've been way worse, man."

I jumped at the second voice, my laughter dying in an instant. My eyes found a guy nearly Jake's height standing at the edge of the kitchen.

"Oh. Hi." I expected Jake to be alone, like he always was.

"Hey," the guy said, taking a step closer, looking at me now. "Should've gone with the pink."

"Maybe next year," I said, forcing a smile, feeling like I'd been caught stealing cookies from the cookie jar.

"This is Micah." Jake nodded. "This is Audra."

"You're the friend," I said, remembering the only time Jake mentioned him.

Micah laughed. "So Jake's talked about me?"

"That's why you're the friend."

"Gotcha." He nodded, scratched his scruffy beard, and looked to Jake. "Glitter looks good on you."

Jake made a face, assessing his glittering arms. "I'll never get all of this out of here. Ever."

Maybe that was part of my plan. "Your place needed some color anyway. And I also brought this." I held up the bag in my right hand. "I skipped the birthday cake." Because I figured he'd hate that. "And I bought you a pie. For eating purposes only."

For the first time since I'd thrown the confetti, he gave me a real smile. "I do like pie."

"I know." The particles in his hair shimmered like pixie dust, and it made me think of fairy tales and Disney princesses.

Thank God he couldn't read my thoughts.

"Thank you."

I smiled and then remembered Micah, who hovered awkwardly a few feet away.

After clearing my throat I said, "Well, I wanted to wish you a happy birthday and give you that. I won't keep you from whatever you have planned."

"Don't go," Jake said. "Micah was leaving anyway."

The two of them exchanged a look I tried not to overthink, and then Micah stepped forward. "Yeah. I'm getting out of here." He pulled keys out of his pocket and took a few more steps, boots heavy on the wooden floor. "Nice meeting you, Audra. And Jake, it was really good to see you, man."

Jake nodded in response, and I shuffled out of Micah's way as he brushed past.

"Why did he leave? It's only two," I asked after Jake and I were alone.

He shrugged, walking to the kitchen. "He just stopped by for a bit. You want a piece of pie?"

I followed, pulled the container out of the bag, and handed it to him. "Of course I do."

He took out a knife from the top drawer, then opened a cabinet to grab plates. After cutting two pieces, we took our ginormous slices to the couch.

"You guys didn't make plans for today?" I asked.

"I told you. He just stopped by." His words were short and low.

"You haven't seen him in a while though, right? He drove forty minutes to simply stop by and say happy birthday?" I thought Micah was his best friend—his only friend. If I didn't count myself.

Jake looked up from his pie, jaw tightening. "He was here for an hour."

Shut up about it. "I got you something else. Besides the pie." I hurried to the bag I'd left near the door.

"You didn't need to get me anything. You know I don't even like celebrating my birthday."

"Yeah, I do know that. But I got you something anyway. And you can't make me take it back." I pulled out the small wrapped box and walked back to the couch. I'd spent hours online looking for gift ideas. I thought about photography equipment but most of it was hundreds of bucks, and if it wasn't expensive, I didn't know *what* it was or if Jake could even use it. "Here. Happy birthday."

He took the gift hesitantly, looking back and forth

between it and my face. "What is it?"

I rolled my eyes. "You'll ruin the surprise. Don't you like surprises?"

With a laugh, he started tearing the wrapping paper off. After the black-and-silver paper fell to the couch, he opened the box and pulled out a small bowl. It was black and had a few cracks down the sides that had been filled in with a gold lacquer.

He stared at it and then looked at me. "What is it?"

"It's a bowl," I said with a grin. "It's kintsukuroi. The art of repairing pottery with gold."

Jake brought the bowl closer to his face, examining it and turning it around in his hands.

"The idea is, the piece is more beautiful for having been broken," I added, watching the gold cracks catch the light.

I couldn't decide on a gift he could use, so I decided on one that meant something. And it was black. Total bonus.

"Thank you," he said. "Art is always a good gift."

My insides turned warm, seeing him smile and knowing I'd managed to do something right.

He returned to gazing at the bowl, and whatever he was thinking, he didn't share with me.

"I'll help you clean up the confetti-slash-glitter," I said.

"No. Don't worry about it." Jake turned around, and I followed him with my gaze as he went to the coffee table and set the bowl on top.

My chest constricted when I thought of the box under the coffee table and what I'd done.

"Is it still raining?"

I cleared my throat, shoved those feelings to the back of my mind. "It stopped for the most part." I inched toward the couch, still staring at his back.

He walked to the window and pulled the blinds open, peering out.

"What, you didn't believe me?" I laughed.

"I believed you."

"Then what are you doing?"

A few moments passed, and I grew more curious as the silence continued. Then he said, "Looking for that."

I frowned until he turned his head, motioning for me to look. When I got to the window, Jake stepped away and pointed.

And there it was—a cascading waterfall of colors shimmering in the distance.

"A rainbow," I said, feeling like I'd just witnessed a miracle, rather than a naturally occurring phenomenon. My fingers released the blinds, and I turned around.

"You want to go?"

I laughed, a burn creeping up my neck. It was one of Emily's done-its. She claimed to have chased the end of a rainbow, though I wasn't quite sure what that meant. "I don't think there's a literal end to a rainbow."

He shrugged, a grin pulling on one side of his face. "How do you know? Have you ever tried chasing the end before?"

I stared at him as my chest tightened, the air in my lungs becoming useless.

If you've never tried it—you don't know.

Kat had been right.

"Let's do it," I said.

Jake parked his truck on a side road near Union Street, only a few minutes from his apartment.

"So," he said, looking at me, then back toward the rainbow high in the sky, "I guess we start walking then?"

I didn't have a better idea.

We walked down the graveled road, toward a more open

area. There was no wind, and the late-October weather was perfect, despite the rain. I didn't know anyone who didn't love fall—it was the best season.

"Did you know there's a word for the way it smells after it rains?" I asked. "The way the dry earth smells so hot and humid you can almost taste the raindrops on your tongue."

"Oh yeah? What is it?"

"Petrichor."

"Interesting word," he said, sticking his hands into his jeans pockets.

"I think it's kind of a sad word." My gaze wandered from the multicolored trees to the mountains in the distance. "But the smell doesn't make me sad." It made me feel nostalgic—and those two words didn't fit together in my head.

"I think it sounds angry. Not sad."

Words held a lot of power, I supposed. Twenty-six letters could be combined in countless ways. I'd be willing to bet words had the power to do almost anything—destroy universes even.

But words couldn't bring back the dead.

Jake stopped moving and lifted the camera strap off his neck. I watched as he aimed the lens at the sky.

"Rainbows are pretty clichéd, huh?" I said.

He lowered the camera and smiled, linking his free hand with mine. Warmth flooded my palm, raced up my arm, and spread through my chest. "Pictures of them are, sure. But the actuality of a rainbow? No way. All you need is the combination of bright sunlight, suspended droplets of water, and the proper viewing angle, and you get to witness one of nature's most famous masterpieces."

I liked that answer.

We continued walking, talking about random things. Pumpkin seeds and sheet music and annoying professors. I lost track of the time, and we moved like we knew where we were going, but neither of us had a clue.

"What do you think she meant by chasing the end of the rainbow?" I asked as we crossed over a bridge.

"Maybe she was trying to say…be optimistic."

"What do you mean?"

"Like a metaphor." He shrugged. "When it's dark, look for stars. When it rains, look for rainbows. Something like that."

"Poetic. I'm impressed."

Jake grinned. "Ah, I'm taking that as a compliment."

"It was meant as one. I've been trying to figure it out for as long as I've had the list. And maybe it is a metaphor. Rainbows are temporary, right? Nothing in life is permanent. All of it will eventually disappear." People would eventually disappear. "Maybe we're supposed to know that…accept it, and live our lives differently because of it. Rearrange our priorities based on the finite number of heartbeats we have left."

I could feel all the words Jake didn't say in the way he squeezed my hand tighter.

Walking in comfortable silence with him might've become my new favorite thing—except for the kissing. That was still winning.

Then I got to thinking—and the realization flattened me, deadened my senses before they returned swiftly like a vengeful knife. Today was Jake's birthday. Tomorrow was Emily's memorial.

She died the day after his birthday.

I looked at his profile, at the strong jawline I wanted to trace with my fingers, at the curve to his lips, and a new crack formed in my heart for him.

No wonder he didn't like celebrating his birthday.

He glanced at me, unaware of the fresh fissures breaking my soul into pieces. I tried to smile, because what else could

I do?

"I think it's fading," he said.

"What?" I blinked, panic clawing at my neck.

He pointed out at the sky. "The rainbow."

I looked at the muted streaks of reds, greens, and blues, strained to make out all the colors. "Oh…it is fading."

"In a few minutes it'll be gone."

I stared at the disappearing kaleidoscopic of hues. "Then I guess in a few minutes, we'll have chased the end of a rainbow."

He slowed his step, smiling at me. "Well, look at that."

Smiling back, I didn't understand the pressure behind my eyes. Jake's warm palm still pressed firmly against mine. It was a picturesque afternoon, complete with the rainbow I didn't know I needed so badly to find. I was *happy*. But all I wanted to do was cry.

Chapter Twenty-Four

I couldn't decide on black or gray—and I was freaking out like it was the most important decision on earth. A memorial service wasn't a funeral, but were you still supposed to wear black? Or were you supposed to wear colors because it was a celebration of sorts? Obsessing over unimportant details kept my thoughts from derailing.

I decided on gray because it wasn't black, but I *could not* be the only person wearing orange or purple.

As I drove, I kept the music off and focused on details. On the plan I had. It's not like I was going to a social mixer, so I wouldn't have to worry about strangers introducing themselves to me. I wouldn't be out of place at the service, and I'd have open access to everyone who knew Emily.

Maybe someone knew more than Jake did. Like Dana. A girl wasn't going to tell her brother *everything*, no matter how close they were. Or maybe Jake was wrong, and Emily did commit suicide. If that ended up true, at least he would know. He could find the closure he needed—though he would never admit he needed anything. If he knew the truth, he could learn to accept it, and her death would no longer be an open wound.

But I didn't know which possible truth was more terrifying.

I arrived at the small church, watched a few people mingle toward the doors. It was Sunday afternoon, and Emily's memorial was the only thing going on. I counted ten cars in the parking lot besides mine.

Stepping inside, I realized how wrong I'd been. All my planning went to waste in the short time it took for the double doors to shut behind me. I was incredibly out of place.

Small groups of people stood or sat, talking quietly with one another. No one paid me any attention, but I may as well have been under a spotlight. My skin burned like too many days spent in the sun, and my feet longed to take me flying out of the room. But I'd come this far. No point turning back now.

I took a few hesitant steps toward the row of benches, scanning the crowd for the only face I knew to look for.

"I didn't realize you knew Emily."

My heart leaped at the voice—so not Dana's. I turned around and blinked at the guy standing behind me, taking in the dark hair and a frame similar to Jake's. He'd shaved the slight beard off his face since I saw him the day before. "Micah."

When he smiled, two perfect dimples pressed into his cheeks. "Audra," he said, stepping closer.

"Uh, hey." I attempted to shake off my surprise, twisting my bracelet with one finger. "I didn't expect you to be here."

"That's exactly what I was thinking when I saw you walk through those doors." His brows lifted in a question.

I swallowed the lump in my throat and lowered my voice, not wanting anyone else to hear me. "Well, I kind of…didn't know her."

"Oh?"

My gaze flittered around the room. "It's a long story."

"How about the short version then?"

I inhaled slowly, focusing back on his face. "I have her heart."

Micah's brows lowered, pulling together as confusion colored his features.

"Literally."

All traces of the smile he'd given me were gone. "No shit?"

"No shit." When he turned his head, obviously uncomfortable, I said, "Hey, you wanted to know."

"It's not that. I—ah, Jake didn't tell me."

And I didn't normally go around telling people I owned someone else's heart, so no surprise there.

Out of the corner of my eye, I saw two girls coming through a door—the bathroom, most likely. I recognized Dana's shining blond hair from the Facebook photos I'd stalked. The other, shorter girl looked familiar, too. They whispered quietly to each other as they walked past me.

"Are Jake's parents here?" I asked, returning my attention to Micah.

"I haven't looked for them, but I doubt it."

So much for that. "I'm going to find a seat. It was good seeing you again."

He nodded, and I spun away, heading in the direction the two girls went.

I found them sitting at the end of an aisle, still whispering to each other. Hesitantly, I walked their way and sat nearby. Tucked my feet beneath me. Pressed my palms together.

After a few minutes, I worked up the courage to talk to them, introducing myself.

"How did you know Emily?" Molly, the shorter one, asked. "You didn't go to high school with us, did you?"

I shook my head, twisted my hands in my lap. "No. I didn't. She was like a second cousin," I said, reconfirming what I'd told Dana.

"Oh, okay." Her smile was soft and easy, like something she practiced a thousand times a day.

"I've never been to a memorial service like this before." I ran my sandpapery tongue across my teeth. Swallowed nothing but stale heat. "I wasn't sure what to expect."

"Molly and I decided to do it last year. And then again this year," Dana said. "It's mostly people from school." She shrugged. "We thought it'd be nice to get together and remember her."

I swallowed, forcing my head to bob up and down. "It is nice."

A year from now, should I be holding a memorial service for Kat? The thought caused a heavy pressure in my chest. Would I still be as sad then as I am now, or would that pain ease? Would I have to carry this ache, reliving her death every year until *I* was dead?

Taking a deep breath, I steeled myself. It was now or never—to ask for what I wanted, to say the things I wanted, and to do what I'd come here to do.

"I don't really believe she killed herself." I whispered it, hoping my voice sounded okay and not like crackled static the way it did in my head.

Molly shifted, twisting her auburn hair around one finger. It reminded me of Kat, sending a fierce slice of agony through my chest. My open wound was oozing blood, sorrow, and regret, but no one could see it, no one could feel it but me. I quickly locked down my memories, storing them for some other time.

She exchanged a glance with Dana, whose eyes had widened for the briefest moment. "What do you mean you don't believe it?"

My cheeks blazed, and I ignored that, too. "I think something else happened to her."

They both stared at me like I'd just grown horns.

"Uh." I fidgeted, wrapped and unwrapped my fingers. "Maybe I'm crazy." I was seriously considering that as an option. "But what if something else happened? I mean...I can't see her doing...what she did."

Every new word I spoke tasted like a slow poison sizzling over my tongue. They weren't lies, but they felt like lies in my heavy chest and burning throat. At this rate, I would croak by the end of the day.

Was I destroying Emily's memory?

Was Jake *wrong*?

The two girls stared at each other for a while, exchanging looks I didn't understand. Finally, Dana leaned toward me and said, "We never wanted to believe it, either. It's been really hard for us."

My heart thumped when her face crumpled. I couldn't help but think I was doing more harm than good. The bracelet on my wrist felt cold and heavy, but seared my skin as though it were laced with acid.

"So you believe that she...you think that's what happened?" I asked, looking between the two of them.

They exchanged another glance. Dana's face turned neutral again before looking back at me. "What are we supposed to believe?"

I gazed toward the front of the chapel when their stares became too much. "I don't know." I forced in air, forced it out again. "Jake thinks their parents might have...maybe they had something to do with it."

"Jake?" Molly's soft voice raised an octave.

"Yeah." I turned back to them.

"We haven't seen him in two years. Not since before Emily died," Dana said.

Molly wound hair around her finger, staring wide-eyed while she pulled hard on the gorgeous strands. "He thinks they did something?"

"Yes," I whispered, my heart pounding between my ears.

"Their parents were really weird." Now Molly was talking to Dana, rather than to me, and I had to lean closer to hear.

"Yeah, but…" Dana's voice trailed off, her eyebrows pinching together. "What does Jake think they did?"

My stomach tightened, fingers twitching. "I don't know."

There was silence between us as we sat awkwardly, all lost in our own thoughts.

Molly shook her head, gaping at her linked fingers. "Emily was always so happy."

More people were filling into the seats around us, shuffling down the aisles. The service would start soon. I only had a couple minutes left to talk to them.

"People can lie," Dana said. "Maybe the happiness wasn't real."

"You don't really think that, do you?" Subtle anger laced Molly's tone. "You think we didn't know her? Our best friend?"

She paused, cleared her throat. "No…we knew her—we did. Maybe…maybe I don't think she killed herself. But if not, I don't have any idea what happened."

Molly nodded, leaning a little closer. "All Emily talked about was graduation and some boy she'd been seeing—we never got the details about him, but apparently he was in college and her parents would've killed her if they found out. She—" Her features collapsed. "I didn't mean—it's just…if we had suspected anything, we would've spoken up."

Dana nodded her agreement. "Definitely."

My stomach turned over. I was more confused than before. "Thank you. For answering my questions. I wanted to get those things off my chest. I want Emily's memory to be an honorable one. And maybe it doesn't matter…because she's not here anymore. But I think she deserves the truth to be known."

I wanted the truth for Emily and for Jake.

After the short memorial, which mostly consisted of stories about Emily, I said good-bye to Molly and Dana and started toward the exit.

I wasn't ready to leave—wasn't ready to admit I'd learned nothing, that all my efforts had been in vain.

My steps slowed and I found a wall and leaned against the wood paneling. I shut my eyes, breathing in deeply. When I opened them, Micah stood in front of me.

"Wow, you like sneaking up on people."

He grinned. "On occasion."

"It's not nice, you know."

His grin only widened. "I know. So why did you really come?"

I gaped at him, taken aback by his directness. "Why were you at Jake's?"

"He's my friend."

"Then where were you before yesterday?"

The grin faded, and he squinted at the floor. "What?"

I resisted a groan. "Nothing. Look, I'm sorry, I'm...I don't know."

"Upset? Pissed off?"

"I'm not pissed."

"You look pissed."

I turned away, watched people filing out of the church just as quietly as they'd arrived. "I'm upset, I guess."

"At least you're admitting it."

I wasn't sure how to feel about his comment.

"So you wanna tell me?" he asked. "Why you're really here?"

I turned back to him. "You want to tell me what you were really doing over at Jake's?" There had been something going on between them when I showed up—I was sure of it.

He gave me the kind of grin that likely got him out of all kinds of trouble. "No."

I dug my keys out of my purse. "Then you don't get an answer, either."

Micah stepped in front of me as I started for the door. "You think something happened to Emily—something other than the story everyone believes."

A chill tingled across my neck. "What?"

"I overheard you. Talking to Molly and Dana."

"You mean you were eavesdropping?"

"If you want to call it that."

"Fine." I sidestepped him, clutching my keys tighter.

"Wait." Micah's fingers gripped my elbow, halting my escape. "You didn't let me finish."

"What?" I pulled away from his grasp but didn't continue toward the door.

"I don't believe that bullshit story, either," he whispered, bringing his face close to mine.

"You don't?" The cold chill itched its way down my spine and froze my feet to the floor. "Then…what do you think?"

He looked away, shaking his head. "Hell if I know."

Disappointment sat heavy in my stomach. "Then why don't you believe the story?"

Micah's blue eyes widened like he'd expected me to drop the subject. He ran a hand up the back of his neck, shaking his head slowly. "I know she didn't— She wouldn't do that."

I chewed on my lower lip, trying to force the puzzle pieces together. "You and Emily…"

His lips parted, and he looked away, but not before I saw panic flash across his features, confirming my theory.

"You were together," I said. "That's why you and Jake don't talk, isn't it?"

Micah lifted his head, and the panic was replaced with something unnamable. When he spoke, regret dripped from every word. "Yeah… So like I said, I know Emily wouldn't have done it."

His words echoed Jake's. They both believed wholeheartedly that she couldn't have done something so devastatingly tragic. Molly and Dana believed Emily had been happy.

I had to believe they were all right. And that only left one conclusion.

Her parents lied.

Chapter Twenty-Five

I hadn't thought this through. It was intentional—my lack of thought. Because if I'd considered the options, weighed out what might happen, I'd have decided this was a bad idea. But this was the only option left.

I'd caught up to Dana on the way out of the church. Told her I lost the Cavanaughs address and wanted to stop by and say hi, keeping the lie about being related to Emily. She gave me a funny look, like *why do you want to talk to them,* but she hadn't questioned it. She believed I was "family."

I knocked on the Cavanaugh's door and waited. Blood pumped violently through my ears while I wondered about the people who lived there. I'd never met Jake's parents, but a part of my soul already despised them.

One breath. Two. Three breaths. Four.

A wave of nausea hit me, and I squeezed my eyes shut. I was about to puke all over the Cavanaughs' porch. One hell of a greeting.

Shit, at least it'd be honest.

The door opened slowly, and a woman appeared. Her

short blond hair was shoved into an almost-ponytail, and her eyes were wide as she blinked curiously at me.

"Hi. Mrs. Cavanaugh?"

"Yes." Her eyes searched the scenery behind me, as if waiting for a guy with a huge check to pop out from behind a bush.

"My name is Audra. I'm a…a friend of Jake's."

"Jake?" Her features collapsed in on themselves for the briefest of moments, and she looked a decade older. The smile reappeared as fast as it had gone. "He hasn't lived here in a few years, since he left for school."

Right.

"Ah." I swiveled around, looking for what held the woman's attention. Seeing nothing, I turned back to her, sliding my purse strap higher on my shoulder. "Actually…my name is Audra Madison."

I waited for recognition or understanding—or anything. But Mrs. Cavanaugh's face remained as still as a statue.

My fingers tingled in anticipation as I shifted my weight from one foot to the other. Oh God, what if she regretted ever writing that letter to me? Sure, the Cavanaughs agreed to exchange personal contact information with me through the donation agency, but we'd never agreed to *meet*. Showing up here was probably against some sort of rule. What if she—

"Would you like to come in for a minute?"

I let out my breath. A light-headedness clouded my vision. "I don't mean to bother you."

"Please. I'll take all the company I can get." She smiled, but since I'd become something of a fake-smile detector lately, I saw the lie in the forced curve of her lips.

I thought of what Jake said, about his mother being ill. "You know who I am?"

"Of course." She moved swiftly through the spacious living room, leaving me to either stand in the doorway or come inside.

I fingered my bracelet and stepped forward, fighting off the swarm of dizziness. Nausea roiled in my gut. There was still a better-than-average chance I'd ruin the spotless floor with the contents of my stomach.

"Have a seat. Please. Would you like something to drink?"

I found a seat on the long white couch, observing the spotless appearance of the house. "No, thank you." Everything was so bright—white and yellows everywhere, like they wanted their interior space to scream *sunshine!* The furnishings were simple and every surface wiped clean. These were the kind of floors you could literally eat off of.

She sat on the matching love seat, clutching her hands against her waist.

I licked my lips, sat back, and tried to get comfortable— which was impossible. Sitting back was too casual. Sitting forward was too aggressive. Sitting there at all was dizzying to my senses.

Mrs. Cavanaugh tore her gaze from the wall. "You said you were friends with Jake?" Her voice was soft and far away.

"Yeah, I…I go to school at Colorado State. We…" The words lodged in my throat, and I rubbed my fingers across the clock tattoo, forcing myself to breathe.

This was a bad idea.

I shouldn't be here.

I swallowed, pressing my palms together.

The way she smiled and then hid it away, like displaying it was a mistake, reminded me of Jake.

"How is he doing?"

Who was I to tell her—when he'd chosen not to speak to them?

But she was sitting right in front of me, and she looked so damn sad when she said his name.

"He's good," I whispered. But the small talk wasn't going

to work. We had nothing in common to talk about besides Jake and the letter she'd sent me—and I didn't want to talk about either.

She clasped and unclasped her palms. Her eyes grew empty and unfocused.

Pressing a palm to my chest, I started counting. *One breath. Two. Three breaths. Four.* The room's bright colors warped and blurred together. I blinked, clearing the haze. "I was hoping…" *That maybe you'd tell me what really happened to Emily.*

As if that was going to happen.

"I thought it'd be nice if I could know a little more about Emily. I went to her memorial service today. But…" I put on a smile—one as real as hers. "I came here to say thank you. For answering my letter."

Mrs. Cavanaugh looked away. Up and over, down and back. Finally, she parted her thin lips. A phone rang in another room, the shrill tone unreasonably loud. Her spine straightened. "Excuse me. I need to see who that is. I'll only be a moment."

I nodded and watched her hurry out of the room. For a single second, I'd seen the real Mrs. Cavanaugh. Not the well-put-together woman wearing lies on her face, but the grief-stricken mother with empty, hollowed eyes.

The longer I sat, the more my skin crawled. The house was beautiful. A few rooms short of a mansion. But it was a purely decorated house, not a collected one. Like an interior designer had been paid a pretty penny.

Most families with two kids would have pictures along the walls or on the mantel. I spotted only one framed image tucked back in the corner of a shelf. If I'd had something better to do than inspect the living room, I would've never seen it.

A standard family portrait. All phony, forced smiles. Maybe that was why there was only one. Their lips turned up into perfect displays of happiness, but their eyes—they were all wrong.

Jake had said it was easy to fake it for a photograph.

Looked like that wasn't true for this family.

I eyed the door, wondering if I could make a mad dash to my car and get out of there before Mrs. Cavanaugh came back. Listening for the sound of footsteps, I stood. The change in elevation threw my balance off. I pressed two fingers to my temple, and before I could make the short trip to the door, she silently rounded the corner.

"Sorry about that." She smiled—more reminders of Jake. Lips partially pulled up, like the effort to do so was all she could manage.

"No. Don't be. I should get going. I don't want to keep you." And I didn't want to make an ass out of myself. Not a bigger ass, anyway.

"When I read that letter you sent us, it reminded me so much of Emily."

I froze, unable to move my feet from the tile beneath them. If I did, the entire world would've come shattering down.

"You were both so young. But not only that. Your letter simply…sounded like her."

Another onslaught of nausea rolled through me violently. Light-headedness threatened to send me crashing to the floor. I couldn't stand in front of her any longer. Not without completely losing it.

"Thank you," I said. "For the letter. And for seeing me today." Uninvited.

I couldn't get outside fast enough, couldn't get enough of the fresh air. My hasty exit verged on rude, but all I could think was *don't cry, don't scream, and don't faint.*

And once I was in my car, I only did the first.

I drove away from the picture-perfect house and all its secrets, ashamed I'd come in the first place.

Chapter Twenty-Six

As days passed by, the information—or lack thereof—ate away at my clarity. What had I been thinking, and who was *I* to go around bringing up the past, digging through secrets everyone else had long ago forgotten?

Wrong became a constant state of being, and I clung so desperately to my belief that I was only trying to do the *right* thing.

The dorms were nearly deserted. Everyone was out at one of the fifty Halloween parties raging on and off campus. I'd almost forgotten about the holiday altogether. It was Kat's favorite. She loved dressing up and making a big show of it. She'd dress sexy. I'd aim for funny. She'd encourage me to show my cleavage, and I'd tell her all those Cokes had officially fried her brain. It was our yearly tradition.

Now that she wasn't here babbling on and on about costumes, makeup, and parties, I had no desire to celebrate.

I'd begun to dread the weekends, because I didn't have enough things to do to fill up all that time. So by Friday afternoon, I'd already completed my homework for all of *next* week. Fucking pathetic.

Jake hadn't responded to my last text—the one I sent hours ago. When six o'clock rolled around, boredom took over, and all I could do was stare at my phone. Waiting.

Annoyed at myself, I climbed off my bed and put on shoes. I needed out. Jake's place was only a fifteen-minute walk, and if he wasn't home, it was still an excuse to leave my dorm.

But Jake *was* home.

"Hey." I stumbled backward, wholly unprepared to see him. "I texted you earlier."

"Yeah, I know." He rubbed under his jaw, averting his gaze. "Sorry. I was planning to text you back, but my mom called. I got sidetracked dealing with that shit. You want to come in?"

I stepped inside, and he let the door shut.

"Your mom called?" Heat flooded my cheeks and tingled the backs of my ears.

"Yeah. She told me one of Emily's friends stopped by today."

I swallowed thickly. Cleared my throat. Sucked in air. None of that helped quell the roaring in my head or the thumping in my heart. It had been days since I'd knocked on his parents' door, so his mom wasn't referring to me. "She did?"

"Yeah...I couldn't understand half of what she said. Just that Dana came over. Something about Emily... I don't know." He shook his head, glancing up at the ceiling. "I asked if she was taking her meds. Said she was." But he didn't believe her, based on the sideways frown he wore. "She's hard to understand when she gets to rambling and crying."

I blew out the fiery air from my lungs and pressed my palms against my jeans, wondering if Dana had asked any of the questions I couldn't. Was my growing list of lies coming back to bite me? "Is everything okay?"

He stood inches away from me, yet he was somewhere else. "Jake?"

After a moment, his eyes refocused on mine. "Good as it ever was. You want to go do something?"

He was evading the subject—but I didn't want to talk about his mom, either. If she'd outed me as a fraud, Jake didn't know it. Yet. "Sure. I'd like that."

Of all the strange and random things on Emily's done-it list, this one seemed the most out of place. Handling a deadly weapon didn't fit with rainbows, and pie-smashing, and hair dye.

The slick grayish-silver metal sparkled in the sunlight. Just looking at it made my heart pump faster.

"Uh. So. Not to sound like a girl or whatever, but I don't know the first thing about what…what to *do* with that."

Jake chuckled, pulling the gun out of its protective box. "Don't worry. I'll teach you."

I'd never been up close and personal with a gun before, so being at a firing range was like a monkey tango dancing with the queen of England. Out of fucking place.

With the earplugs in, everything sounded fuzzy, like it does underwater. I still understood what Jake said, but the effect left me slightly off-kilter. A shot went off two rows past us. The sound seemed to echo in the distance forever.

Jake ran through the basic rules of gun safety. One: always treat a gun as if it's loaded. Two: don't point a gun at something you don't intend to shoot and aren't willing to kill. Easy enough.

I watched him fire a magazine of bullets at the target out in the distance, wiping my palms against my jeans. A pointless gesture. The sweat kept coming back.

"I don't know," I said when he asked me if I wanted to try. "I'm…scared. I think."

He gave me an easy smile, like he understood. "If Emily

could do it, you can do it, too. There's nothing to be scared of. You're the one with the loaded weapon. And you're only aiming it at a piece of paper."

I tried to laugh, but it only made me more nervous. "Uh. What if it backfires? Guns do that, right?"

"Only if you don't clean them. And even then, the chances of that are rare."

I stared at the metal could-be-killing machine, unconvinced. "Rare is not the same as impossible."

Jake laid the gun on the small wooden table in front of us and turned, dipping his head close to mine. "I promise it's not going to backfire on you."

I switched my attention from the gun to his face, half hidden in shadow. The other half, lit with the falling sun, smiled, and the lines near his eyes crinkled.

"You can't promise me something like that."

A burly-looking guy—with a contradictory ponytail— shot something much bigger than Jake's handgun. The sound was new. Like an explosion that was only getting started. My body twitched, and I fumbled back.

He put one hand on my shoulder. "I can. You'll be fine. I swear. And you might even like it."

I eyed the guy's handheld cannon again. It made me squirm to look at it, but I couldn't stop looking, even though Jake was talking to me, touching me, and I was supposed to be paying attention to him.

"Um." I couldn't force my eyes away, and my hands started to shake.

Jake's hand moved down my shoulder and down my forearm, and then he slowly intertwined his fingers in mine. My heart fluttered, but his gesture was calming somehow.

"I would never tell you to do something that would hurt you. Do you trust me?"

One hell of a question.

I didn't need the thirty seconds it took me to respond. I knew my answer as soon as he'd asked. But it took all of those thirty seconds to accept that trusting him would mean firing that gun, proving him right.

"Yes. I trust you," I conceded, and a thousand violent butterflies exploded in my stomach. He deserved my trust. He'd proven himself trustworthy. Me, on the other hand? Not so much. I squeezed his fingers, shoving those thoughts away. "I'll shoot the stupid gun. But…I want to watch you do it one more time."

He grinned, seemingly satisfied. "I can get behind that deal." Then he kissed me once, softly against my forehead.

I closed my eyes and exhaled louder than I meant to, my skin tingling where he'd touched it. I focused on that while he reloaded the pistol, and I stared at the subtle muscles snaking around his forearms and biceps. Anything to get my mind off a backfire that would melt my face.

It was working, too.

The proper gun-firing stance looked good on him. Easy and casual. Unassumingly dangerous. He fired off ten more rounds. When he finished, the place where the bull's-eye had once been was now a singular hole — thanks to the ten bullets that had ripped it open.

I didn't know which was more impressive: his no-holds-barred smile or his aiming skills. "How'd you get to be so good? You're *seriously* good."

I couldn't hear his laughter, but I saw it on his face and in the tilt of his head. "Just like everything else. Practice."

"Oh, whatever. That's your answer for everything."

"Practice is the answer to a lot of your questions."

Maybe he had a point.

Jake nodded down the field, toward the target. "We'll change the paper, and then it's your turn."

The hyperventilating was back. I tried to slow my breaths,

steady the fierce beating of my heart. But Jake returned from replacing the target, and all my procrastination time was up. I nodded, mostly to convince myself I was ready.

And when I finally put my fingers around the cool metal, felt the weight of it in my hands, I'd forgotten all about my measured breaths.

"Like this," he said, moving my hands into position. One underneath, steadying. The other wrapped around the side, close to the trigger. "Hold your arms out straight. Ah, not that straight."

Then he said, "Perfect, just like that," and so I tried to stay just like that. Harder than it sounded. I aimed the barrel of the gun down the field and shut one eye to focus the sight on the target.

Squeeze the trigger slowly.

Breathe. In and out. In and out and start squeezing.

Once I pulled the trigger far enough, the shot fired, sending the bullet rocketing out of the gun. All of my senses were on an ultrahigh setting. Pulse pounding. Gun blasts echoing. Fingers tight around the metal. And then came the relief of it *not* backfiring and blowing my face off, and holy shit, I couldn't keep the grin off my face.

I set the gun down and spun around toward Jake, who smiled. "So, how was it?"

Something like a giggle escaped me. "It—oh man. It was great. But I still feel, uh, I don't know. Wired?" I shook my hands in the air for effect.

"Probably your adrenaline. Shooting a gun does a lot of interesting things to your brain."

I nodded, still grinning. I'd read somewhere that firing a weapon releases the same chemicals as a passionate kiss does. I was no scientist, but it seemed pretty damn accurate. Maybe Emily had also read that somewhere and wanted to find out for herself if it was true.

Chapter Twenty-Seven

Back at Jake's apartment, I was still high from the adrenaline—tingling and floating.

"We can do whatever you want. As long as it's not Disney."

I spun, ready to fire off about how there were *other* movies I liked to watch, but Jake's unexpected closeness tied my tongue up in knots. My sudden stop put us only inches apart, but he didn't step back.

"Uh. Anything but Disney is fine."

He grinned. "Well, that narrows it down."

Instead of leaning forward, like I wanted to, I inched back. He stood stationary, tracking my slow movements with storm-colored eyes. "Let's play a game."

"Like what? My game collection is pretty scarce. I've got *Resident Evil* and *Call of Duty*."

I laughed, slipping off my shoes, still inching toward the couch. "As much fun as today was, I don't think I'd be any good at a first-person shooter. What about…Yahtzee?"

Jake shrugged out of his jacket. "Do people still play that?"

"I think it's one of those games that'll never die. Like Battleship."

"No, I'm pretty sure that game is dead."

"Aw." I pulled my lips into a pout and sighed dramatically. "You sank my battleship."

He set his shoes against the wall and shook his head. "I'm going to pretend you didn't turn that into a joke."

"It wasn't *that* bad."

"Depends on your definition of 'that bad.'"

I stopped my retreat and admired the smile lines pressed in around his mouth. Maybe it was the leftover aura of badassery from the shooting range that tempted my feet in his direction. Or maybe it was simply my desire to touch him. To feel the heat of his skin on mine. To feel his energy and drink it in.

To finally ask for the things I wanted.

I twisted my fingers against his. When I spoke, my voice came out as a whisper. "Do you believe in clichés?"

His lips quirked into the smallest possible version of a smile. "Which one are we talking about here?"

The warmth flooding my face rivaled the warmth emanating from our joined hands. "Do you think there's a reason behind everything that happens to us? And I mean us as in the whole wide world. Not just...you and me."

Jake stayed silent, but his eyes contained pages of unspoken words.

I grew dangerously close to overthinking.

"I don't think I believe that," he finally said. "I think things just happen, and people make what they want out of them."

"Maybe."

My instinct was to pull away, but when I released his hands, he inched closer. His hands found my waist, successfully keeping me from running.

"You know what I do think?" he whispered, leaning his

forehead toward mine.

My heart reacted like I'd had a cattle prod to the chest, and my whole body thrummed from the sensation of his fingers moving gently along my sides. I raised my eyebrows, trying not to act like a fifteen-year-old who'd never been touched before. I was neither fifteen nor saintly.

His head dipped until his mouth neared my ear, hot breath trickling down my neck. He gripped my lower back. Pulled me against his solid chest. "I think you're good for me."

My pulse spiked with one part guilt and two parts desire. More than I wanted for that to be true, I ached for him to want me the same way I wanted him.

He leveled his gaze with mine again. "I'm still not sure if I'm any good for you."

He was wrong. He had to know that by now.

I kissed him. My right hand snaked up his neck. His hands tugged me toward him—though there was nowhere else for me to go. I felt every hard plane of his body against mine.

I'd seen him shirtless before, but I desired nothing more than to admire his muscled chest, feel its warmth against my own. More than just our hands. More than just our lips.

My fingers wound their way into his hair, and when I let out a soft sound of longing, he twisted our joined bodies sideways, and my back hit the wall. I arched into him, my hips pressing against his. He groaned. "I'm serious, Audra. I don't want to hurt you."

I ran my hands down his arms, appreciating the corded muscles there like he was art. Jake was art. Captivating and mysterious. Unique and beautiful.

I leaned my mouth toward his, bold from the longing and desire churning in his gaze. "I told you, I trust you."

The corners of his mouth lifted slyly. "Careful not to say something you might regret. I can promise you a gun won't backfire in your face, but I can't promise I won't end up hurting you."

Even though a slow burn worked its way from my gut to my cheeks, I smiled sheepishly, moving my hands from his arms to his waist. His back muscles tensed beneath my touch. Then one hand cupped my jaw, gently but firmly. His breath was uneven, and his eyes darted across my face, sending a thrill through all of me. It had been so long since I'd been touched like this, since someone looked at me like this.

Since I'd wanted something so much.

His lips dropped to mine again, and I welcomed the taste of his mouth, the feel of his tongue. It was every one of my wildest dreams come true, and I wanted this moment to last all night.

Something rattled against my hip. An electronic melody followed, and I pulled my head back, sucking in a breath. "Your phone."

He backed up but only enough to reach into his pocket and pull it out, never once looking down. "I've got voicemail for a reason."

An instant after dropping the phone to the ground, his mouth assaulted mine again. But this time he didn't press me into the wall. Instead, he pulled me forward, inching backward. My heart boomed with anticipation and desperate longing.

A few moments later, my chest filled with a different feeling. The anticipation no longer felt light and giddy. It was heavy now. Overwhelming.

Jake's fingers brought the hem of my shirt up, the rough pads sending shivers dancing up my spine. He'd seen me in a swimsuit before, seen a portion of the scar running between my breasts, but it hadn't mattered then like it did now. Before, it was two semi-strangers hanging out in typical poolside clothing. Now it was intimate. Meaningful. Intense.

But I didn't stop him from taking it off.

When his shirt lay on the floor in a crumpled pile next

to mine, he placed his hand on my belly, and with one finger, very gently traced the line of my scar between by breasts and up to my neck. My chest heaved against him.

He looked at me like his room was a museum and I was the art. "You're beautiful."

The invasive melody from his cell phone yanked me out of my dreamy euphoria again. I tensed, angling my head.

"It doesn't matter," he said against my lips.

But I knew how often Jake's phone rang. Two calls in a row weren't normal.

Stranger things had happened, so I let the thought slide out of my head, forgotten and unnecessary.

I got lost in him again, in the way his lips moved against mine, like they'd been designed solely for kissing me. It felt like drowning. And I loved every second of it.

My bra was somewhere between the living room and the bedroom, and my brain was in another world.

His phone rang again. This time, he tensed.

"Maybe you should answer." My voice sounded breathy and unfamiliar. "It could be important."

Jake sat back and groaned. Raked one hand through his hair. "Fuck. I'll be right back."

I was alone on his bed. Topless. Awesome.

I strained to catch what he was saying, to find out who was blowing up his phone.

"Are you sure?" he asked. "Yeah. Yeah, I know." A pause. "Where is he now?"

More silence.

"I'll be there as soon as I can."

My heart jumped at the idea of Jake leaving. I slid off the bed and crept toward the door until I saw him running a hand through his hair again.

"What's going on?" I picked up my clothes and clutched them to my chest. The modesty was unnecessary. Jake wasn't even looking at me. "What's wrong?"

"My dad's wasted. My mom, she's flipping her shit."

Nakedness was so not appropriate anymore. I snapped on my bra and yanked my shirt on. "You're going over there?"

"To make sure my dad doesn't hurt her, yeah." He shoved his shoes on. Grabbed his keys from the coffee table. Finally moved toward me. "I'm sorry. I can't explain how fucking sorry I am. But I have to go."

"I'm coming with you."

"No."

"I—"

"*No*. I don't have time to argue about it."

I barely felt the sting of his words through all my panic.

"I'm sorry. I'll text you later." He kissed my forehead so briefly, I could've imagined it.

I followed him out the door, stunned and reeling. He was halfway down the hall.

And then he was gone.

I counted out my breaths while I stared at nothing. *One breath. Two.* Jake hadn't seen his parents in two years, so he must've been compelled by whatever his mom said… *Three breaths. Four.*

Tracing the cracks in the baseboards with my gaze, I thought of everything he'd told me, everything I'd learned.

She's freaking out.

Where is he now?

Understanding sank its grimy claws into me. A sickness settled low in my gut. Hearts weren't supposed to beat this fast—not even replacement ones.

I pictured the possible scenes playing out at the Cavanaughs'. Easy to do with the stock footage ingrained into my memory. The picture-perfect house. The smile his mom wore to hide her fear. Everyone's insistence that Emily didn't end her own life. And thanks to Jake's stories, *drunken asshole* wasn't an image I had to work hard to imagine.

The scene grew dimmer when I added more detail. Me showing up to my heart donor's memorial service. Me pushing everyone to talk about her. Me tearing open the wounds everyone was either trying to heal or trying to hide. When I added Jake to the movie I'd created in my head, the image went dark.

I bolted down the hallway, hopped down the steps, and sprinted toward the dorms to get my car. Whatever was happening in that house—whatever was about to happen—it was my fault.

Chapter Twenty-Eight

Jake expected me to go back to my dorm and sit around, wondering and worrying. Of course he did—he didn't know I'd gone to Emily's memorial, or that I'd gone to his parents' house afterward. He didn't know I'd riffled through his belongings and found his journal, that I was the one interfering and tempting fate.

My feet were on autopilot once I parked my car and climbed out. I walked across the road to the house glowing in streetlight. Like last time, the two-story building screamed of all things normal and perfect. I glanced left and right while I strode toward the door. The rest of the neighborhood remained quiet and empty. Everyone else cozily tucked in their beds, unaware of the horrors inside 264 Bracket Street.

The door was unlatched—not quite closed—and my hand hesitated a few inches away.

Knock? Would anyone come to the door?

Would Jake even let me in?

I strained to hear something, *anything,* but all I found was silence. It was a big house. They could be anywhere. I lowered my hand. Stared at the door.

If I'd caused this—if all of this was *my* fault—why did I think I could fix it?

Maybe I should've left well enough alone.

A loud *clang* sounded from inside the house, followed by the tinkling *clink-clink-clink* of what must've been shattering glass. I yanked open the door and nearly fell when I stumbled inside.

I stood absolutely still and listened, blood rushing through my veins.

Muffled voices.

Moving through the pristine living room, the sounds became louder. Still no one in sight. I walked around a corner, through the kitchen, and did a three-sixty.

Where were they?

I found a set of dark stairs, leading to a dark upper hallway. Taking them one at a time, my hand skimmed the ice-cold railing.

This could've been considered breaking and entering. Or maybe it was wrong on an entirely different level.

A deep voiced boomed from the other end of the house. "It's your fault, isn't it?"

Whatever response was given was overshadowed by another loud crash. I rounded the top of the stairs, shuffled faster down the hall, toward a light at the end.

"*Stop.*"

I couldn't tell who'd said it—or if I'd even heard it. Could've been my own delusions. My feet moved faster, and my heart pumped quicker until I thought for sure *this* was the time it would break.

Shouts filtered through the air. Mostly indistinct obscenities. I turned the corner, my mouth going dry. I quickly assessed the room, instantly pegged it for a teenage girl's room. Emily's. Of all the places in this big house, they'd ended up in here.

Light teal walls. Yellow comforter. Shimmering pieces of a broken lamp on the hardwood floor. Jake's back to me, hands clenched into fists.

His dad barely inches in front of him, still screaming. "Worthless piece of shit." And then his hand shot forward, slamming into Jake's shoulder.

He stumbled back, and I stepped forward, a high-pitched squeak the only sound escaping my opened mouth. My hand reached out uselessly.

A raspy growl came from Jake. His spine straightened. He pulled his arm backward, and a heartbeat later, one of his rocklike fists collided with his dad's jaw in a sickening *crunch*. Bone on bone sounded louder when there weren't fifty people standing around making noise.

"Jake." My voice was barely there, his name barely a word.

His dad clasped Jake's shirt, twisting and slamming him into the closet door. The frame and drywall shuddered and creaked from the impact. I caught a glimpse of Jake's face. Only a fraction of a second, but it was enough to see it—the fiery hatred and anger burning in his eyes.

His fist shot forward again, this time smashing into his father's cheek.

A tangle of fists. Rough, painful noises. Sharp inhales. Exhales. Grunts and groans. The violent popping noises turned my insides to acid, which bubbled in my throat.

I was a coward. Because I couldn't watch anymore. Because all I could do was press against the wall and cover my mouth with my hands, and wish I had the power to disappear. Wish I had the power to change this.

Something shattered to the floor.

I squeezed my eyes shut to escape the madness of the room. When I opened them again, his father's head jerked backward. He dropped like a boulder to the floor.

I stopped breathing.

Jake didn't stop punching him.

Over and over and over. The crack of bone against bone, flesh on mangled flesh.

Stop.

Spatters of red marred the teal walls. Red covered Jake's fists and his father's jaw.

STOP.

So much red.

I'd lost count of how many times Jake hit his father since he'd been knocked out, lying limp on the ground.

"Stop." I barely heard my voice over my thundering heart.

How many more punches before Jake's dad stopped breathing?

How many before he killed him?

"Jake. Stop. No. *No.*"

Fear and adrenaline exploded within me, and I pushed off the wall. My body collided into his side. It was like slamming into concrete, but he moved, rigid muscles shifting sideways.

"Stop," I croaked. "Please, please, *please.*" Fat teardrops dripped from my nose. Acid burned my tongue. "Jake, stop."

Eyes partially covered by hair locked a steely gaze on me. "What the hell are you doing?" His chest heaved up and down, his bloodied fingers twitching.

The growl in his tone sent my heart to my feet. "It's all my fault." The words combined with my heavy cries. "I'm so sorry. I never meant for this to happen. I couldn't let you do something you'd regret. I'm—God, I wish I could take it back, take it *all* back." I wiped at my tears, blinked through the haze clouding my sight.

"What?" he snapped, backing up onto his knees, away from me.

I stifled a sob, looked down at his unconscious father—wrong choice. A slice of fear split through my chest.

Was he dead?

"If I hadn't gone to the memorial service and talked to Molly and Dana—if I hadn't told them—"

"Told them what?" Jake stood, shoulders back, fists clenched.

"I..." Scrambling backward, I fought for a standing position, wishing I could stop crying. Wishing, wishing, *wishing.*

"You told them about Emily?" His voice was low and laced with pain. "About what I said?"

"I thought..." I couldn't talk over the sound of my heart beating wildly, my lungs expanding too quickly or not enough—couldn't be sure. "If you knew what really happened—"

"Did you figure it out?"

I backed up as he advanced toward me—not out of fear—well, maybe a little fear. But I wasn't afraid of his fists still balled into knots, or his tense and ready shoulders.

"Did you? Did you fucking figure it out?"

I sucked in air, breathed in the metallic tang of blood. My throat closed. Fingers shook. That look in his eyes.

Cold. Empty. Dead. All aimed at me.

"Jake, I—"

"Get out."

My words became bombs in my mouth, detonating and traveling down my gut, burning like fire. Nerve endings, already on edge, exploded and ignited my soul.

He brushed past me so quickly I felt the air moving. "You were right. This is all your fault."

Burning.

I hurried after him, surprised I got my shaking legs to move.

"I need to find my mom." Jake stopped his descent down the hall and said, "You remember where the door is, right?"

His tall, lean frame disappeared.

The vise around my chest tightened, denying precious oxygen to my lungs. My heartbeats sped up, warning of more violent detonations. Tears rushed to my eyes with an intensity I never thought possible.

That's how I knew my heart was truly breaking.

I nearly fell down the stairs. And that might've been perfect—I longed for unconsciousness. Anything to take the pain away. I couldn't get to the door fast enough. The fresh air outside smelled like leaves and perfect campfire weather, which was the universe's sick way of kicking me in the gut. Fumbling with my keys, I managed to unlock my car and climb inside.

The sounds coming out of my mouth were amplified in the tiny, enclosed space no matter how I tried to stifle them.

I ruined everything. Now Jake hated me. I did everything wrong when I'd only been trying to do the right thing. Look where it left me.

I guess what they say about no good deeds was true.

Pulling my phone out took a lot of effort. And seeing the screen was proving to be difficult.

911. I needed to call them.

No. *No, no, no.*

Did I?

Should I be allowed to decide something like that? Interfere more than I already had?

But what if Jake's father was dying and my phone call saved his life? What if he woke up and turned his rage on Jake again? Or maybe the cops would show up and arrest Jake.

I buried the strangled cry escaping my lips and let my phone slip through my tear-soaked fingers.

Maybe I deserved to burn forever.

Chapter Twenty-Nine

Jake no longer had an active Facebook or Instagram page. As far as I knew, he might've thrown his phone into a lake by now.

Days turned into weeks, and then I stopped counting, tried to focus on classes and the upcoming holiday break. But I was alone. Completely, truly alone.

I'd depended on Kat. We'd been friends for so long I didn't know anything different. I expected her to always be there. Nothing could come between us.

Except death.

Maybe because I'd cheated death, I deserved this.

Maybe this was my fate: to be a girl with someone's stolen heart. To be without the two people in the world who meant something to me besides my family. To be the girl who wanted to honor Emily's name—but only managed to disgrace it.

I didn't deserve to have her heart.

I never would.

"He's going to catch you sleeping."

My head swiveled when someone whispered beside me.

The girl sitting two seats down from me in the psych auditorium stared at me, half smiling, half frowning.

"I wasn't sleeping."

"Looked like it to me. Thought I'd save you the embarrassment of getting called out."

Maybe my head in my hands made it look like I was sleeping, but it was far from accurate. I'd forgotten what normal sleep felt like anyway.

I straightened. "Thanks."

The lines on her face disappeared, and she gave me a real, worry-free smile. "No problem."

Friends. Was it moments like this that led to friendships?

The girl whose name I didn't know turned her attention back to the lecture. I couldn't focus on anything but what she'd said.

After my class, I returned to my dorm—my new one. I'd gotten a single. There was no way I would share that room with some stranger, not after Kat.

I'd texted Jake my new address, just in case…

That would take a miracle, and I'd pretty much reached the cap on lifetime miracles.

This dorm, the small space I shared with only myself, it emphasized my loneliness. No one to talk to. No one to see. That kind of silence was so incredibly loud.

I stared at my new bedspread—plain light blue—and the undecorated white walls. Nothing about the room was dark, but it was still the most depressing place I'd ever seen.

The heavy silence crushed me, consumed me. That's when the numbness subsided, and it took all my willpower to not scream.

I snatched the keys from my dresser and fled the room. Maybe I never had to go back.

Thirty minutes went by. I wandered around campus, paying little attention to what I passed, *who* I passed. I had no one to look for, no one to see.

I was alone in a place full of people.

• • •

I listened to Professor Otto babble on about depression and sadness, regret and loss and all the things I didn't need to hear.

It was torture.

While I tried to tune the lecture out, I pulled my phone from my purse and furthered the torture by scrolling through my Tumblr, stopping at the photo of Jake and me. Couldn't say when I became a masochist.

But there were still other done-its I needed to complete, and I needed to continue without Jake. Maybe doing so would distract me—at least a little. But I was down to slim pickings, and I wasn't necessarily looking forward to the rest.

Graffiti with hot-pink paint.

I'd never been one to break the rules—at least not obvious laws like graffitiing the town. In hot pink nonetheless. With the way my luck was going, I would get caught. Wind up in jail.

Jake.

I didn't know what happened to him. Or his father. And since he hadn't answered my calls or responded to my texts, I'd never know.

My guilt twisted in my gut like a dull knife. But I'd grown used to the pain.

I shoved the phone back in my purse and tried to forget the way Jake had looked at me that night at his parents'.

I'd been so close to everything I wanted, and I'd wrecked it. Thanks to one stupid decision after another. After another. *After another.*

Sinking down in my seat, I cautiously browsed my phone, looking up the penalties in Colorado for spray-painting the town pink. As it turned out, it was an act of vandalism and none of the consequences sounded worth the risk.

"Do you have the notes from last class?" the girl two seats down from me whispered.

I paused. She was hunkered down in her seat the same way I was. Talking didn't bother Professor Otto like sleeping did, but it was still frowned upon.

"Um, I've got my notes. But I don't think they'll help. I haven't been paying attention the past couple weeks so my notes are...mostly blank pages." I offered an apologetic smile.

"No worries," she said, waving her hand. "This material is simple. We probably don't really need to pay attention to the lectures."

I nodded. That was the only reason I was still passing the class. And if attendance didn't matter, I would only show up on test days. God, why couldn't I have gotten a professor who didn't give a shit about attendance?

The girl—whose name I still didn't know—went back to scribbling on her pad, a smile still on her face. I stared at her profile for longer than I should have, contemplating what her name might be and if I should ask.

Would I simply find someone and go *oh, I like you—I pick you, let's be friends.*

I didn't know which was worse—considering how to make friends, or plotting out a crime all in the name of a dead girl's done-it list. They were both weird, I finally decided.

I tapped my foot against the sticky floor, rubbing my pen between my palms slowly, staring out at nothing. Come to think of it, Emily's entire list was weird—to some degree. Not in a bad way. Because I believed "weird" to be a synonym for "awesome."

And then I had a thought.

I leaned toward the girl with long dark hair. "I know this seems like an odd question, but do you have any idea where I could find hot-pink spray paint?"

She stifled a giggle, which surprised me. I'd expected her to send me a look like I was speaking in tongues. Guess I had a habit of anticipating the worst.

"I actually bought this spray paint for cars last year—for my sister's birthday. It's like car art or something," she said, wrinkling her nose as she tried to remember the details. "You can get a can for less than ten bucks. I don't know if that's what you're looking for, though."

I was so stunned by her answer that it took me too long to respond. "Well, maybe." Did spraying a car count as graffiti?

The girl gave out smiles like they were food and we were the hungry. But I liked it. It made me want to smile back, even though I didn't feel like smiling.

"Thanks. I think that just might work."

I tapped on my phone, pulled up Merriam-Webster. Graffiti: pictures or words painted or drawn on a wall, building, etc.

So painting on a car with temporary hot pink *would* totally count.

Maybe I did have a friend after all. Good old Merriam-Webster.

And then I realized that was the equivalent to having imaginary friends—which hadn't been socially acceptable since I was seven.

Guilt was a reliable friend, too, sitting in my lungs and firing through my head.

But maybe I needed to *friend* a person. I leaned to the right again and whispered, "I'm Audra."

She beamed. "Katie."

I fought to keep my smile in place even as the blood drained from my face. Of all the names in all the world, her name was fucking Katie.

Images of Kat swam in my head. Emotion clogged my

throat, and I longed for the numbness to return.

Staring at my Facebook feed did little to help my sadness. But I kept scrolling, clicking on funny videos, hoping to laugh. I never did. I opened news links and movie trailers. Anything and everything to keep my mind on something easy, something other than the thoughts wreaking havoc on my brain.

Man Cooks, Feeds Ex-girlfriend Her Dog for Dinner.

Oh my God, the world was coming to an end. With news stories like that, how could it *not* be?

Fourth Graders Suspended after Plotting to Kill Teacher with Hand Sanitizer.

Coming. To. An. End.

I'd had enough of the internet and was about to shut my laptop, maybe open a book, but I paused when I skimmed the next headline.

House Fire Kills Two. Murder-Suicide Suspected.

Underneath the words was an image of a house half eaten away by fire. Charred remains lay along the grass and in the driveway.

I clicked on the link and read the first few lines of the report.

Greg Cavanaugh and his wife, Rachel, were found dead yesterday morning inside their home after a house fire raged late last night. First responders to the scene initially believed the fire to be an accident. Upon further investigation, it has been ruled as an intentional act. Accelerants were detected inside the couple's bedroom.

I looked back to the picture of the half-eaten house.
The Cavanaughs' house.
Murder. Suicide.
My heart seized when I considered the possibilities.
No. No. *No.*
"Oh, Jake." I said it as if he could hear me.
I wanted to see him, to know if he was okay, to be there for him, the way I always *tried*. But he didn't want anything to do with me, and I couldn't blame him.

Chapter Thirty

I spent the next week reading through every news article about what happened at the Cavanaughs. No one knew *why* Mrs. Cavanaugh supposedly put gasoline around the bed while Mr. Cavanaugh slept and then took a handful of prescription pills and set a candle next to the bedroom curtains. But that's what they suspected happened.

Did the pills knock her out, or was she awake to watch everything burn?

It felt sickeningly real, that these were people who'd stood feet away from me. They were just people, like everyone else.

But were they?

The image of Jake's dad on the floor haunted me. Now the pictures of their burned house was an image I couldn't lose. Funny how people burned photographs, like you could burn away the memory. Burn away the hurt. You can't.

If I had died instead of being saved that day I got a new heart, I wouldn't have ruined Emily's memory. Jake could've been happy. Kat might've still been alive.

If not for me, everything could have been different.

Chapter Thirty-One

My heart pounded, rattling my chest—a sensation I'd grown accustomed to over the past couple months. But this time was different. This time, there was no trigger. No thoughts of Kat, or Jake, or my own grief over the way things had all played out. I'd been staring at Professor Otto's gray hair, half-listening to his lecture, when it suddenly became harder to breathe.

I sat back, but the movement made me dizzy. Drawing long, slow breaths of air did little to stop the room from spinning. The fluorescent lights of the auditorium—the kind that did nothing good for anyone's complexion—blurred and dimmed.

I was going to be sick.

Shoving my notebook into my backpack, I dragged in a desperate breath and stood. All one swift movement. Surely the other students would notice my sudden exit. Professor Otto, too. I could hear his voice in my head now: *it is rude to leave while someone is talking, hoping to teach you something.* But it was either suffer the wrath of my grumpy psych professor or vomit all over the empty seats in front of me.

I hopped over feet as I hurried down the aisle. My stomach churned, and I moved faster. But the faster I moved, the more my heartbeat sped up.

I made it to the bathroom, blissfully empty, just in time. After I'd lost my meager lunch into the toilet, I sat back on my heels and stared at the green-tiled wall.

"Audra?"

Bracing my hand on the metal safety bar, I slowly pulled myself up, too nauseous to feel any embarrassment.

"Are you okay?" the voice asked again.

Who would be out there? I didn't have any friends left, so there should've been no one coming to my aid. Not here, in a public, university restroom. Who else—besides a teacher, maybe—even knew my name?

I unlatched the door and tapped it open.

The fluorescent lights in there were even more awful. The hazy whitish beams burst when I looked at them, like exploding stars. I blinked, and the girl came into focus. Short. Mocha-colored skin. Long, narrow face.

Katie.

"Pink graffiti," I mumbled. Forming words on my lips shouldn't have been so hard.

She cocked her head, stepping closer. "Are you okay?" Without warning, she laid her palm against my forehead. "Good God, you're burning up. You're sick."

I nodded my head and pressed one hand against my throbbing chest. "I-I feel…terrible."

"Here, let me help you. Do you need a ride home? To the doctor?" Katie asked, swiveling one arm behind my shoulders.

My knees buckled as we moved forward and the room spun, green tiles blending together with eggshell-colored walls. I lost my balance and pitched toward Katie's petite frame before the blinding lights evaporated.

"Food poisoning?" I repeated.

"Yes. Given the precarious state of your immune system, it's not altogether surprising." Dr. Lane folded one hand in front of the other, her brows pulling inward. "But I'm worried about the intensity and the rapid onset of your symptoms."

I avoided her concerned gaze, wriggling my toes beneath the lightweight blanket.

"Had you been feeling sick before today? Any nausea, dizziness, or rapid heartbeat?"

All of the above. But I'd blamed each occurrence on emotional stress, not physical health.

She stepped closer to the hospital bed. "We're going to do a biopsy of your heart, to ensure your body isn't rejecting it. We'll adjust your medications as necessary after we get the results." Her voice remained soft and soothing, the way my mom's voice usually sounded. "Regardless, you'll need to start being more cautious. Make sure you take your medication. Continue eating a healthy diet, exercise, and try to keep stress at a minimum."

I closed my eyes and fought the urge to cry. My diet had always been healthy—aside from the occasional pizza and Twizzlers—and I took my pills religiously. But I buried myself under piles of stress, drank more alcohol than I should've, and only went on the occasional hike. In my frenzy to honor the gift I'd been given, I'd neglected aspects of my health and ignored the obvious signs.

A few minutes after Dr. Lane vacated the room, someone rapped their knuckles on the door. Since Mom would've bypassed the knocking, I expected a nurse.

But it wasn't.

Katie stepped into the room as if it were riddled with land mines. "After you passed out, I saw the bracelet around your wrist. Called 911. Once they got you into the ambulance, I decided to follow. To make sure you were okay."

Swallowing thickly, I pushed myself backward on the bed. "You don't even know me."

She smiled. "No. But I'm a nursing major. Couldn't help myself."

I stared at the shiny metal bracelet, a stark contrast from my pale skin. "Thank you."

"If you ever need anything, let me know. I'm from Ohio, so I haven't made many friends yet since moving here for school. And my classes this quarter are easy, so I've got plenty of free time."

Pain ripped through my chest, and tears threatened to fall. I didn't deserve her smile. Her words. My heart. My life.

. . .

On the drive from the hospital to my parents' house, Mom stayed silent, allowing the devastating thoughts to consume my soul.

"Mom," I said when she opened the door. After that, I started crying and words fell to pieces from there.

She sat me down on the dark purple couch—the same way Jake did after Kat died. And then she asked what she did when I started sobbing more.

It was ugly.

But I finally stopped sniffling. Maybe I'd officially run out of tears.

I told her everything. Seriously, pretty much every single detail of what happened with Jake.

"Honey, you can't honestly believe you're responsible for what happened to that family," she said, rubbing her hand across my back.

"How can you see it that way?"

"That family… Whatever chain of events took place that led to this, it started long before you came around. It wasn't something you could change. And sad as it is, it would've still happened regardless. You don't factor into the equation."

"But you don't *know*." I wiped fingers across my wet cheeks. "You don't know it still would've happened if not for me."

If I hadn't opened my mouth and made Dana interested in talking to the Cavanaughs, maybe Jake wouldn't have beaten his father half to death. Maybe then his mother wouldn't have set their house on fire.

"Honey, listen to me. It's not your fault. You have to believe that."

I laid my head back against the cool leather couch. "Why do I have to believe that?"

"Because I'm your mother. I'm never wrong."

I thought it was impossible, but I laughed. For only a second. "But Jake…he hates me. And that *is* my fault."

She didn't have a quick reply for that.

"I doubt he hates you."

Why did all moms think that simply saying something made it instantly true? "You're only trying to make me feel better."

"'Hate' is a serious word, Audra. I sincerely doubt he hates you."

I stared at the black TV screen, lips pressed together. She didn't know, didn't understand. Jake hated me. And that was that.

"I'm going to drop out of school," I said.

Mom shifted, the leather squeaking beneath her. "Are you sure that's what you really want?"

"I might as well. I don't know anyone there." *Who doesn't hate me.* "Kat isn't there and…I don't know why I should even go to school when I don't have any idea what I want to do. All being on campus does is make me think of Kat. And Jake. I don't know if I can do it."

Her hand squeezed my shoulder gently. "What about that girl from your class? The one who was at the hospital with you?"

"She just happened to be there when I passed out. A bit of luck and coincidence."

Mom's narrowed eyes said she knew it was bullshit.

"If you really don't want to go to school at CSU anymore, you don't have to. But will you at least give it until the end of the quarter to decide?"

"I guess...I can probably do that."

"Good. I know you've had a lot going on. Losing Kat's been hard on you. And honey, love is always going to be hard. But I also know you're a tough girl. You'll get through this just fine."

I didn't want to be tough anymore.

"Why don't you try thinking about it like this..."

I turned my gaze on her, curious to hear what crazy idea she'd pulled out of the sky.

"Jake lives by campus, too. And if he really does have no friends, like you say, then now he has no friends *and* no family. He's much more alone than you are."

"That doesn't make me feel better."

She smiled halfheartedly. "The only person he has is you. And maybe you should take advantage of that, if you still want him around."

"Mom, I looked through his box of personal things when he wasn't around. I went to that memorial knowing he wouldn't want me going. I was trying to *help* him, and I only lied to him and hurt him. Jake doesn't want anything to do with me."

The wrinkles on her face deepened when she gave me a look I knew well. "You didn't do any of those things out of the meanness of your heart. I think if you give it time, he'll see that. He'll forgive you."

The words sounded nice, but I didn't believe them.

"You should give yourself some time, too. Focus on something else for now. What about the rest of that list you're re-creating?"

Maybe I can curl up under a blanket and sleep off this feeling for a few years. "That's the whole reason for this…" "Mess" seemed like such an understatement.

"Honoring that girl is a good thing. You shouldn't stop because things got hard and something went wrong along the way. It's still a good thing." She put a hand on my head and brushed my hair back. "Finish the list. You'll regret it one day if you don't."

"I don't understand," I said, tears rolling down my cheeks again. "Any of it. Why Kat? It's not fair… Why her? It hurts so fucking much all the time. And Jake…I cared about him. *Both of them.* They're both *gone.* What was the point? All of that for what? All this pain?"

Mom continued stroking my hair, a sympathetic smile pulling at her lips. "Sometimes grief is the price you pay for love."

Chapter Thirty-Two

Maybe Mom was right—about some things—and I needed to finish the list. I could do the rest by myself. Including the pink graffiti.

Before I'd left to go back to school, Mom suggested I write my feelings down. She thought it'd be therapeutic, and at this point, I would've tried anything to make any part of me feel better.

Back in my dorm, I pulled out a few sheets of notebook paper and spent a solid ten minutes doing nothing but chewing my bottom lip.

My first two attempts were angry scribblings on a sheet of paper. I crumpled my notes and threw them away. They only consisted of fuming remarks and snarky comments.

For my third attempt, I tried to funnel my inner optimist. The words were slower coming out, but they made their way onto the paper.

The thing I've learned about life—it isn't about facing your fears. Well, it's that, too, but it's not solely that (or even mainly that). Of course you should want to conquer your fears, be better than them, better than what terrifies you to the center of your being.

But life is about living.

We don't have a guaranteed future, a promised tomorrow. Maybe tonight will be the night our broken heart decides to stop beating for good, and we won't be lucky enough to have a new one put in its place. What then? What if tomorrow never comes?

Then all of those unspoken words, unlived dreams, and unconquered fears disappear. Poof. Just like that. Gone in an instant.

And the past? Well, we both always have it and simultaneously don't have it. It's gone, too, just like our could've, would've, should've things. But it's always there because once you've lived something, you can never forget it. You can never forget the pain of crashing your bike and needing eight stitches in your chin. You won't forget how someone's careless words speared your heart, crushed your soul. You'll carry all the things that've ever happened around with you until the day your too-fragile heart beats its last beat and you cease to exist.

So life is about the in-between. Between the beginning and the end, between the past and the future.

It's about the now.

What I'd written may have been optimistic and full of sunshine and daisies, but it didn't make me feel a damn bit better. I stared down at my handwriting, reading over the words again and again. I'd written them, *created* them, and I wanted to believe them, but couldn't.

I scribbled a PS at the end.

Pain can't last forever. It just can't.

I folded the piece of paper and stuck it in a drawer. Therapeutic, my ass.

Poising my pen over a new sheet of paper, I hoped inspiration would hit me. When it didn't, I turned on music and set my playlist to shuffle. After three songs of mindless pen-tapping and staring at the blank paper, I had an idea.

I scribbled out uncensored words. One after the other. A few minutes later, I folded the note I'd written and before I could lose my nerve, pulled on my shoes and headed to Jake's. I wasn't going to ask him anything, I was simply going to tell him.

Chapter Thirty-Three

Two days passed since I'd left the note under Jake's apartment door and before he showed up at my dorm.

"Jake," I said, wondering if maybe this was a dream, because in every reality I knew, he hated me.

He stared, hands shoved into pockets as always, expression unreadable.

I never thought I'd get to see his face again.

"Do you…want to come in?" I asked when he still didn't speak.

I shifted out of the way. He hesitated, but finally stepped inside, looking around the room.

"Jake." I waited for him to turn.

"Why did you do it?" His back was still facing me. "Why did you talk to them about Emily? Why couldn't you leave it alone?"

His voice was different—or maybe it had just been so long. "I thought you wanted to know what really happened to Emily."

Jake spun around, took a quick step forward. "No. *You*

wanted to know what really happened."

"For *you*. I thought if you knew the truth, you could find some peace. I care about you, about what happens to you and how you feel. I only ever wanted to *help* you. Not hurt you."

I only ever wanted to be worthy of Emily's heart.

Light strands of hair fell across his brow when he spun. The I-need-a-haircut look always suited him. "I also told you not to care, because I wasn't good for anything."

"But you are, Jake." I strode forward, wanting to touch him, knowing I shouldn't. "You're good for lots of things."

"Like what?"

I tried to imagine what advice Kat would give—because I surely would've asked for it by now. She was always better with things like this. She knew how to be honest, how to say what needed to be said.

I managed a steadying breath. "You're...you're a good person. You can play the piano—teach the piano. You make this beautiful art that I wish the *entire* world could see. You make me so...*happy*, and it breaks my heart that I hurt you like I did." I swallowed, needing a moment to keep my voice from cracking.

I tried to be as straightforward as possible, to not worry about appearing desperate. I *was* desperate, and I didn't want to pretend not to care.

"I should have told you how much you meant to me sooner," I said, blinking at the ceiling. "And I shouldn't have gone to the memorial, shouldn't have talked to them about Emily." I could've, *should've* done so many things differently. "I'm sorry. And I wish it was enough. Enough to matter. Enough to change what happened."

His lips stayed pressed into one thin line, but his eyes softened, and then they shut. He scrubbed a hand over his face, through his hair, and then looked at me again, not saying a word. I shoved away my hurt feelings from his lack of response. He didn't know what to say—I could understand that.

"I'm so sorry," I whispered. "For everything. For going behind your back, for what happened to your parents. For keeping things from you." My heart thumped against my rib cage. "For finding your journal in the box under the coffee table. I flipped through it, read some of it, and I don't know why and—and I'm *so* sorry." I turned my head, fought against the stinging in my eyes. It was a pointless fight. The tears would win. They always did.

"You...looked through that box? I would've never known."

"I know." But the guilt consumed me, and if I was trying to be honest, he needed to know. "I don't blame you for hating me. I'm sorry it was all for nothing."

Jake heaved a sigh, shook his head once.

The silence grew to be too much. "How are you doing?" It was a stupid, pointless question I immediately wished I hadn't asked.

But he answered it. "This is going to sound horrible, I think, but I'm a little relieved. Now that they're dead."

His words sent tingles racing along my arms. "What do you mean?"

"Now...none of it matters. Not if my parents were to blame for Emily's death. Or what they did to me—to us. I never knew what happened to Emily. Not for sure. And now I never will. It's a finality I can't ignore. So maybe the truth is overrated. Something about that is...peaceful to me."

I rubbed my fingers across my chest, feeling my wild heartbeat pounding beneath my skin. "Peaceful sounds nice."

He smiled for the first time since he'd walked in the door. "It is. Even if it makes you look at me like that."

"I am not—"

"You make it so easy," he said with a short laugh.

"Wait." We were joking around like it was old times and everything was fine, and I hadn't destroyed all that we shared? "You're really okay?"

It didn't seem possible that a guy could lose his parents by murder-suicide and be fine a few weeks later.

Maybe I was biased because I would never be okay if that happened to my parents—but his parents were not the same people. They had different lives, destined to live out different fates, or whatever. Maybe Jake truly could find peace in their deaths. Maybe for him, it could all be over, allowing him to move on.

He shook his head, and all the laughter disappeared from his face. "I'm better. I think okay would be a lie. And I still don't want to lie to you."

I breathed in—a raspy, painful act. Tried to smile. "I'm glad you're better."

Jake shoved his hands into his pockets. "That was you, the day in the quad. The ambulance and paramedics."

His reminder of my bathroom shutdown warmed my cheeks. "How did you know that?" There were thousands of other students who could've been in need of an emergency response team.

"I was on campus. Sirens and paramedics with stretchers aren't something you see every day. I'm not immune to the 'train wreck you can't look away from' effect." His lips quirked. "And spectators like to talk. I heard 'heart transplant recipient' thrown around. There can't be more than one of you at CSU."

So, great. I was a train wreck.

He angled his head with a pained stare. "Seriously, though, how are you?"

I looked down, hugging my elbows. Digging my nails into my skin, I squeezed my eyes closed. Breathed in once. Twice. "My heart biopsy came back clean. They changed my medication a bit. I haven't felt like throwing up or passing out in a few weeks. And I may have made a friend out of the girl who called 911. So I guess that means I'm good."

When I returned my gaze to Jake, his eyebrows pinched together. "I wanted to call you. Almost did a few times. Wanted to see if you were okay. But I couldn't figure out what to say, so I didn't." He pulled one hand free and rubbed it across the back of his neck. "I've missed you."

My heart stuttered, warmth spreading through my aching chest. "Thought you said you didn't want to lie to me? There's no way you— Don't you hate me?"

All the parent pep talks and handwritten letters in the world couldn't convince me otherwise.

His eyes cast downward. "I stopped getting close to people because I didn't want them to have to deal with my shit. It's my fault that my shit became yours." He paused, looking up again. "I shouldn't have expected you not to care. And I'm sorry I made you think this was your fault. I'm sorry I told you it was. None of this was your fault. That day…if you hadn't shown up, I would have killed him."

Jake stepped closer, a serious look in his eyes—one that sent a shiver through my fingertips.

"But—"

"I would have killed him, and I would've had to live with that my entire life. I don't know if I could've forgiven myself."

I shook my head, still unconvinced. "You ignored all my calls, all my texts. I thought—I don't understand how you don't hate me, because even if that's true, they're still…dead."

No crying. Not today.

His fingers pressed into my shoulders, his head dipping to level with mine. "Not because of you. And not because of me. You did nothing but make my life better. I didn't even deserve it." His hands ran down my arms until his fingers met mine, filling the empty spaces between them. "I couldn't have saved

Emily no matter what happened to her. Same way I couldn't save my mom, like you couldn't save Kat."

Pressure built up behind my eyes, but I blinked fiercely, begging the tears to stay away. Jake was touching me, and a handful of minutes ago, I thought I'd never see him again. I was waiting for the floor to be whipped out from under me. There was a catch, right? Jake couldn't really be here, really be touching me and telling me it wasn't my fault.

And then he dropped his hands away and *there* it was— the beginning of the end.

Instead of leaving, like I expected, he pulled something from his pocket and held it out to me.

I took the folded piece of paper and quickly recognized it as the note I'd written and shoved under his door. My scribbly handwriting came into view as I opened it.

If you let me, I could love you.

I think maybe, even if you didn't let me, I could still love you.

I think maybe I already do.

When I looked up he whispered, "I'm really bad with words, so…"

So he kissed me.

Warm hands found my cheeks. His lips pressed against mine. My heart went cliff-diving into a different universe, and it was the kind of kiss that made me believe maybe Jake could love me, too.

He pulled back, leaving me breathless and in so many pieces, I didn't think I'd ever be whole again.

"I thought I knew what loneliness was," he whispered, mere inches from my face. "But you can't know lonely until you've lived the opposite."

I was afraid if I breathed, if I spoke, the image would fade, like a wax statue melting into a puddle of colors on the floor. But the muscles beneath my fingers felt real; his lips had felt real.

Jake's chest rose and fell with a heavy breath. "I haven't spoken to anyone that I haven't been obligated to since that night. I've had a lot of time to think. A lot of time to be alone— something I thought I wanted." He paused, looking down at our interlocked hands. "I thought about you a lot. And death. My life seems to be shrouded by it." His gaze raised again, and he shook his head slowly. "Wondering how soon that day would come for me…it felt inevitable for so many years. Then Emily died."

I squeezed his fingers tighter instinctively. My heart thumped fiercely.

He asked, "That beautiful place we talked about, do you remember?"

A beautiful place to photograph?

In a way.

I gasped a breath that stung my lungs. "What were you really looking for?"

He gave me a smile I'd seen so many times, but never once made me so nervous. "I thought about dying, and I thought… if it's going to happen, maybe I should choose how it ends. Choose the place, the time. The idea was peaceful to me. I've never believed the world owed me anything, so I could either let the world decide or I could decide for myself."

He'd taken me to those places, places that meant something secretly truthful, somber, and achingly real for him. And he'd chosen to share those beautiful places with me. I never realized it, could never appreciate it.

"Oh, Jake." I couldn't find the right combination of letters and words to respond with anything else.

"Don't look at me like that." He leaned in a little closer. Gripped my hands a little tighter. "I never set out to do it. Only thought about it."

That he even considered it broke my heart.

"I don't want to die, Audra. I don't think I actually did then. I wanted to disappear. So I did. And that was my life. Before you. Then after you were gone, I realized…I didn't want to disappear." Brushing my hair away from my face, his gaze dropped to my lips and back up again. "I'm not used to letting people in or letting them love me, so I've done a lot of shit wrong. I'll likely still be wrong sometimes, but…I want to be with you."

Hot tears scattered down my cheeks, breaking apart my promise not to cry. He wiped them away with his fingers, but the contact only brought on new tears.

I needed to say something, to respond in any way other than soundless sobs. So I whispered the one coherent thought I had. "You don't hate me?"

His crooked smile brightened his eyes. "After all of this, you still think I hate you? What do I have to say to make you believe me?"

I shook my head, unable to find an answer.

"Guess you'll have to trust me then…"

I gaped at his face, blinking furiously as my eyes filled with tears. A weird laugh climbed out of my throat. "I can't believe I ever said that."

He put his hands on my cheeks, tenderness, laughter, and seriousness fighting for control on his face. "I don't hate you. I never did. Never will. Now, tell me you believe me."

My cheeks burned where his fingers lingered, and it took several seconds to respond. "I do. I believe you."

Jake kissed my forehead and tugged me against his chest. It gave me a feeling I thought was out of my grasp. One that filled me up, sealing some of the cracks throughout my soul.

One of hope, and forgiveness, and *love*.

"I do have something to show you," he said, skimming his hands down my back, pressing our bodies closer together. "But…you might hate *me* for it."

"I think you'd better cut the surprise and get to it. Before I make some crazy shit up in my head."

He laughed, the sound vibrating against my chest. "You're right. No surprises."

Pulling away from me, he reached into his pocket for his phone. A few taps later, he turned it around and handed it to me. "I never printed the picture, but I saved the image onto my phone."

I stared down at the screen, tried to keep my fingers steady. "You…you *asshat*."

But my own light laughter joined his deep chuckles.

"I'm sorry."

"You're not sorry," I said—and he grinned. "You took a picture of me by the pool. With the glow sticks. I told you not to!"

He moved closer, reaching for the phone, but I yanked it back. I wanted to look at it, now that I was over the initial shock of what he'd done. What a traitor.

"You looked beautiful. How could I not take a picture of you?"

I looked away from the picture of me backlit with the faint glow of reds, greens, and blues, smiling at seemingly nothing. Happy as a clam—even I could see that. "You took this before you even came back from getting your camera, didn't you?"

"Creepy in the name of art."

I handed his phone back. "I think I'm too flattered to be creeped out."

"Good." He smiled, closing the distance between us. "So you don't hate me for it?"

"Definitely not. I could never hate you."

"Same way I could never hate you."

Euphoria and disbelief flooded my veins. "That's not at all the same."

In lieu of a response, he kissed me, guiding my body close to his. Close enough to feel his heart pounding in rhythm with mine. When his lips broke away he whispered, "You're crazy for thinking I could ever hate you. I know I said I don't think I understand the concept of love, but I think...I think I could."

My heart increased its manic cadence, and I was never so grateful to feel it. I placed my hand on Jake's chest and felt his pulse beat in time with mine, thinking maybe the point of life wasn't to live—maybe the point was to love.

Acknowledgments

Writing may be a solitary act, but it's utterly impossible to finish a book alone. This story wouldn't exist without the help of countless wonderful, inspiring people, and I'm still in awe about how lucky I am to have found so many awesome individuals along my journey.

First off, I want to thank you—yes, *you*! Thank you for reading Jake and Audra's story, for recommending it to friends, for writing reviews, for *everything*.

An enormous thanks goes to my editor, Jenn Mishler, for being SO enthusiastic about this story from day one. The love and excitement you've shown me has been beyond anything I ever fantasized. From your help with brainstorming, your (necessary) nitpicky comments, to all the exclamation points your emails contain—you've helped shape this story and these characters in ways I could never have done on my own. And another massive thanks to Jessica Snyder—your in-line comments had me laughing and made editing a bit easier. Eternal virtual hugs to you both!

And to the entire Entangled team, from the copyeditors,

publicists, production editor, and everyone who played a hand in making *The Heartbeat Hypothesis* a possibility, thank you. You've made my dream a reality.

To the writing community: if I named everyone I wanted to thank, the list would be endless. Having you all in my corner makes me one happy girl. You're the BEST. And a special thanks goes to Brenda Drake, who does *so* much for other writers. If not for her and her writing contests, I never would've found Jenn and ended up being a part of the awesomesauce Entangled family.

To my wonderful CPs and Beta readers: you've kept me going. You've reminded me why I write and why I shouldn't simply throw in the towel when things get hard. You've kept me from jumping off the ledge on multiple occasions. Katie Harris—you deserve an award for reading this book *at least* five times, as well as brainstorming, listening to me rant, rave, and moan. For being my biggest cheerleader and second writerly brain! I adore you. Colleen Oefelein—so many thanks for your continuous encouragement and love. I know you'll always have my back and that you'll always be there to answer my many random writerly questions at all hours of the day. KD Proctor—on top of critiquing this story, you still continue to gush over it, and I could never find the right words to express how much that kind of love means to me. Judi Lauren—you might not have read this story before its publication, but you've been there for me since the moment we met. You've always listened when I had my editing freak-out moments, and you're always there to help ease me off that ledge. You're a rock star. *Jazz hands*

Thank you to my family and friends. You might not fully understand what it's like to write and publish a book, but you've been rooting for me the entire time (and joining in on my jazz hands celebrations)!

And lastly, but *certainly* not least, Trent Iffland—you've

dealt with my crazy moments (or days, or weeks) of writing purgatory, showing me love and compassion all along the way. If I thanked you for all the things you've done, this could go on forever. I love you so much, and I intend to spend all my finite heartbeats with you.

About the Author

Lindsey writes romance, though sometimes there's an added sci-fi or magical realism twist. She lives in Columbus, Ohio (where the weather is never quite right). Her Fine Arts degree has granted her a wide assortment of creative knowledge that serves as inspiration (and not much else). When she's not crafting YA and NA stories, you'll likely find her spending *waaay* too much time on Pinterest, playing a video game, or performing in a burlesque show—because she enjoys giving her introversion a worthy adversary. (Plus, it's the closest to Broadway she'll ever get.) *The Heartbeat Hypothesis* is her debut novel.

Discover more New Adult titles from Entangled Embrace...

A Star to Steer Her By
a novel by Beth Anne Miller

Ever since her last dive ended in bloodshed, Ari Goodman's been terrified to go back into the water. But the opportunity to spend a semester at sea is too good to pass up. So is Tristan MacDougall. Rugged, strong, and with demons of his own, Tristan heals her with every stolen moment they share. But when a dive excursion goes wrong, their only hope for survival is each other.

Silver Edge
a *Straight Edge* novel by Ciara Knight

All I've ever wanted is to fit in. But no one can ever see past how weird I am. Bright lights? Can't stand them. Loud noises? Definitely sends me over the edge. And touching? Forget about it. At least, until I met Drake. From the moment I walked into that nightclub, I finally felt like I belonged somewhere. But now someone wants to close the club down and I'm going to have to find a way to tap into whatever that inner strength thing is that everyone always talks about. And fast. But what happens if I can't?

Last Wish
a novel by Erin Butler

Nothing feels right. Not since my best friend died and I fucked up the one promise asked me to make. Now my life is so fucking empty. Then *she* walks into the bar, all bright beauty and sweet lips made for kissing. Em Stewart is a complication...one I need to avoid. No matter how hard I try, I can't resist her, and our unexpected road trip sure as hell isn't helping my cause. But I'll be damned if I screw up my first chance at something real...

CPSIA information can be obtained
at www.ICGtesting.com
Printed in the USA
LVOW12s1539230317
528243LV00001B/43/P